# *Secret Baby for the Navy SEALs*

*A Military Reverse Harem Romance*

Krista Wolf

Copyright © 2022 Krista Wolf

All rights reserved. No part of this publication may be reproduced, distributed, or transmitted in any form without prior consent of the author.

Cover photography stock models only.

### KRISTA'S VIP EMAIL LIST:

Join to get free book offers, and learn release dates for the hottest new titles!

Tap here to sign up: http://eepurl.com/dkWHab

# ~ Other Books by Krista Wolf ~

Quadruple Duty
Quadruple Duty II - All or Nothing
Snowed In
Unwrapping Holly
Protecting Dallas
The Arrangement
Three Alpha Romeo
What Happens in Vegas
Sharing Hannah
Unconventional
Saving Savannah
The Christmas Toy
The Wager
The Ex-Boyfriend Agreement
One Lucky Bride
Theirs To Keep
Corrupting Chastity
Stealing Candy
The Boys Who Loved Me

Three Christmas Wishes
Trading with the Boys
Surrogate with Benefits
The Vacation Toy
Nanny for the Army Rangers
Wife to the Marines
The Switching Hour
Secret Wife to the Special Forces
Secret Baby for the Navy SEALs

# Chronicles of the Hallowed Order

Book one: Ghosts of Averoigne
Book two: Beyond the Gates of Evermoore
Book three: Claimed by the Pack

# One

## JULIANA

The interior of the building was warm and inviting, not the least bit as cold and clinical as I'd expected it to be. It could've been the back end of a museum, or even a library. Carpeted floors and strategically-placed plants guided us down another hallway, as I followed the primly-dressed woman in front of me.

"Sorry to make you wait so long, Ms. Emerson."

She paused at a frosted glass door, rapping sharply three times while wearing her best plastic smile. After poking her head inside for a moment, she eventually opened it wide.

"The director will see you now."

'The director'. It sounded so important, so official. The term was also starkly meaningless, especially in the context of why I was there.

*Could you please come to our main office? The director has something important to discuss with you.*

That cryptic email had forced me from my

conference room mid-presentation, out of my office, and into the nearest cab. Sixteen blocks later, here I was.

"Ms. Emerson?"

I was ushered into what could've been a doctor's, lawyer's, or even a dean's office, the three made completely indistinguishable by the sheer number of bookshelves around me. Each was stacked floor to ceiling with a thousand leather-bound books that might never get read in today's digital age, but sure as hell looked impressive.

"Ah, Ms. Emerson."

A gaunt, balding man with wire-rimmed glasses smiled weakly at me from across his desk. He stood up halfway, gesturing to one of two leather seats in front of him.

"If you please."

I took the chair he didn't point to, just to set him off guard. Not that there was a *need* to set this man I'd never met before off guard, but old habits died hard.

"Thanks for coming so quickly," he said in a soothingly, velvety voice. "I appreciate you taking the time to —"

"I'm here. Just tell me."

His eyes registered surprise at my bluntness, but also a little concern. It was the concern that concerned me.

"Alright then," he leaned back. "Straight to the point."

The man took a moment to clear his throat. When he spoke again, he looked a lot less comfortable.

"The donor you selected with us is unfortunately

unavailable."

It took a few seconds for the words to register. When they did, my heart sank.

"And why the hell not?"

"Because the samples were destroyed," the director replied coolly.

The sentence was like a punch to the gut. It felt exactly like I'd gotten the wind knocked out of me.

"W—What? How?"

The man steepled his fingers together across his scrawny chest. In his white labcoat and glasses, he looked like some skinny cartoon professor.

"The long version of that story involves an unforeseen mechanical failure, and an oversight in transferring certain samples to our backup freezer," the director said. "The short version is that some samples reached degradable temperatures. They became nonviable, and unfortunately had to be discarded."

My mouth was suddenly bone dry. All those weeks of searching through profiles, reading bios, looking at photos. Of pouring over pros and cons. Of making lists, and narrowing things down.

All of this work was now gone in an instant. Before I'd even gotten started.

"And you decide to tell me this *now?*" I seethed. "After spending months in your database, and when I finally chose someone to—"

"Again, another oversight," the director jumped in.

"This donor's record should've been taken out of our database months ago, when the event happened."

*Event.* Holy shit.

"He wasn't, and of course that's entirely our fault."

"You *think?*" I snapped.

The man stared back at me somberly, then slowly removed his glasses and set them on the desk between us. For some reason it made him look even older, more vulnerable.

Maybe he knew it, too.

"Again, we're very, *terribly* sorry."

*Six months!*

That's how long it had been since I started looking at profiles. Two-dozen weeks of pouring over what I knew full well would be the most important decision of my life.

*Not to mention another three months before that of waffling back and forth,* I reminded myself. *Gathering and then losing the courage. Starting and stopping with two different agencies, then starting all over again.*

It was only last week that I'd finally settled on the man who would — biologically, at least — father my child. He was the full package, the perfect specimen. A man who was tall, dark, and physically outstanding, with a good intellect, a sharp wit, and immaculate blood work.

This one nameless donor had seemingly everything: a squeaky clean genetic carrier test, with a high sperm count and impressive motility rate. And then of course there was his essay, which put him over the top. It fleshed out that final piece of a very anonymous puzzle; how incredibly sweet and thoughtful his personality was, to go along with that gorgeous, blue-eyed face.

"If you have a second pick for a donor..." the director was saying nonchalantly.

*No.*

"We'd be happy to expedite the process in any way we can. Put you right at the top the calendar for—"

*NO!*

I snarled, shaking my head. This donor was supposed to be the cherry on my sundae. The one decision that had taken me more than year to make, in a world where I normally made decisions so fast and on the fly I'd become somewhat of a legend for it.

"Of course you should take as much time as you need," the director continued carefully. "Think about what you—"

"No. I'm done."

I grunted the words harshly, like they tasted foul in my mouth. They still echoed hollowly in my mind as I shoved back from the desk and tore out of the office.

# Two

## JULIANA

The elevator doors opened smoothly, dumping me into the sixteenth-floor, glass-enclosed lobby of Shameless Marketing. People scurried left and right, disappearing in and out of more glass doorways. They carried laptops, folders, even entire presentations tucked under their arms.

And all of them were there because of *me*.

Normally I'd get a kick out of this little fact, accepting it as a well-deserved shot in the arm. I might even pause to revel in the sheer size of the marketing firm I'd built entirely from scratch, or stop for just a moment or two to smell the proverbial roses, and enjoy the fruits of my hard labor.

Not today, though.

Aric glanced at me curiously as I passed into my office, one well-manicured brow arching high on his handsome forehead. My expression told him not to follow. Not even with the second cup of coffee that rested on his desk, and it already being an hour later then when I usually took it.

*Fuck.*

I sank into my chair, being careful to keep my shoulders high and my head from falling into my hands. That was the problem with a glass-walled office. As the boss you got to see what everyone else was doing, at all times. But the other edge of that sword was equally as sharp: they also got to see you.

The road to get here had been a long and winding one. Nearly eight years ago I'd lucked into my first big account, through an all-or-nothing gamble that ultimately paid of in spades. From there I'd built things outward, expanding whenever I could, putting every dime right back in. Taking risk after risk to keep people on, often making payroll from the bottom of my own pocket.

At nearly thirty, I'd sacrificed just about everything else in my life to further my career. Maybe that's why my mid-life crisis was a little earlier than most. It arrived when I least expected it, in the form of an extremely loud and obnoxious biological clock. But there were other reasons I wanted children, too. More practical reasons that had everything to do with filling my house with love and family and laughter, at a time in my life when I could most fully enjoy it.

And now I was back to square one.

There were other options, of course. Other pathways that would get me to motherhood just as quickly. Only I didn't want 'other' options. I wanted the one I'd carefully and painstakingly selected. Anything else was second place, and second place never mattered.

And so I sat there, thinking about the director's bad news. Mentally flipping through the same five gorgeous profile photos of my future child's sperm donor. It was something I'd done dozens, even hundreds of times before, both online and in my head. Only now that I knew I couldn't have him, I found those images slowly fading away.

Aric waited twelve whole minutes before entering my office, which was exactly perfect. Anything before ten minutes and I would've snapped his head off. Fifteen minutes would've been too long.

"I don't know how to call and pre-report a murder," he said, "so I figured you should probably have this before somebody dies."

He slid the tall latte across my desk with a strong, practiced hand. I took it and drank deeply.

"You probably just saved a life," I admitted.

"That's what I do here," he smiled. "Save lives."

My second-in-command pushed a pair of stylish glasses higher on the bridge of his Roman nose. Fresh from his afternoon workout, he looked broad-chested and big-armed and absolutely amazing. Like a slightly less-nerdy version of Clark Kent.

"You know if you weren't gay and happily married, the two of us would rule the world by now," I declared with a wistful sigh. "You understand that, right?"

Aric chuckled. "I know. But we'll rule it anyway."

"You got that right."

He regarded me with a practiced eye, then slid into one of my chairs. Aric *never* slid into one of my chairs. He was a stand up kind of guy.

"What's bugging you, boss?"

"Not a thing."

His eyes narrowed suspiciously. "We didn't *lose* anything, did we?"

I paused a little too long at the question, then shook my head.

"The De'Angelo account still good?"

"Rock solid," I replied.

"And Rocket Pizza? They're still on board for the dropping coupons all over the city thing we talked about?"

I snorted. "They'd damned well better be. I've got thirty-seven drone operators on standby this weekend."

"It's this place then," he joked, looking around. "All this crazy glass. All the prying eyes. It's like living in a fishbowl!"

I frowned, waving my hand dismissively. I liked the glass most of the time. Being able to see everyone gave me a sense of control.

"Fine then," he said. "What could possibly be bothering the Viral Vixen?"

I exhaled slowly, letting my sigh out through clenched teeth. "I asked you to stop that."

"Bullshit," Aric countered. "You earned that nickname. It comes with instant recognition, and we all know how important *that* is." He shook his handsome head. "Like it or not, it's your brand."

My brand. It was the one thing I definitely had going for me right now. But I'd already decided, as I almost did, that I wanted more.

And this time around, a *lot* more.

"Aric, do you and Jason ever talk about having children?"

The man sitting across from me blinked. I had to admit the question really did come out of left field.

"We're *scheduled* to talk about it," he answered carefully. "Sometime next year."

"Next *year?*"

"I mean, he's brought it up a few times, but I've always tabled it."

"And what made you table it?"

My second-in-command's lips pursed together as he scratched the back of his head. "Lots of things, I guess. We're still young for one, or so I keep telling him. But that excuse is only going to work for another year if I'm lucky. Two, tops."

"He wants kids and you don't?"

"Oh I didn't say that," Aric answered. "I want a bunch of kids, actually. I want them very much."

"Well you've got a beautiful place," I said. "A good partner. Plenty of room. And I know you make *more* than enough money."

At the last comment, he delivered an obligatory smirk.

"So what's stopping you from doing it now?"

"Want the truth?"

"Always."

He extended a finger, inverted it, then tapped my desk. "This place."

I was floored. Thinking about it however, I probably shouldn't have been. "Really?"

"Yeah, well right now there's just too much going on here," he shrugged. "Too many irons in the fire. Maybe once things calm down a little—"

"But things never calm down," I countered. "They only ramp up."

Aric wasn't just my right-hand man, he was my whole right arm. He ran every single thing at Shameless that I didn't, and maybe even some that I did.

"I guess that's why I'm still waiting," he said. "You know. For the right time."

*The right time...*

He was looking over my shoulder now, at nothing in particular. Or maybe he was looking through the glass walls at something or someone else.

"Aric?"

"Yeah boss?"

"I want you take the rest of the night off," I told him. "Use the black card. Take your husband to a really nice restaurant, on the company's dime."

His eyes lit up. "Seriously?"

"Fuck yes," I smiled. "A good steakhouse, that new Asian Fusion place over on Seventh Avenue; whatever you guys want. You know you damned well deserve it. Without you, this place is just a pile of glass."

His face deepened to a bright scarlet under all the praise. I had to turn away for fear of turning a matching shade.

"Well shit, boss," he said. "I don't care what people say about you, you're—"

"And while you're at it, tell Jason I'm sorry."

"Sorry?" Aric scoffed. "For what?"

"For getting to see more of you than he does."

# Three

## JULIANA

There were good decisions and bad decisions, each with their own set of unique consequences. For the bigger ones, I did my due diligence. I agonized, I researched, I studied data until I was sure I was making the right moves, and not a potential mistake.

And then there were decisions like Wayne.

"A little more?"

He smiled as he held out the wine bottle, and I almost extended my glass. I'd had enough wine for tonight, though. Probably a little more than I should've, although I'd made the Wayne decision hours ago, even before I'd popped a cork.

Plucking the bottle from his outstretched hand, I sauntered over and set it on the bar. The music drifting down from my bluetooth speakers was nice. Nice enough that I was swaying my hips, dancing through the dimly-lit living room to where my ex-boyfriend sat happily on my new leather couch.

*Mmmm. He looks good.*

He did, really. Although I hadn't seen him in nearly a year, Wayne had apparently been keeping in shape. He sported the same well-groomed beard and immaculate haircut as when we'd been dating, and his shoulders seemed broader than I remembered them.

"C'mere, gorgeous."

He reached out for me, and I danced playfully away. Draining the last inch of wine still in my glass, I set that on the bar as well.

*You sure you know what you're doing?*

The thought nagged at me a little more, but I pushed it away. Inviting Wayne over had been a spur-of-the-moment decision. Even so, it was a spur-of-the-moment decision with ulterior motives.

"You ready for me?"

I breathed the words more than said them. Wayne simply nodded, sinking deeper into the cushions as he set his arms up on the back of the couch.

"You know what to do."

He did, which was nice because I sure as hell wasn't going to tell him. I continued my sultry, sexy dance as Wayne unbuttoned his shirt, pulled off his socks, and unbuckled his belt. He dropped his expensive slacks around his ankles and kicked them off, just around the time I climbed into his lap.

*Mmmmmm...*

His body felt warm and inviting, but that could've just been the wine. Or the fact that it had been... well... quite a while.

"God, baby. I missed you..."

I shushed him instantly, shoving a finger against his lips. "Don't ruin it."

His eyebrows knitted together with a silent question. *Ruin it?*

Squirming into his lap, I set my cheek against his shoulder and began planting soft kisses up and down his neck. He smelled like a mixture of cologne and bourbon. Wayne responded in kind, his hands piercing the hem of my dress. Slowly, tentatively, they glided upward, until his palms rested high on my bare thighs.

I let him have that little victory for a few moments, fighting the urge to let my hands wander the warm expanse of his chest. I didn't want to wander. I wasn't here to catch feelings.

No, I was here for something a *lot* more specific.

I felt it before I saw it — Wayne's growing bulge, just beneath me. I reached down to confirm, giving it a gentle squeeze before leaping up from the couch and spinning away.

"Juliana!" he chuckled in exasperation. "What the—"

His sentence died as I turned around, hiking my dress up over my hips. Sticking my ass out I began swaying it back and forth, in perfect rhythm with the music. When I was satisfied I'd hypnotized him with the slow, sultry movements, I began rolling my panties downward. They glided smoothly and easily over my well-rounded ass.

*Juliana.*

Down and down they went, rolling across the heated flesh of my upper thighs...

*Juliana!*

Inch by glorious inch the dropped. Until they were almost at my knees...

Awww, shit.

I stood up quickly, pulling everything back and smoothing my dress down. I grabbed the remote. Killed the music. By the time I was undimming the lights, I already felt like an asshole.

"Ummm... what just happened?"

Wayne looked like a kid on Christmas that just had his best present yanked back from him. Which he pretty much was.

"I'm sorry," I told him.

"Sorry?" He blinked. "Sorry for *what?*"

"For having to ask you to go home."

I grabbed the wine bottle again, and poured the remainder into my glass. I might've just finished the rest straight from the bottle, but I wasn't that type of girl.

"Juliana, what the actual fuck?"

And this wasn't that kind of night.

"I'm very sorry," I said again. "This... isn't what I want."

"Sure seems like you wanted it a minute or two ago,"

Wayne frowned. "When you were climbing all over me."

"Yeah, I know. And that's why I'm apologizing. I screwed up."

"Screwed up?"

I nodded firmly. "This whole thing was a mistake, Wayne. You really have to go."

My ex-boyfriend stared up at me, utterly dumbfounded. His eyebrows knit together in anger.

"You're serious?"

"Dead serious."

He was still mostly naked, sitting there helplessly with a lump in his boxers. I grabbed his slacks and threw them onto his lap, to cover it up.

"C'mon," I urged. "I have to get up early for work tomorrow."

"You *always* have to get up early," Wayne countered. "I don't think I've ever seen you sleep past six o'clock."

"Good. Then you're making my point for me."

"Even when we took that trip to the Maldives all those years ago," he went on. "I'd wake up and you were already in front of your computer, already working—"

"I know."

The words sounded bitter. Hell, they *tasted* bitter.

"How was the sunrise, I'd ask. But you didn't know because you'd already missed it."

"I said I KNOW!"

Wayne's own anger reflected mine. He sighed in frustration and leap from the couch, pulling his clothes on piece by piece.

"Wayne look, I *am* sorry," I told him. "I called you here for all the wrong reasons."

"There's only one reason you call your ex-boyfriend at midnight," he snarled.

"I know," I admitted. "And you didn't do anything wrong. It's just... it's just that..."

*It's not what I want.*

I frowned, thinking hard about the internalization.

*No, that's not right. It's not WHO I want.*

Wayne grumbled some more, cursing as his fingers stumbled through the buttons on his shirt. I got one last wistful look at his chest before it was put completely away, and then he was fumbling with his belt.

*You would've been tied to him forever, you know that right?*

Yeah, I knew. And it would've been a nightmare.

"You're never happy with what you have, Juliana," my ex-boyfriend barked abruptly. "You know that, right? That's your problem."

"I know," I agreed. "It is."

"No matter where you are or what you're doing, your mind is always somewhere else."

He fought his way into his shoes, as I contemplated what almost happened. It didn't make sense. It just wasn't me.

*What were you going to do, wait until after he'd finished inside you? Let him know a few weeks afterward?*

The voice in my head was mocking now. Harsh and merciless.

*Or would you tell him right before? Let him know you haven't been on birth control since–*

I bit my lip, letting the pain obliterate everything else. Yes, what I almost did was pretty fucking despicable. Yes, I was a complete asshole for it.

*But you didn't actually do it,* another more reasonable voice said.

Heavy footfalls indicated my ex-boyfriend was finally done. He stomped toward me, grabbing his jacket from the nearby rack as he headed in the direction of the door.

"Thanks for coming anyway, Wayne."

"Coming?" he laughed harshly, pausing at the threshold. The sound of the slamming door coincided with his final two words: "If *only.*"

# Four

## JULIANA

"Fine, then. If you won't help me, get me someone who will."

The man behind the desk shook his head slowly. He had the condescending look of someone about to explain something simple to a small child, and that part was maddening.

"It's not that I won't help you, I *can't* help you," the man said. "I'm sorry Ms. Emerson. I simply don't have access to—"

"Get. Me. The. Director."

I'd asked three times, and three times I'd been rebuffed. Now I stood up. I turned in the direction I knew the director's office to be.

"Please sit back down," the man implored. "I'll do what I can."

He left abruptly, taking his overly-creased shirt with

him. At least his tie was ironed, but the rest of him looked like he'd stepped on a wrinkle-bomb.

*This place could be run a hell of a lot better.*

It was one of the many curses of owning your own business: too often you saw fault in everything and everyone. I'd tried to calm down, to be patient and understanding. But the more ineptitude and unprofessionalism I saw, the harder it was to bite my tongue.

Forcing myself to relax, I settled back, unfolded my arms, and went over the *almost* unfortunate events of last night.

Booty-calling Wayne had been a bad idea from the start. Not because of the sex, which I desperately needed, but because of the attachment on his end that would inevitably come along with it.

But no, even worse was the idea that I should somehow utilize an ex-boyfriend to bring a child into this world. It was lame, it was stupid, and it was fraught with a thousand future problems. Not to mention trying to get pregnant without even discussing it with someone felt wholly shitty and undeniably wrong.

I'd tried blaming the wine, but the wine was only part of the problem. The real issue was I felt slighted. The clinic left me feeling wronged; cheated out of my choice of sperm donor, to the point where I almost did something cataclysmically stupid.

Luckily I'd had the sense to send Wayne home. After that I'd called up the old profile pics of the man I suddenly *couldn't* have, and I'd stared at them with all new levels of obsession and infatuation.

I couldn't stop gazing at the young, gorgeous hunk attached to the donor's bio. Who was he? What was he doing right now? If he donated sperm here in the City, it stood to reason he probably lived here as well.

True or false, *that* little deduction sent me down an endless rabbit hole until the wee hours of the morning. Did this guy live only a few blocks away? If so, did we visit the same restaurants? Ride together on the subway? Had I unknowingly jogged past him in Central Park, while he was reading a book?

All these fantasies converged on me at once, heightening my other, more baser needs at the time. Soon I was stretched out on my bed, staring up at the ceiling. My eyes fluttered closed as I'd allowed my fingers to wander, giving myself at least some of the pleasure Wayne hadn't... while calling up the best angles and favorite images of my now mysterious father-to-be.

Of all the in-depth bios and corresponding medical histories I'd studied, the one thing that got me was the really sweet essay attached to this one man's file. It was written by the donor, and intended for his future biological offspring. He talked about his own childhood, and growing up shy. Very gently, he told his potential son or daughter that if he or she were also shy that they shouldn't worry, because they'd eventually grow out of it.

The rest of the essay talked about friendship, and family, and confidence — all good things, with positive spins on each. He ended it by telling his future offspring how excited he was for the amazing journey they had ahead of them, because the world was full of so many incredible, wonderful things.

It was this essay that truly resonated with me, and really sealed the deal. Any man who could write something like that would pass on traits of love and happiness and laughter. Whoever he was, a man like that undoubtedly had a very big heart.

"Why hello there!" a sugary-sweet voice called from my left. "Ms... Emerson, is it?"

The tall woman who'd entered the room was already wearing a saccharine smile. She slid into the chair wrinkle-man had left unoccupied, then stared at the screen for several moments.

"You're not the director," I stated flatly.

"No," she continued, her smile not fading a single centimeter. "But I'm the assistant director, Sarah Fields. I'm told you had a question?"

I punched my phone to life, then slid it her way.

"This man," I said, tapping the screen. "I was wondering if you could tell me his name."

She didn't even look down. Instead she folded her hands.

"You realize that man is no longer in our system," she said coolly.

"He shouldn't have been in your system at all," I shot back. "But being that he *was* in your system, I was wondering if maybe he'd donate again."

"That's up to him," the woman said. "Not us."

"Fine," I agreed. "Did you contact him to tell him his sample had been thrown out?"

"No," the woman allowed. "That's not part of our protocol."

"Was accidentally defrosting the specimen part of your protocol?"

Her saccharine smile devolved into a frown. "Of course not."

"Then why not go a tiny bit out of your way for me and contact him?" I asked. "The worst he can do is say no."

"But—"

"Or let *me* contact him. I'm sure if he donated once, he'd be fine with donating agai—"

"This man donated eleven years ago," the woman stopped me. "He never returned. I can tell you these things only because they're part of his profile. That information is open to all clients, like yourself, who are looking to conceive."

"So you can give me his DNA, but not his name?" I scoffed. "You can plant his seed inside me, but you can't give me his last known address?"

"All donors' personal information is strictly confidential," the woman said. "You know that."

"But this was *your* mistake. *Your* error."

"I'm aware."

"Why not just call him to let him know what happened to his sample," I reasoned. "And while you've got him on the phone, maybe mention there's someone else who'd already decided upon—"

"No and no," the woman shook her head. "It's not

how we operate."

A scathing string of curse words rose to mind, attached to phrases that might send a woman like this running from the room. Rather than unleash them, I choked them back. I was too depressed for even that little measure of fun.

"Fine then. Forget it."

I stood up, using the last of my willpower to keep my shoulders held high. Silently, I slid the phone back into my hand.

"You've been a gem," I told her, scrolling through my contacts. "A real diamond."

I hit the call button, waving the woman off dismissively as she tried to say something else. On the third ring, my friend picked up.

"Addison!" I boomed, loud enough to be heard all throughout the office. "I'm going to send you a series of photos of someone. Four of them, in fact."

I turned to look back at the assistant director, who was still looking on incredulosly.

"I need you to find out who this guy is."

# Five

## JULIANA

Addison was one of my oldest New York friends — a city cop who'd pulled me over the first month I was here. She cited me specifically for 'driving like an asshole'; a term I later learned was used to describe any driver *not* from New York.

Growing up on the small town roads of rural Maine, I had to learn the glory of aggressive New York City driving the same way everyone else here did: by baptism through fire. I fought my citation down to a small fine, and after leaving the courthouse, took Addison to lunch to pick her brain.

We'd been fast friends ever since.

In the decade that followed I'd been her mentor, her financial adviser, her maid-of-honor, and her eldest daughter's godmother. I'd been the shoulder she'd cry on, when her mother was sick. I'd been the one person she chose to confide in, when she was unexpectedly stricken by debilitating panic attacks. Addison was strong, fierce, take no prisoners — she reminded me exactly of myself. I loved her like a sister. I'd do anything in the world for her, and she for me.

Which was why asking her to use the newly-launched NYPD facial recognition network to find my mystery donor seemed like no big deal at all.

"Give me a few days," she'd said. "If this guy's walked down a sidewalk in the last sixteen months, I'll find him."

I wasn't exactly sure she'd succeed, but I knew she'd try like hell. For those reasons alone, I shouldn't have been surprised when my phone rang two days later and I picked it up to a single, spoken word.

"Devyn."

I blinked in confusion, still licking the chocolate frosting from a Funfetti cupcake off my middle finger. "Wait... what?"

"The man you're looking for is Devyn Bishop."

An alert preceded the image coming over my phone: a single driver's license photo of the man that had been burned into my brain. He was a little older, but somehow even *more* handsome. His eyes had wisdom now. His stubbled jaw exuded a more experienced, yet still rugged sex-appeal.

I dropped the knife I'd been using to frost the cupcakes. My heart, beating excitedly, threatened to hammer itself right out of my chest.

"W—What else do you know about him?"

"I know he grew up local," Addison went on. "South

Brooklyn. He lives in the Arizona desert now, but about a year ago he came back for a few days for his mother's funeral."

"How the hell do you know *that?*"

"I checked his old address against the obituaries database."

"*Fuck,*" I swore.

"Yeah I know," spat Addison. "It's invasive. Cameras on every damned street corner. I hate this whole fucking system, but it's not going anywhere anytime soon. Might as well use it for something good."

My mind was reeling now, spinning with possibilities. I knew his name. I knew where he lived. This man *existed*, and not just in terms of the eleven year-old photos I'd been holding in my greedy little hands. He was *real*. He was flesh. He was blood! He was—

"I have a whole file on him," said Addison, "believe it or not."

"Come over," I told her quickly. "Bring it."

She balked. "Ummm... why don't I drop it off tomorrow, on the way to—"

"I have cupcakes."

On the other end of the phone my friend sighed, then cursed, then sighed again. Sugar was Addison's weakness, and Funfetti cupcakes were her Kryptonite. I just so happened to be making them for her as a thank you, whether she found this guy or not.

"Have you seen my ass, Juliana?" Addison grunted.

"Of course. Lots of times."

"Lately, I mean."

"Look, you can eat the cupcakes or you can roll up your sleeves and squash them with your fists," I told her. "I don't care which, and I won't even be offended. But I need to see that file."

"Squashing them sounds like fun, actually," she chuckled. "But with my luck, I'd probably end up absorbing the calories through the pores in my fingers."

"And your husband will thank me," I shot right back at her. "Evan doesn't like your ass tiny, anyway. He told me so, half a hundred times."

"Bah," my friend scoffed. "My ass hasn't been tiny since he put the first of three babies inside me."

"All the more reason to eat a cupcake."

There was a measure of silence, during which I already knew I had her. I used the precious few seconds to conjure up the seeds of a plan, now that I knew where my potential donor was.

"I'll be there in forty minutes," Addison said finally, "and I'm stopping for milk. We're going to need milk for what I'm about to do to those cupcakes."

"I have milk."

"No, you have one-percent milk," my friend corrected me sharply. "I'm not sure what planet you're from, but *that's* not milk."

I smiled and rolled my eyes. "Fine."

"No, it's not fine Juliana. It's outright criminal!" In

the background, I could hear her grabbing her keys. "Why don't I pick up some white food coloring, and we can just dye some water and call it 'milk.' It'll taste the same as the shit in your fridge."

"Do they even *sell* white food coloring?" I giggled.

"Maybe," my friend surmised. "Oh, and do me a favor?"

"Yes?"

"Fuck off."

# Six

## JULIANA

Addison had eaten three and a half cupcakes, then wrapped up another four for her 'husband and kids' (not that I believed her). The rest she squashed with her fists. That activity had been strangely satisfying to watch. She'd enjoyed the experience way too much.

"You've got problems," I'd chuckled, as my friend went through the process of washing and drying her hands. "*Big,* deep-seeded problems."

But Addison was too good at ignoring me.

"You're flying out there, aren't you?"

"Of course," I'd shrugged.

My friend's smirk widened. "Tomorrow, if I know you."

"Is there any better time?"

Addison left soon afterward, and I'd spent the rest of the evening staring into the driver's license photo of this man who was no longer so much of a mystery. His file told me why he'd left New York: immediately after his eighteenth birthday Devyn Bishop had joined the military – the Navy, in fact. He was twenty-nine, like me, only he'd moved from place to place so many times it was almost impossible to count. There didn't seem to be a Mrs. Bishop, or any children, at least none that his file revealed. That last part was disappointing. I would've loved to see a reflection of what my own son or daughter might look like, if I could somehow convince him to re-up his sperm donation.

*This is weird.*

Maybe, I thought to myself. Maybe not.

*Even for you.*

It struck me how strange the whole thing might seem, at least to an outsider. But in the end, it boiled down to a simple yes or no. Either this guy was still optimistic and eager to provide the gift of life for someone else, or the past decade on the planet earth had jaded him as much as it had jaded me. One way or the other, I was going to find out.

Aric didn't even stop typing as I barged into his office, dragging my carry-on luggage with me. He finished his train of thought, pushed his glasses higher on his nose, then settled back into his chair to regard me coolly.

"Did I miss a memo?"

"No, wise-ass," I smirked. "But I am leaving town for a day or two."

"Hmmm. Business?"

"Personal."

Aric cleared his throat, then shook his head slowly. "I don't remember you giving us any notice," he teased.

It felt a lot like he was my boss and I was answering to him, which of course was what he wanted. Aric and I played this little game all the time. It was fun thinking of him as an equal, which he was, even if he wasn't a full-fledged partner.

"I need you to hold down the fort," I said needlessly. "Keep this train from derailing while I'm gone."

"Is it a man?"

His question was abrupt — too abrupt for me to deny it right away. My hesitation spoke volumes. By the time I'd decided to shake my head, his eyes had already lit up like the Fourth of July.

"It *is* a man!" Aric gasped. He rolled his chair forward and gripped his desk. "Holy shit, I can't believe—"

"Pipe down," I snapped, looking left and right, then over both shoulders. In my head, I silently calculated how much it would cost to convert all the glass walls in the office to something less see-through. "This isn't what you think. It's not like, well..."

"Are you going to see a man or not?" Aric asked simply.

Begrudgingly, I nodded.

"Well that's all I needed to know!" he smiled. "Kudos to you, boss. I'd been wondering when you'd get around to cleaning out the cobwebs in the womb-room."

I stopped in my tracks. "Excuse me? The *womb*

*room?"*

"Yeah, you know, crushing buns. Buttering the biscuit." He tapped a long finger against his dimpled chin. "Batter-dipping the corn dog."

The last one seemed to really please him. I made a face.

"Yuck. That's gross."

He winked at me. "Only if you're doing it wrong."

Aric and I didn't often talk about our personal lives, but when we did there were very few boundaries. He'd been there to help me through dry spells, calm me down through monsoon seasons, and to support me during my breakup with Wayne. When it came to this one topic however, I wasn't ready to share just yet.

"Whatever," I eventually sighed. "I'll be out of town for two days, three tops. And I certainly won't be... buttering any biscuits."

"Getting a visit from old one-eye?" he pressed. "Taking a trip to bone town?"

I shook my head and smirked. "You know I really should fire you."

"Oh God please, could you?" he pleaded. "Jason's constantly chewing me out for never being home as it is. We canceled two weekend trips already." I watched as his face broke into his biggest, whitest smile. "You're not gonna believe this, but he says I work too much."

I couldn't help but laugh. "Has he *seen* you work?"

Aric dismissed me with the wave of one hand.

"Look, there's nothing wrong with glazing the donut from time to time." He smiled. "You're an adult, and adults have needs. It's perfectly okay to enjoy these things, you know."

"I know I'm an adult!" I declared sharply. "I don't need you to *tell* me I'm an adult. And for your information —"

"I'm just glad you're finally letting someone conquer the pink fortress."

Our eyes locked, and our smirks clashed. Still, we both knew victory was his.

"Goodbye Aric," I said, gripping the extendable handle of my bag with a white-knuckled fist.

"Call me when you're done opening the Gates of Mordor," he shouted after me, on the way out of his office. "I wanna know how it went!"

# Seven

## JULIANA

The address wasn't even accessible by standard GPS mapping; a sprawling house at the end of a dirt road way out in the Arizona desert. It had taken me more than two hours to reach this place from Phoenix, and another thirty minutes to figure out where the turnoff was. But now I was here, in the shadow of the mountains. Just south of a place called Queen's Valley, in the middle of fucking nowhere.

If I *did* conceive with this man, it would make one hell of a story to tell my child one day.

I passed through a set of wrought-iron gates then rolled to a dust-choked stop. Co-existing perfectly with the desert landscape, the house was asymmetrically beautiful. Its Italian-style architecture blended with the desert colors and materials, looking as if it were built and added onto for generations.

As old as it looked however, I could see it had been built with cutting edge materials and an exotic, modern flair.

My nerves got the best of me as I exited my rental car and clip-clopped across the flagstone walkway that lead to the massive, square-relief teak doors. They were decorated all over with bolted metal fittings. Two giant iron rings hung from sand-blown hinges, but were well-oiled enough that I could easily use one to knock.

*This is it.*

I squeezed my hands into fists, trying my best to keep from looking nervous. I'd dressed for the desert so I wouldn't be sweating, but it turned out the desert was a lot cooler than I thought it would be. Especially with the sun setting.

*This is—*

The door opened inward with a rush of motion. Standing barefoot on the terra-cotta tile of the home's massive foyer, a man in a sleeveless T-shirt was spooning cereal into his mouth from a large, blue bowl.

"Well hey," the man smiled. He used one thick, corded forearm to wipe milk from his lips. "Hello there."

Whoever he was, he was absolutely *gorgeous.* Tall and broad and powerful, the man's bare arms were rippled with acres of beautiful, well-sculpted muscle.

"I— umm..."

He continued eating, casually crunching away. I remained at a loss for words. Eventually he brought one hand to his spiked, dirty-blond hair and scratched his head.

"Hang on a second."

He disappeared through an archway, into the cozy-looking home. I was still looking after him, watching him go, when someone else stepped into the doorway from another part of the house.

"Hi, can I help you?"

Oh my God it was *him!* The object of my quest. The center of my recent universe. And yes, the most recently unwitting subject of some of my more far-flung fantasies.

I'd pictured this same handsome face countless times in my mind. And now he was actually standing before me, in the flesh. Leaning against one beautiful, well-built arm as he regarded me with an iron jaw and a curious, mischievous smirk.

"Yes?"

"H—Hi," I eventually choked. "I... umm..."

It was a living nightmare — the one time in my entire existence I was actually at a loss for words. I'd spent my entire adult life giving high-pressure sales pitches before large gatherings while internally scoffing at people who had a fear of public speaking. Right now however, I understood each one of them fully and completely.

"You're trying to sell me something, aren't you?"

The man arched an eyebrow, then crossed two powerful arms over his massive chest. The muscles flexed as he moved, surging to life beneath his tanned skin.

*Fuckkkkk.*

My helplessness was amplified by his mere presence. Yet somewhere in the back of my mind, I fell even deeper in love.

"Alright," he smiled, and his smile was radiant. "Go on. I'll listen."

Shifting in the doorway, he cleared his perfectly-formed throat.

"I'm probably not going to *buy* anything," he advised, "but since you drove all the way out here, you might as well practice your script on me."

His face wasn't just handsome, it was kind as well. And his voice! It was even deeper than I'd imagined, but not rough or gravelly in any way. In fact, it was quite smooth and pleasing. Just like he was.

"You're Devyn Bishop," I finally managed to say.

The man's whole expression changed. He was more guarded, more suspicious, as he looked me up and down.

"Maybe."

"No, not maybe," I countered. "You're definitely him."

I put out my hand, which felt a little silly. Almost like I *was* trying to sell him something.

"I'm Juliana Emerson."

Those cornflower blue eyes studied me for another moment, then a big, calloused hand closed over mine.

"Nice to meet you, Juliana."

Oh my God, we were *touching*. Actually touching! Electricity flowed through me like we'd completed a circuit. We were flesh to flesh now, skin to skin. I still couldn't believe it.

"So if you're not selling me anything," he went on, "what is it you actually want?"

"The truth?" I asked.

"Always."

I took a long, deep breath, searching for my usual confidence. Somehow, I found it.

"I need your sperm."

The man in the doorway raised a fist to his mouth and let out a sharp cough. "Come again?"

"I need your sperm," I repeated plainly. "Your seed."

His arms dropped to his sides now, his hands opening and closing mechanically. He cocked his head.

"My... sperm."

"Yes," I smiled sweetly. For a brief, hysterical moment I had the absurd vision of pulling out an actual collection cup. "Please."

Our eyes locked for the first time, and I felt myself melting right there on his porch. By the time his face cracked into a smile, I was almost a puddle.

"Well that's *definitely* a new one," he admitted. Stepping aside, he gestured me into the foyer with an open hand. "I'm guessing for this, you'd better come inside."

# Eight

**DEVYN**

Its not every day that a beautiful stranger shows up on your doorstep, asking to have your baby. Especially when you live out in the middle of the desert, and aren't even sure how she found you in the first place.

But hey, the least I could do was serve her coffee.

It was adorably cute how nervous she was, as I guided her along the tiled floors and into our kitchen. Gage was still there, pouring himself another bowl of cereal. He began strategically eyeing her over, as I pulled out a chair and tried to make her comfortable.

"Gage, this is Juliana Emerson. From New York."

They shook hands awkwardly, the two of them. But Juliana's eyes were still locked on me.

"How'd you know I was from New York?" she demanded.

I laughed. "Your accent for one. It's almost the same

as mine." I dropped a fresh paper filter into the coffee maker. "Sounds like you grew up somewhere else though, and you've only recently adapted it."

"Maine," she acknowledged. "Ten years ago."

"Ah."

She folded one delicate hand beneath her chin and stared up at me. "Anything else?"

"Yes, actually. But first..."

I shot Gage the universal look for 'why don't you go take a walk?' At first he scoffed at me, but I persisted. Slowly, begrudgingly, he rose to his feet.

"You know we have that thing in a few minutes," he reminded me.

"I know."

"Maverick's got the connection set up by now. All we're really waiting for is—"

"I *know*."

He rolled his eyes dramatically before giving up.

"Nice to meet you Juliana Emerson from New York."

He ogled her a little more, not that I blamed him. The brunette sitting at our kitchen table was fiercely beautiful. Eventually Gage took her hand again, kissed the back of it, then bowed out of the room trailing droplets of milk behind him.

"Sorry," I apologized. "He's harmless."

"Don't be. He seems nice."

The coffee maker began its drip cycle, filling the room with its rich, delicious aroma. Leaning back against the counter I looked her over some more, trying to determine anything else I could about her.

It also didn't hurt that she was fun to look at.

"I also figured you're from New York because you've obviously been to the clinic," I told her. "It's the only reason I could think of that you'd want my... well..."

"Sperm?"

The word could've come out crass or outrageous, but somehow it didn't. Instead she'd said it smoothly, and with total confidence.

"You *can* say it, you know," she chuckled. "It's not like its a dirty word."

"Fine then, sperm," I agreed. "But what happened? Did they run out of my sample?" A thought occurred to me, causing me to grin. "Wait, was I really *that* popular?"

Juliana shrugged, her long hair dancing across her pretty shoulders. "Actually I don't know how popular you were. They don't give any information on other potential siblings unless you conceive."

"Ah," I nodded. "I vaguely remember something about that."

"As the donor you could call and ask, though," she said. "They'll tell you how many biological children you have. I know that much."

I felt inwardly guilty all of a sudden. In all these years, I hadn't even thought about wanting to know. Was it wrong that I felt that way? So much had happened in the past decade. So many things between then and now.

"I only donated once," I said, struggling to remember. "Had to be more than ten years ago."

"Eleven."

I nodded in acknowledgment. "I needed a little cash so I went with a friend who'd done it before, on a whim. It seemed righteous to me at the time. Like a good thing to do, helping people who couldn't have babies of their own."

"It *is* a good thing to do," she said. "Which is why I hope you'll do it again."

I scratched at my chin. "For you," I stated plainly.

"Yes," she smiled politely. "For me."

It was the last thing in the world I expected when I woke up this morning, but here she was. Strong. Determined. Blunt. I recognized these traits immediately, because they were also my own. Whoever she was, I could tell Juliana Emerson was someone used to getting her way.

"Alright, so what happened?" I asked.

"Your samples were destroyed, accidentally," she replied. "But there was an oversight. You were still in the database at the time I picked you."

"You picked me, huh?"

"Yes. But then I was told I couldn't have you."

"Hmmm."

I grabbed the coffee pot and began pouring.

"Why 'hmmm?'" she frowned.

"Well you came all this way," I said. "For me. For... this."

I almost looked down at my balls. I fought the urge not to.

"Yes."

"Why not just use someone else?" I asked. "Another donor? There have to be hundreds."

"Thousands actually."

"So why me?"

The question seemed to set her back a little. But only a little.

"You appeared to have a lot of great traits," she shrugged. "That's all."

I pushed a mug her way, along with some milk and sugar.

"Such as?"

"Well you're tall, for one. Your bio said you were six-foot two, but looking at you in person you have to be at least two inches more than that."

"I was a late bloomer," I acknowledged. "I had one last growth-spurt."

"And not to be superficial but you *are* good-looking," she said without batting an eye. "You're strong. Very well-built."

I noticed she used that last part as an excuse to really look me over. Her eyes lingered as they crawled my chest, my shoulders, my arms. Unapologetically, too.

"Anything other than physical?"

Juliana picked up her mug and drank, her light brown eyes flashing dangerously over the brim. She took a moment before speaking again.

"I know you're very intelligent," she went on. "Your bio mentioned you graduated at the top of your class. It also said that you were athletic, social, artistic."

"Ah, my 'artistic' phase," I sighed fondly. "I remember when I had the time for things like that."

"And I happen to know that you're very, very sweet."

The last one knitted my eyebrows together. It didn't seem like something I would've put down in my bio when I was nineteen years old and trying to make a few quick dollars. Then again, who knew? In the grand scheme of my life, all of this seemed like a thousand years ago.

"Well, it certainly seems like you've thought this through," I said finally.

"I have," Juliana replied. "I've also made arrangements with a sister clinic in Phoenix. If you're willing to provide a sample, they're ready to cryogenically freeze it and ship it back to the sperm bank in New York for me."

"Phoenix, huh?"

"Yes."

She had it all worked out in her pretty little head. All the bases covered. Except one.

"I'll have to think about it."

Juliana flinched visibly. It wasn't what she was expecting at all.

"*Think* about it?"

"Sure," I told her. "I mean, it's a big decision isn't it? Plus I don't even know you."

"B—But you were willing to donate without knowing who was getting—"

"That was a long time ago, when I was nineteen. Don't you remember being nineteen?"

I laughed, and the laughter made her angry. Her anger made her even more beautiful, as she shoved her coffee away.

"C'mon, you have to admit this is a little funny," I said. "You flew clear across the country with the equivalent of a collection cup. Before I, uh, do the deed," I flushed, "can you really begrudge me wanting to know who you are first?"

My guest tapped her foot on the floor rapidly, restlessly, while trying to compose herself. After a few moments of awkward silence, I extended an olive branch.

"Where are you staying, Juliana?"

She hesitated a few seconds before answering. "The Renaissance. Downtown."

"Not bad," I smiled. "Why don't you head back there, get some rest. I'll pick you up for lunch tomorrow. You can tell me all about yourself."

"Tomorrow," she repeated flatly.

"Sure."

"Fine," she sighed. "And if all goes well? We'll already be in Phoenix. If you catch my drift."

She smirked at me, and even that was cute. A minute later we'd exchanged phone numbers. Two minutes after that, I was walking her to her car.

"I guess I want to know more about you, too," she said before getting in. "Who in the world *are* you? And how did you end up all the way out here?"

We looked around together in silence, at the purple desert sky. The stars were just starting to emerge. In just a little while, there would be tens of thousands of them.

"I'm nobody," I told her plainly. "And this is no place."

She looked genuinely confused sitting in my driveway, staring back at the house behind me. Everything was silent. The windows glowed from the inside with a warm, orange light.

"Devyn, what exactly—"

"Goodnight Juliana Emerson from New York," I said, before turning and walking away.

# Nine

## JULIANA

"Marketing, huh? Tell me about that."

The man I knew as Devyn Bishop still hadn't touched his lunch. His piercing eyes — and whole demeanor, really — seemed totally fixated upon me, as if studying or assessing me in silent, secret ways.

"Well I always liked funny commercials," I explained. "As soon as I was old enough to handle a camera, I started making my own parodies."

His Adam's apple bobbed sexily up and down as he sipped his drink. I couldn't stop staring at his perfect, beautiful mouth.

"So how'd you end up with your own company?"

God, he was so fucking *amazing*-looking! I could admit that now. Last night I'd wondered if it were merely my own months-long obsession over his photos that had inflated his obvious good looks to epic proportions. But here in the restaurant of my Phoenix hotel, with the golden afternoon light kissing his handsome, stubbled face?

I could see my infatuation was well-deserved.

"I suffered through two semesters of college before I realized it wasn't for me," I went on. "At that point I took the remainder of my savings and student loans and decided to run my own agency instead of working for one. I dumped it into a single project for a fledgling software company who were trying to put out a radical new game."

Devyn leaned back and smiled. "Sounds chancy."

"Yeah, you could definitely say that."

"So what happened?"

"I bought the mother of all zombie flash mobs," I explained proudly. "Right in the heart of New York City. Full-blown professional makeup artists. No expenses spared. I had zombies bursting out of the dressing rooms at 5th Avenue stores. Zombies stomping through high-profile restaurants..."

"Holy shit, I remember that!" he exclaimed. "That was *you?*"

Tracing the rim of my glass with one finger, I nodded.

"There were zombies crashing the steps at City Hall," cried Devyn. "Zombies chasing people up the stairwells at subway stations!'

"And don't forget Central Park," I beamed proudly. "The whole thing was a commercial for a new first-person shooter, by a gaming company no one had ever heard of. Never mind that zombies were played out by then. Or that first-person shooters were a dime a dozen."

"That commercial *rocked*," Devyn declared. "They played it everywhere."

"It went viral as viral can be," I nodded. "On YouTube alone it pushed past two-hundred million views in the first two weeks. And now that gaming company is a household name. We handle every ounce of their marketing needs, everything from design and packaging to radio ads, television, and of course, online presence."

"I still can't believe that was you," he breathed. He looked me over again, this time with all new eyes. "Shit. You're famous!"

"Sort of," I shrugged. "My company took off after that. They started calling me the Viral Vixen."

"Viral Vixen," he repeated, tasting the words slowly. "Well you certainly deserved it. You kicked ass."

"Yeah," I agreed. "I definitely got lucky."

Devyn's eyebrows knitted together as he shook his head. "Luck had nothing to do with it," he disagreed. "Your concept was creative, and you were the one who took a chance on it. You were the one who risked everything on a single idea, and that idea panned out."

Silently I contemplated his words. Shit, was he right? I'd always prided myself on being lucky, but now I wasn't so sure.

"That's not luck," he went on. "Luck is being in the right place at the right time. You *created* the right place. You created that moment in time." He nudged me from across the table and smiled. "That's skill, Juliana. It also looked like a shitload of fun."

"Filming it was fun," I agreed, "but the hard part came afterward."

"Hard part?"

"Chasing down people to sign release forms. Editing a hundred and sixty hours of footage down to minute-and-a-half segment."

"Ouch."

"Yeah, nobody ever considers that part. My editors are the real unsung heroes." I shrugged. "Still, I did the whole thing without permits. Without telling anybody."

"That's why all the reactions were so genuine," Devyn pointed out.

"True," I agreed. "But I could never pull something like that off now, as big as I am. The City would have my ass."

Silence descended, and we both took the opportunity to sip our drinks. Devyn scanned me unabashedly, his lingering eyes betraying the fact he was probably still hung up on the words 'my ass.'

"So I've been doing some thinking," he said abruptly, "and I have a question for you."

"Shoot."

"How do I know it's me that you actually want, and not someone else?"

I set down my drink. My expression quickly turned to one of pure astonishment.

"Are you kidding me?"

"No, I'm being serious," he pressed. "I mean, this is a pretty big decision, don't you think?"

"Yeah. So?"

"So what makes you want *me* in particular? You could've moved on to any other number of similar donors."

"But—"

"They told you my sample was unavailable, right? That it was destroyed?"

"Yes," I replied. "And your point is?"

"Any normal person would've picked her second or third choice."

I didn't know whether to be pissed off or flattered. In the end, I let out a sarcastic laugh.

"Yeah, well I'm definitely *not* a normal person."

"True enough," Devyn grinned. "But maybe you only want me because you *can't* have me?"

He was searching me for anger, and that was probably good. Maybe he wanted to see anger. Anger was decisiveness.

Still, game-playing just wasn't my thing.

"I flew all the way to Phoenix, then drove all the way out to the middle of the desert," I told him. "Just to find you."

"Which brings up another point," he reasoned. "How the hell *did* you find me?"

Our eyes locked. My smirk widened.

"The truth?"

"The truth would be nice, yeah."

"I bribed a friend of mine who has access to every street camera in the five boroughs," I said. "You came up as being in New York about a year ago, for your mother's funeral."

He looked floored. Flabbergasted. Downright fucking impressed.

"Sorry about your mom, by the way."

"Err... thanks."

"Don't mention it."

Devyn flexed involuntarily. It was like watching a sea of hot muscles rolling and shifting beneath his tight, camouflage T-shirt.

"You tracked me down," he said at last. "You must really want this."

"That's what I keep telling you."

He squinted hard, his eyes narrowing as he sized me up. I wanted to ask him more about his own life, where he'd been, what he'd done. I wanted to know about the Navy, and the places he'd been stationed. From the limited information Addison had gathered for me, it seemed he'd led quite an exotic life.

"Alright then, let's go."

I shot up hopefully. "Really? To the sister clinic?"

"Back to my place first," Devyn answered, pulling a stack of bills from his back pocket. He flipped a few onto the table, along with his napkin.

"I need to know what the guys think."

# Ten

## JULIANA

The ride out to the desert seemed only half as long this time, maybe because of the company. Devyn's electric blue Raptor devoured the road smoothly, sending a V-shaped plume of hot dust billowing out behind us. But on the inside, nestled into the air-cooled, racing-style leather seats, we were cool and comfortable.

He spent the ride asking me about New York, and telling me how many things had changed in the time he'd been gone. It occurred to me I'd probably arrived in the City around the same time he'd left it. We'd missed each other by a matter of months; two random ships passing in the night.

*Two ships destined to one day make a baby together.*

Hopefully.

When we arrived at the house the sky was uncharacteristically dark, but the place looked just as warm and inviting as yesterday. I noticed it incorporated seamless indoor and outdoor spaces, including atriums and open-air walkways complete with interior cacti and rock gardens. Flagstone paths connected different parts of the house, whose wood surfaces were warm and polished.

Greeting us at the door was Gage, the spiky blond eye-candy I'd devoured yesterday, and another equally good-looking man I didn't recognize. He had short, dark hair and a strong, masculine jaw covered in light brown stubble. But his smile...

It was his smile that made my stomach do a sexy somersault.

"This is Maverick," Devyn nodded in the direction of his friend. "He might just be the brains of our operation."

At that, Gage laughed merrily. "Him?"

"Well it sure isn't you," Devyn shot back.

"Hell no," Gage agreed, "but *this* guy can't be the brains."

Looking his friend up and down, Gage ran one hand through his ocean of spiked hair, which didn't move an inch.

"Maverick it's not your flying, it's your attitude," he spat, poking his friend in the chest. "The enemy's dangerous, but right now you're worse. Dangerous *and* foolish."

Devyn and Gage spun inside, leaving me alone with the newcomer. He finished greeting me with a handshake, while rolling his eyes at his friends.

"What's that all about?" I chuckled.

"It's a quote from the movie Top Gun," he sighed. "I'm Maverick. Get it?"

"Yeah, I get it," I smiled back. "And hey, with all

that spiked blond hair Gage *does* look like Iceman."

"It's annoying," Maverick apologized. "All these years and they still never let up."

I looked him up and down, from his well-sculpted chest to his gorgeous hazel eyes. Eventually I flicked the pair of mirrored sunglasses that hung from his neck.

"Well these aviators probably don't help," I smiled.

Maverick shrugged. "I'm an aviator."

"Yeah," I laughed, "that's probably not helping either."

I followed him inside, past the kitchen I already knew and through an archway into the back part of the house. The hallway opened into a sprawling living area, complete with state-of-the-art entertainment system, sleek flat-panel televisions, and a breathtaking, fully-stocked bar. Somehow it all blended into the same desert architecture, despite all the bells and whistles.

"You shoot pool?" Gage asked, handing me a cue stick.

"8-ball maybe."

"Good," he nodded approvingly. "You're on my team, then."

He guided me through another arch, where a red felt pool table dominated another giant space. There were arcade games here too; everything from foosball to pinball machines, and a few upright consoles that lined the walls. Most of them I didn't recognize, but I eventually picked out a Ms. Pac-Man cabinet similar to the one I'd dominated for a few years, back in high school.

"Who *are* you guys?" I laughed, as the others chalked up. "I mean, this place is like Neverland for twenty-something alpha males. All it needs is a basketball court, and maybe a hot tub."

"The hot tub's out back," Maverick smiled. "And the basketball court goes in next week."

I couldn't tell if he was kidding about one or the other. Maybe both.

"It had to be expensive as hell," I noted, "dragging all this stuff out into the middle of the Arizona desert."

Devyn racked the balls, using his fingertips to make them tight before lifting the triangle away. He didn't answer one way or the other.

"So what do you guys *do,* anyway?"

I watched silently as Gage leaned out over the pool table, his thick, corded arms stretching the limits of his plain white T-shirt. There was a definite swagger in the way he held himself. A confident, borderline cockiness that stayed just on the right side of charming.

*CRACK!*

The pool balls scattered abruptly in a dozen different directions. I saw at least three balls sink their way into three separate pockets, as the ones still on the table slowly rolled to a halt.

"We're military contractors," Gage said simply, not even looking up. "As for what we do..."

He lined up his next shot, pushed smoothly through

it, and sunk the thirteen ball in the opposite corner. The look on his face was pure satisfaction.

"I guess we're stripes," he smiled.

I glanced to Devyn, who seemed to be watching me more than the pool table. Eventually it was his turn, then mine, then Maverick's as we alternated through the playing order. Everything the guys did seemed to happen effortlessly, and that didn't just apply to the game, either. The way they talked to each other, even the way they *moved* — it was all very practiced, yet very natural. There was a sense of them being a team, of acting together as one. And right away, I knew it went back a lot further than a few games of 8-ball.

Music started up, and somewhere along the line wine got poured. In the meantime, the game progressed. Gage and I were handily ahead of the others, leaving him with enough bragging rights to mercilessly tease his friends. I on the other hand was able to kick back, relax, and enjoy watching the dynamic between them.

At one point Devyn bumped me playfully out of the way to take his shot, then smirked back at me as he leaned on his stick. I noticed the silver chain around his neck was finally outside of his T-shirt. A single dog-tag dangled from the bottom. It wasn't flat, though. It was far from perfect.

No, this one was twisted violently. Maybe even blackened...

"Your turn."

I was still calculating whether I needed the bridge for my next shot, when all of sudden the guys put their sticks down. It happened quickly, silently, without explanation. To my dismay, the trio wandered off in perfect unison, leaving the game room altogether.

*What the—*

I followed after them, still clutching my pool cue. They walked through the next room, through a pair of glass doors, and out onto a giant stone patio that stretched across one side of their entire side yard.

It should've been warm. It wasn't. The sky had gotten even *darker* somehow, though it was still early in the afternoon.

"Guys?"

Their faces were tilted upward, fixated on the sky. They looked like cult members under group hypnosis. Or like experienced ghost hunters, sensing something that only they could see.

And then I *heard* it: a slow, rhythmic thump, somewhere off in the distance. It grew louder, the rhythm faster, as whatever it was drew nearer the house. And then slung low in the sky, I could see it too.

*A helicopter.*

# Eleven

## JULIANA

The military helicopter swung in fast, its twin rotor blades sweeping in opposite directions as it maneuvered our way. Devyn had his hands on his hips. Gage and Maverick were shielding their eyes with their hands, while squinting at the dark shape in the air.

"That one's not based at Luke," I heard Gage say. "It's from Ventura. Or maybe Los Alamitos."

The chopper grew louder, the shape even more distinct as I tracked it through the sky. Not far away, the guys shifted in their positions.

"A Chinook," Maverick said. He clapped Devyn on the shoulder. "This one's all you. One hundred-percent."

If Devyn heard him, he didn't even flinch. He only stared ahead as the helicopter flew straight toward us. Eventually it swung its tail around, hung in the sky for a moment, then flared smoothly before landing. The rotors slowed, the whine of the twin motors dying down as the machine whirred to a halt.

The guys lowered their arms as the chopper's side door rolled open. A man in full uniform hopped out and ran immediately over to Devyn.

"Commander Bishop!"

Devyn returned the man's salute. As I watched, Gage and Maverick exchanged a twenty-dollar bill behind their backs.

"You're to come with me immediately, by order of—"

"Save your breath," Devyn interrupted, turning back toward the house. "Just give me five minutes to gather my gear."

"You have three," the man answered apologetically, before adding the word: "Sir."

It was wildly humbling, staring up at this enormous piece of military hardware. The Chinook was swirled with greys and blacks, presumably painted to blend in with the sea. Only the sea was quite a distance away.

"Storm's coming gentlemen," the man in the uniform said to Gage and Maverick. "Nasty one, by the look of the weather map."

Together the rest of us gazed up at the sky. It wasn't just dark it was also angry now, the clouds swirling violently above us like a stirred-up hornet's nest.

"Dust storm?" I asked.

"Sand," Maverick said. "Big one."

Not even two minutes later Devyn rushed from the house, trailing what looked to be three full backpacks of very heavy, expensive-looking gear. Two other men hopped down to grab his things, then jumped back into the chopper. That left him standing before me, holding my hands in his.

"I'm very sorry about this," he said, his voice genuine. "I would've liked to... well..."

"Another time," I told him. "Another place."

I still had no idea what was going on. Only that he was being called away for something important. So important, in fact, that the US military had flown a Chinook through a sandstorm to pick him up from his house.

Shit, it only made me want him more as the father of my child.

Just *as the father of your child?*

"Hey! Julia!"

I whirled and saw Gage, who was ushering me in the direction the house. The chopper was getting ready to take off.

"Juli*ana*," I corrected him, running back. "Nobody calls me 'Julia'."

"Fine," he winked. "We'll go with Jules, then."

I rolled my eyes, but with the noise of the enormous rotors spinning up it was too late to argue. Besides, the tall blond was far too cute to argue with.

Instead we cowered just inside the doorway, watching the big machine spin itself into the darkening sky. It nosed west, in the direction it had come, then flew off directly into the storm.

"What the hell just happened?" I asked, when it was

relatively quiet again. "Why did they just—"

"We'll tell you *all* about it," Maverick interjected, nodding back inside. His eyes were full of concern as he stared at the sky. "But first you'll need to help us batten down the hatches."

# Twelve

**GAGE**

She worked fast, I'd give her that. Even better, she caught on extremely quickly.

"Hand me that pole?"

The woman who'd shown up asking for Devyn's baby pulled the aluminum pole from the wall mount and handed it to me. I gave it a twist and extended it to its full length, then used it to close the skylights in the ceiling, high overhead.

"Good, now do those two also?"

Juliana took the pole to the other side of the room and followed my lead. She worked smoothly, turning the handle at the bottom that would pull the skylight closed with the hook at the top. By now, the wind had picked up considerably. Already we could hear it whipping through the atrium, which of course we'd sealed first.

Maverick jogged into the room just as Juliana finished. He saw the skylights and nodded his approval.

"Is the back of the house all buttoned up?"

"The sand shields are down, if that's what you're asking," I replied. "This is our first real test of them, so who knows if they'll do the job?"

"They'll definitely do *some* kind of job," my friend replied. "But in a storm like this, who knows?"

We'd spent the first fifteen or twenty minutes dragging out the heavy plastic lluevers and hanging them from the many different mounting hooks. They were designed to seal off the open areas of the house, keeping the dust and sand from blowing in during a situation such as this.

The storm was nasty — maybe even too powerful for the heavy curtain of laminated plastic. By now though, there was nothing more to be done. Either the system would work or it wouldn't.

"What now?" asked Juliana.

Her face was still adorably flushed with the exertion of running around, helping us close all the windows and lock all the doors. Right now her eyes shone with an inner light that made them seem alive. They were extraordinarily beautiful too: the light-brown color of coffee mixed with cream.

"What now?" I repeated, smiling. "Well, there's nothing else to do but wait out the storm."

I lifted the glass of red wine she'd been drinking earlier and handed it back to her. But not before topping it off from the open bottle.

"Oh I wouldn't say there's *nothing* to do," she

smirked devilishly, as she thanked me with an appreciative nod. "But you boys promised to fill me in about what's going on. And that includes telling me why Devyn just got kidnapped by a giant, scary helicopter."

She took a sip, and I watched as the wine slid down her lovely, unblemished throat. Juliana's movements were lithe and feminine as she made her way across the room. Eventually she settled into the couch, crossing one leg sultrily over the other.

"So you're *all* military?" she guessed with a sigh.

Maverick stared back at me for a moment, and eventually nodded.

"Yes," I told her. "We are."

"And you're all Navy, like Devyn?"

"SEALs actually," Maverick replied, without fanfare. "We go all the way back to BUDS school together. Did our Tactical Air Operations down in San Diego, as well."

Juliana's mouth curled a little at the corners. She seemed impressed.

"If the three of you are Navy SEALs, what are you doing all the way out here in the desert?" she asked. "Shouldn't you be traveling the world, completing missions? Inserting yourselves into conflict? Running *toward* danger, instead of—"

"We did all those things already," Maverick pointed out. "For more than ten years now, we've put in our time."

Juliana's eyebrow arched. "So now you're done?"

"Far from it," I told her. "Nowadays we just have a

different... contract."

Maverick crossed the room, then bent to grab a pair of beers from the fridge under the bar. He popped both caps and handed me one.

"You live out here with the caveat you could be called in to work," Juliana guessed.

I nodded and drank. "That's right."

"At any time," she continued, pointing outside. "Like Devyn."

"Just like Devyn, yes," I answered. "Alright it doesn't usually go down like *that*."

Maverick sat down on the opposite couch, cradling his beer in both hands. He was looking our guest over every bit as much as I was. Which if we were being honest, was quite a lot.

"We have different skillsets though," Maverick cut in. "Different jobs. Gage and I here do mostly Reconnaissance, with Special Ops mixed in."

"Special Ops with the occasional support team mission," I added. "Joint SWCC forces. Multiple branches, engaging in—"

"English please?" Juliana smiled sweetly, setting her lips back to her glass.

"Fine," I sighed, watching those lips intently. "Let's just say the Navy puts us down someplace and we take it from there. Night missions, mostly. Hostage recovery, too."

She sipped her wine and nodded slowly, staring back at us. The house creaked as the wind began howling even more loudly.

"And what about my handsome sperm donor?" she asked, nodding in the direction the Chinook had just flown off. "What was so important that they grabbed him so quickly?"

"Devyn's specialization is deep search and rescue," Maverick replied.

She looked confused, so I sank into the seat beside her.

"Ever heard of the Kursk?" I asked.

Her hair danced and shimmered as she shook her pretty head. "No."

"It was a Russian submarine on a naval exercise back in 2000," I explained. "A couple of torpedoes went off in the forward compartment, and the whole thing sank to the floor of the Barents Sea. Russians wouldn't admit they had an emergency for several days. By the time they were finally willing to accept some help, all one-hundred eighteen souls on board had perished."

Her expression was genuine. "That's horrible."

"It really was," I agreed. "Especially since half the crew could've survived. Someone like Devyn would've helped in a situation like that. He's one of the most skilled deep-sea divers in the entire world, much less the US Navy." I glanced at Maverick. "And trust us, he's seen some real crazy shit."

There was a whooshing sound off in the distance, as a rush of sand was flung against the plastic storm barrier. I saw Juliana shiver. The whole house had gone abruptly cold.

"So right now, somewhere out there, someone's in a lot of trouble," she murmured softly.

"Unfortunately yes," I told her. "But with a little luck, and a lot of speed..." I shrugged. "Maybe Devyn works some magic."

Maverick read my mind by grabbing the remote that operated the fireplace and turned it on. The gas ignited in a rush of heat and noise, as a warm blue flame erupted across the stonework insert.

Juliana sipped her wine, then stood and moved instinctively closer to the fire. She turned to look out one of the windows, and into the coming storm.

"I've never seen it so dark for this time of day," she marveled.

"Neither have we," Maverick pointed out.

"I'm not getting out of here for quite a while, am I?"

"Nope," I replied, tipping my beer back. "Looks like you're stuck with us."

Juliana turned her back to the fire, then stuck her ass out, warming it. There was a gleam in her eye though. A definite sense of satisfaction at being where she was, safe inside with us, with a glass of wine in her hand.

"Or maybe," she suggested coyly, still bent sexily at the waist. "You boys are stuck with *me*."

# Thirteen

## JULIANA

The first hour with the boys had been informative, the second one relaxing. By now though, three and a half glasses of wine into our killer sandstorm, I was feeling pretty damned good.

"Show me that one."

Maverick pointed to where one of my tattoos peeked out from my left upper arm. I rolled it up obligingly and sauntered over to him.

"That's a Valkyrie, isn't it?"

I stared down into his handsome, attentive face and gave him an impressed nod. "It sure is."

The tattoo was one of my favorites: a black-and-grey portrait of a fierce viking woman in a winged helmet, soaring through the sky. Interlaced throughout, and spreading down my arm, was the word 'Invincible.'

"Alright, let's hear it," smiled Gage.

"Hear what?"

"The story of that tattoo."

I strutted over to the mantle, then used Maverick's phone to change the song again. Something soft and melodic began playing — one of my favorites from Natalie Imbruglia. So far I'd been in charge of the music all night, and the guys hadn't seemed to mind.

"Not much of a story," I said, finally turning to face them again. "I turned twenty-nine a few months back. Went through a little bit of a mid-life crisis."

"You Jules?" Gage asked. "Seriously?"

I shook off his playful use of my nickname. "Why, does that surprise you?"

The blond SEAL sent up a shrug of his massive shoulders. "The way you carry yourself, I guess I just can't see you giving in to a crisis."

I smiled at him for a few moments, letting my body sway slowly to the rhythm of the song. It was a damned good song. One of my favorites.

"Who said I gave in to it?" I replied finally. I tapped the Valkyrie. "This felt more like... embracing it."

"Is that your only tattoo?" asked Maverick.

My eyes shifted his way, enjoying their view of the ripped, beautiful body so casually sprawled out over the couch. Without even thinking, I winked at him.

"Maybe."

The storm had come and raged and gone, but the memories of it still lingered in my mind. The whole thing had been violent. Almost vengeful. Yet with the room warmed by the fireplace and the music playing in the background, I'd been very comfortable.

More than comfortable actually, surrounded by these two hunky, flirty saviors who kept plying me with wine.

In all honesty I'd been drinking them in every bit as much as they had me; the guys were beyond gorgeous, and they both turned out to be great company. The flirting and innuendo was something I'd urged on throughout the evening, even initiating it at times.

I kept reminding myself I should've felt bad for still being here, or somehow even guilty. Fortunately I felt neither of those things.

In fact, maybe even just the opposite.

"Truth," Gage said abruptly.

I turned to face him. "Go on."

It was a little game we'd started before the storm even hit; sort of like truth or dare, only there were no dares. At least not yet, anyway. We'd used the game to break the ice. To learn about each other in a no-bullshit, can't-lie environment.

"Did your little mid-life crisis have anything to do with you wanting a baby?"

I paused, taking an emboldening sip of my wine. Answers sprung quickly to mind, and half of them were already lies. All of them were defensive.

"Yes," I said finally, surprising myself with the stark truth of my answer. "It did."

The song changed to another on the same album. Still dancing with my shoes off, I glided a little closer to the fire.

"That's understandable," Maverick allowed.

"You boys really think so?" I challenged. "You don't think it's silly, or even foolish, to bring a life into this crazy world? At least not without the benefit of two solid parents, or without—"

"No," Gage said abruptly, standing up. "Actually, we don't."

He looked at me with those big blue eyes, and his expression softened. There was empathy there. Empathy and understanding.

"You need to realize we've been out of the loop for the past decade," he said gently. "None of us have had time to give proper attention to our existing families, much less think about starting our own."

"But you have?" I asked, actually surprised.

The two men glanced at each other — something they did a lot — and shrugged in unison.

"Recently, sure," said Maverick simply. "It's not like the thought hasn't crossed our mind."

"Fine then, truth," I said, knowing they both had to answer. Gage smirked.

"Go for it."

"Would it make either of you jealous if Devyn got me pregnant?"

They took surprisingly long to answer. For a few

long seconds, I didn't think they would.

"No, not really," Maverick eventually said. "You're not looking for a father, you're looking for a *donor*. That's different."

Gage scratched at his chin as he nodded his agreement. "It wouldn't be like he had a child, except biologically," he answered. "So there really wouldn't be anything to be jealous of."

The guys were on their feet now, and together they came over by the fire. They smelled absolutely incredible — all musky and salty and faintly of sweat, the way men always should. As they sipped the last of their beers, I became hyperaware of the proximity of their bodies in relation to mine.

"Why no girlfriends?" I asked abruptly.

Together they shook their heads. "No time."

"That can't be true," I frowned. "Obviously you've got time. I mean you're *here*, aren't you?"

"For now," Maverick acknowledged.

"But—"

"Ever try explaining to your girlfriend that you got called away for three, six, nine months at a clip?" Gage murmured. "Not be able to contact her for weeks at a time, and yet somehow expect her to be there waiting for you when you got back?"

I frowned again, imagining the scenario. In the meantime, every nerve ending in my body seemed to be coming alive.

"Sounds lonely," I said at last.

"It *is* lonely," Maverick answered. "Especially the coming home alone part."

We stared into the fire some more, letting the heat absorb into our bodies. I felt warm. Cozy. Eventually the boys emptied their bottles and set them down on the mantle.

"What about you?" asked Gage. "Why haven't you been scooped up by some savvy, New York City–"

"Same reason as the two of you," I cut him off. "There's just... no time."

I felt a tingle as an arm slid around me, and a hand clasped mine. Before I knew it I was swaying to the music again, only this time Gage was leading.

"No time, huh?" he murmured, his nose buried in my hair.

The music was perfect. The feel of him against me, even more so.

"No," I practically choked. "None."

I'd surrendered to the enjoyment of dancing with him when another body slid up behind me, pressing softly against mine. Maverick's chin was over my shoulder, his stubble tickling the skin there. His lips were mere inches from my ear.

"So you know something about loneliness yourself, then?"

I shivered involuntarily as we swayed in unison, the three of us, gliding gently back and forth through the living room. I was sandwiched between them now. Pressed firmly and quite willingly against Gage's beautiful chest, as Maverick folded his body around me from behind.

"Yes," I said at last. "Loneliness and I go *way* back."

Maverick's stubble disappeared, replaced by a pair of warm lips on my neck. He kissed me hotly, wetly from behind. My body exploded with happiness, even as a tiny voice screamed in the back of my mind.

*Juliana!*

There was no time to think, no time to protest. Not that I could've anyway. Especially not when a second pair of lips closed over my own, and Gage's hot tongue pushed its way into my mouth...

*Holy fuck!*

That tongue swirled and played, gliding effortlessly and wonderfully against mine. In no time at all, I was kissing him back. Rolling my breathless mouth against his, as I wrapped my hands around his two big upper arms and pulled his body even tighter against mine.

*Oh my GOD.*

A distinct bulge had formed against the small of my back, and in an instant I knew what it was. Maverick's hands had slid around me from behind. They cupped my breasts, lifting them gently. Causing me to gasp into Gage's sweet, open mouth, as Maverick's fingers spread and his thumbs dragged tight circles over my shirt, right around the edges of my areolae.

I sighed, squirming backward against something I hadn't had in so very long. I used one hand to squeeze Gage's gorgeous bicep, marveling at its hardness, while reaching back with my other hand to pull Maverick against me.

*Yes...*

My hand clawed a very tight, extremely well-formed ass. My fingers dug in...

*Is this what you really want?*

Shit, seriously? I'd been unwillingly celibate for what seemed like forever! Totally and completely without release, except for whatever limited pleasure I managed to grant myself a few nights per week before bed.

Right now I was stuck in Arizona of all places, on a now-failed mission. Stranded by a violent storm. Forced to hole up in some beautiful yet cozy house in the middle of the desert, with two hot Navy SEALs and a bottle of wine to keep me company.

Two SEALs who were now kissing me into a wet, wonderful oblivion... while their four big hands began roaming my eager body.

*Fuuuuuck...*

"Please tell me you've got a bed big enough for this?" I murmured, pushing back to look them both in the eye.

My hands wandered upward, to the backs of their warm, manly necks. Extending my fingers, I sifted my painted fingertips sensuously and lovingly into their hair.

"Hmmm..." Maverick chuckled softly. His eyes were half-lidded as he looked down at me. His voice was breathless, and choked with lust.

Gage's wicked grin however, was a mile wide.

"Come upstairs and find out," the blond grunted, hoisting me easily over one boulder-like shoulder.

# Fourteen

## JULIANA

The room at the top of the stairs was warm and dim and wholly inviting, the king-sized bed covered with a white, pillowy comforter made of the softest down.

I didn't find out for several minutes, though. And that's because the boys stood me up to disrobe me, kissing me all over as they slowly peeled the clothes from my shivering, shuddering body. I arched my back as my shirt hit the floor, and two warm mouths closed over my exposed breasts. They fed on me for a long time, feeling me all over, taking turns piercing the thin, delicate waistband of my satin thong, which by now was so soaked through you could've wrung it out like a washcloth.

*Holy.*

*Fucking.*

*Shit.*

There was nothing I wouldn't do for them. I knew that the instant Gabe rolled my panties down over my thighs, pausing only to bury his beautiful face between my legs and inhale deeply.

"Get her on the bed."

It happened without even a sense of movement, almost without motion. One second I was standing there shaking with lust, clutching Maverick against my chest, and the next I'd been lifted and somehow gently deposited right in the center of the enormous bed, my back feeling momentarily cool against the linens.

I wanted to close my eyes. To just lay back and enjoy the epic adventure that was about to happen. But even more, I wanted to *see*. I needed to witness every last detail of this night because I might never get another one, not like this.

*Two guys, plus me.*

It was a fantasy. A crazy, ridiculous dream I'd always wondered about, and whether or not it could ever happen. There were times throughout my adult life when I thought I could do it, but there were too many rules I'd already set in my head. For example, it couldn't be anyone I knew. No friends, or ex-boyfriends even. It had to be strangers for it to work. But not *total* strangers either.

No, I needed two men I trusted enough to be comfortable with. Two men who would take the reins, yes, but still leave me with some semblance of control. They needed to be strong, gorgeous, powerful. The type of men who'd plunder me in all the ways I'd ever dreamed, while giving me the opportunity to use them, as well.

It had to happen someplace far away, where no one would ever know me. With lovers that were discreet enough that I could totally let go, mentally and physically, and never have to worry what someone else thought of me when the fantasy was ultimately fulfilled.

And now somehow here I was with all the planets aligned; stuck in the perfect place at the perfect time. I sat up on my elbows, watching as two of the most ripped, beautiful men I'd ever seen stripped their clothes off on either side of me. They did it slowly, sensually, exposing every inch of their skin. Allowing me the enjoyment of it as their boxers dropped and two thick stranger's cocks sprang into full, glorious view.

*Wow...*

Their eyes remained locked on my naked body as they approached the bed. I let out a sharp gasp as they joined me on the soft surface of the down comforter, their hands sliding back to my thighs and spreading them wide.

*Oh WOW.*

Gage pushed his way between my legs, then lowered his mouth to kiss my stomach. He dragged his hot tongue around the flat of my belly, tracing my navel as his lips continued planting softer and softer kisses, all the way down to my pubis.

"Hey..."

I turned and there was Maverick, cradling my face in one big hand. His strong jawline was sexy as all hell. His stubbled face, impossibly handsome.

"You good?"

I nodded dreamily and he lowered his mouth over mine, drinking deeply from my lips as he inhaled my every heated breath. Over and over he kissed me, letting the palm of his other hand glide down over my chest, my breasts, my quivering stomach. He didn't stop until he reached the very top of my honey-coated mound, where two thick fingers brushed the hood of my clit with an electric jolt.

*Ohhhhh...*

And then he was rubbing me. Kissing me. Devouring my mouth with his, as his friend's hands pushed my legs even further apart. Gage's tongue had been lightly tracing the insides of my thighs. He buried that tongue inside me now, causing me to cry out in happiness and wonderment and near-instant ecstasy.

*Oh my—*

It was wholly overwhelming, being eaten and kissed at the same time. I forced myself to relax and let my body thrash happily against Gage's questing tongue, all while clinging onto Maverick for dear life. I kissed him back with total wanton abandon, letting him know how much I wanted and needed what was about to happen. Down below, his fingers parted me like a pretty pink flower. Working in tandem, it gave his friend even greater access to the warm, wet world between my legs.

"MMMmmmMMMmmm..."

I let out a shuddering moan, not even caring what I sounded like. All that mattered were these two hot mouths, working their magic. Another pair of fingers — this time belonging to Gage — slipped achingly deep inside me, right alongside his tongue. They drove in and out with a slick, effortless rhythm, causing me to throw back my head as they curled delicately into my G-spot.

*FUCK!*

I was already close to coming. Unexpectedly close to just giving myself over, and putting an end to the building torment of my first real orgasm in so many long months.

"Do it."

Maverick smiled against my lips, his hazel eyes flaring wide as he assessed my dilemma. He knew exactly what was happening. With his fingers spread wide, pulsing against my lower belly, he could sense how close I was.

"It's okay," he kissed me. "Just let it go."

Our eyes locked, and for a glorious few seconds we forged a bond so raw, so intimate, it was like our souls brushed against one another's. My whole body stiffened at once. My mouth opened in a perfect 'O', at the same moment my toes curled.

And then I was screaming like a banshee, coming and creaming around Gage's talented mouth and thrusting fingers.

*Fuccccccccccccck!*

My orgasm was one for the record books, and not just because it had been so long. The intensity was magnified by where I was, who I was with, and of course, what I was doing. It freed me to let completely loose, flooding Gage's tongue with a hot splash of sweet nectar as I grabbed his head with both hands and convulsed, over and over again, against his gorgeous blond face.

It was life. Love. Heaven and earth. Anything and everything all at once, wrapped up in the pure, brilliant light of white-hot ecstasy. I cried and thrashed and screamed against the softness of the cozy bed, while Gage kept devouring me and Maverick kept fingering me, and both men kept holding me down. Gage's own fingers eventually left my quivering channel, and in a moment of heat he pushed them past my eager lips so I could taste myself as well.

*Ohhhh...*

They gave me the freedom of my afterglow, kissing and caressing me softly as I came down from cloud nine. But there was so much lust in their eyes. A pent-up, almost animalistic arousal in the way they were looking at me now, lying on either side of me upon the sex-soaked sheets.

I reached down to stroke them for the first time, wrapping my fists around what felt to be double-sized thickness. They felt utterly spectacular. These were big men, with big, powerful bodies. It only stood to reason that they'd be big where it truly mattered.

"Pick one," Gage chuckled, nuzzling my ear.

I gave him a squeeze with my fist, then did the same to his friend. Stroking them up and down, I said a silent prayer of thanks to whomever was listening.

"Both," I sighed contentedly, spreading my legs.

# Fifteen

## MAVERICK

She was perfect in every way. Perfect face, perfect ass. Perfectly amazing attitude too, as she chuckled coyly and spread her incredible thighs for both me and my friend.

*Me* and *my friend...*

It was unbelievable that we were doing this, especially since it was the one thing we'd never done. Gage and I had shared so much over the course of our lives. Devyn, too. We'd crawled through frozen muck and lay against each other for body heat in the dankness of the most pitch-black cave. For five days we'd suffered malaria in the jungles of Panama, delirious to the point of madness, while sharing a single canteen of water.

Yet at the same time, it was somehow totally believable, too. Not just because the naked, exotic woman spread across our bed was absolutely gorgeous, but because we'd always acted as a team, working together on so many, many things.

In that respect, teaming up on *her* seemed the natural thing to do.

I moved before Gage did, grabbing one pretty ankle and gliding between her outstretched legs. Juliana was in heat, her chest still heaving from the enormity of her climax. Her lips were full, her face flush and beautiful. The air in the bedroom was absolutely pregnant with the delicious scent of her.

"Go easy on me," she whispered, as I dragged the head of my manhood thorough her warm, wet folds. "Please."

"Easy?" I scoffed. "You really want *easy?*"

"At first, yes," she smirked back. "It's uhhh... been a while."

I pushed forward, and we both watched as I parted her like a flower. As my first couple of inches disappeared inside her, she bit her lip.

"You're *big*, too," she breathed. "And I'm little. And it doesn't help that—"

Her sentence ended in a gasp as I shifted forward, burying myself even further inside. God, she felt so good! Snug and slick and indescribably hot, especially with those legs wrapping themselves around my ribs like they had a life of their own.

"Damn..." she swore, but it was a good swear. "This... this is—"

I drove into her slowly but smoothly, guiding her thighs upward and over my shoulders. Eventually I bottomed out. Our eyes met, and a connection was made: we were lovers now, wholly and irrevocably. Juliana was wrapped tightly around my throbbing shaft, which was buried so wonderfully deep inside her.

"Oh my *God,* Maverick."

I could tell she'd take some getting used to, or at least I would. For that reason I went slowly, sawing back and forth with long, deep strokes. It took every last ounce of willpower to stay in control, but somehow I forced myself to keep things rhythmic, when all I *really* wanted to do was just wrap my arms tightly around those two supple thighs and start plowing away toward sweet oblivion.

I leaned down to kiss her, crushing her beautiful tits against my chest. Juliana's mouth was warm and willing. I could sense her eagerness, taste her sweetness on her own tongue. And then that mouth was pulled away, as Gage guided her back in his direction. We took turns on her, passing those lips back and forth between us. Kissing her through her moans and whimpers, as I fucked her deeply, slowly, her body bouncing gently between us in perfect, sensual rhythm.

*What the hell are we doing?*

There were probably a thousand reasons why the three of us shouldn't be up here right now — in Devyn's bed of all places! At the moment though, I couldn't think of a single one. The beautiful woman screwing down on me right now wanted this every bit as much as we did, and possibly even more. There was hunger in her eyes. A heated desperation in the way she kept grasping our arms, our legs, our shoulders...

No, Juliana needed this too, and in all the same perverse, carnal ways that Gage and I did. It had happened too naturally, too organically to be wrong. The mutual intensity of what we were doing was inevitable.

"Mmmm..."

I'd rocked back on my legs to plow her more efficiently, driving myself faster and deeper on every thrust. When I looked down again, Juliana's head was lolled to one side. She had her lips locked around Gage's shaft and was blowing him, and the sight of that little act somehow made me even *more* excited.

*Wow, just look at her...*

She had one hand wrapped around him, and Gage had five thick fingers entangled in her hair. They moved in unison, with Juliana guiding him deep down her beautiful throat. Her head bobbed eagerly up and down in rhythm to my thrusts, hypnotizing me in ways that left me dazed and awestruck.

*Unreal!*

It was like watching a live sex show. Witnessing something hot and forbidden and taboo, yet being *involved* in that something, too. Juliana rolled sideways, and I scissored one sexy leg and kept pumping away at her. She propped herself up on an elbow and continued going down on my friend, while Gage sifted her hair back so we could both get a good look at the amazingly hot view.

*Devyn.*

The third member of our trio jumped into my head, but only for a moment. There was no guilt, no worry on my part. I knew if our friend hadn't been called away he'd be exactly where I was, buried balls-deep inside this beautiful, writhing creature. Devyn was our comrade, our brother-in-arms. We'd shared everything and always would; just the three of us, together against the world.

Even something like this — as crazy as it seemed — would be no exception.

My arousal peaking, I became fixated on Juliana's perfect, bouncing ass. She was so tight around me now, and the friction was driving me crazy. I wanted so very badly to bury my hands just above that ass, right in the curve of her feminine hips. To dig my fingers into that warm, supple flesh, plowing away without a care in the world until I finally exploded, deep, deep inside her.

"Switch."

Gage's voice was music to my ears. If he hadn't said anything, who *knows* what would've happened.

# Sixteen

## JULIANA

I was floating in the delirium of being taken from both ends. Drunk from the sheer wonderment of having two men plunder my body at once, and not just two ordinary men either, but two hard-bodied Navy SEALs who were in peak physical and cardiovascular shape.

"Switch."

The word itself felt deliciously dirty, especially in the context it was being used. It meant that these men would trade places. That the one I'd just been so expertly licking and sucking would crawl around behind me, only to lift my hips with his strong hands and glide right back into the warm, wet place his friend had just exited.

*YES.*

As filthy as it all sounded, I couldn't fucking wait.

To call the experience incredible felt like a gross understatement, yet that's exactly what it was. I'd been double-kissed into a literal puddle of wetness. Fingered and devoured and now fucked so deeply and beautifully I'd all but screwed my fists into the comforter until it exploded into a pile of feathers.

I'd been spitroasted back and forth between two hard bodies, as my fingertips happily roamed every breathtaking ridge and muscle. Both Gage and Maverick were weapons built for combat, each shaped to form and honed to a razor-sharp edge. But they were also different weapons, in different styles. Maverick was shorter and broader, his chest and shoulders swollen with raw strength and power. Gage on the other hand was tall and imposing, with long, well-formed arms that sported granite-like biceps and triceps.

Together they worked as a team, delivering pleasure from either end of my body. I couldn't spread my legs wide enough. I couldn't get them far enough down my throat, or deep enough inside me…

"Fuuuck."

Gage swore the word like a curse, as he guided himself into me from behind. My God, he felt *big!* Maybe even thicker than Maverick, and that was really saying something.

"Oh, man. She's so fucking *warm.*"

I let out a shuddering gasp as he filled me from within, leaning over my back to let the full weight of his body drive himself all the way home. He paused inside me for a second, enjoying the moment. Wrapping an arm around my waist for leverage, he guided my head back with his other hand so he could plant his mouth over mine.

*Mmmmm… fuck yes.*

I kissed him back eagerly, tasting myself on his tongue. Savoring the pleasure of having him so deep inside me, while still reveling in the feel of his mouth on mine. He was fucking me differently from Maverick, but in many ways still the same. Later on it would be fun to focus on the comparison. But now...

Right now I was reaching for Maverick, to give him some of what his friend had received earlier. I made eye-contact as I licked up and down his glistening shaft, moaning as Gage drove into me. He had a way of grinding his hips in a tight, beautiful circle at the end of every thrust, and I loved the way his hands felt on my ass.

*So strong. So commanding.*

Again and again they switched, each man eagerly taking his place back between my thighs. They flipped me onto my back. Rolled me onto my stomach. One man took my ankles, spreading my legs wide, bracing me against his hard body so the other could have the leverage to screw me physically and emotionally senseless.

And thankfully, that happened over, and over, and *over* again.

I was bent over the bed and drilled hard from behind. Shoved against the nearest wall and taken while standing up, face to face, kissing and caressing and moaning the whole time.

At one point Gage lifted me from behind, sliding his long arms beneath my knees and holding me suspended in the air against his chest. I was spread eagle. Completely helpless and open...

"Fuck her."

He grunted the words at Maverick, who walked straight over and guided himself inside me. It was the perfect height. The most incredible position imaginable. I was held utterly weightless, back arched, thighs open as Maverick plunged into me again and again, screwing me hard and fast in front while Gage chewed my shoulder from behind. He whispered things into my ear while his friend fucked me. Nasty things. Dirty things. But also, unimaginably hot things that they planned to do to me, that melted me on the spot.

He told me how many times they were going to take me tonight, and how they planned on going until I passed out from pleasure. Nestled between them, with one hard body in front and behind, I exploded again. My climax was hard, almost violent in its intensity, surging and churning around the strong, thrusting cock buried so deeply against my womb. My orgasm must have triggered his, because suddenly Maverick was grunting and groaning and clenching me tightly against his fully-embedded member.

"NNNNGHHH..."

The noise he made was sexy, beautiful, animalistic. He lowered his face and I clenched him between my breasts as he pumped me full, his shaft pulsing and twitching inside me as it unloaded every last ounce of his hot, life-giving seed.

*HOLY SHIT, Juliana!*

This incredible, gorgeous man had just come inside me. So much so that I could feel it running out of me, down the insides of my thighs. The whole thing was crazy, spreading my legs for these guys I barely knew! Giving myself completely over to them in any way they wanted, to do with my body whatever they chose.

Beneath all the false outrage however, I knew I *loved* it. I sure as hell loved fucking them. I loved the way they took charge of me, moving wordlessly and in tandem. I imagined it was like a mission for them, one they took on together. There was a measure of communication that existed silently between these men, built by long years of training together and combat and God only knew what else.

Eventually Maverick withdrew, and the three of us looked down on his handiwork. I was still being held by Gage. The muscles of his arms were stretched deliciously tight, until he dumped me back on the bed.

"C'mere."

I extended both arms, wriggling my fingers and spreading my legs even further to invite him in. I didn't have to wait long. The tall SEAL pounced on me in an instant, burying himself all the way to the hilt in my warm, come-soaked essence.

*You're out of your fucking mind.*

Yeah, maybe. Or maybe I was just cashing in on a lifelong fantasy, while putting an end to an epic dry spell at the same time. What was it that Aric had said about buttering my biscuit? Opening the Gates to Mordor?

Hell, I'd just about blown the Gates clean off.

# Seventeen

## JULIANA

"Here, finish this."

Maverick's arm muscles flexed beneath his tan skin as he scraped the rest of the eggs onto my plate. My eyes couldn't help but follow his ass on the way to the sink. The perfect bubble shape shifted beneath his thin mesh shorts, as he ran a mixture of soap and hot water into the pan.

I couldn't believe it was the same ass I'd clenched so tightly in both hands, with his body buried between my legs. There were probably fingernail marks on that ass right now, put there by me. Before I left this place, I was determined to find out.

"And the government really puts you up here," I continued, "as part of your contract?"

Gage shook his head over his coffee. "We put ourselves up," he corrected me. "Uncle Sam subsidizes us in certain ways, as part of our agreement. But this is our place. Our stuff."

"Most of it, anyway," Maverick called back.

I watched him glance over his shoulder, and out through the window. Fifty yards from the house was a massive, familiar-looking shape covered in a sand-colored tarp. I'd noticed Maverick checking it last night, just before the storm.

"That's a helicopter, isn't it?"

He turned and leaned back against the counter, smiling. "Not bad."

"Technically it's an attack helicopter," Gage said, setting his mug down. Casually he shoved another piece of bacon into his mouth. "As long as we're being honest."

"You have an *attack* helicopter parked outside?" I swore.

"An Aérospatiale Gazelle, yeah," said Maverick, his expression turning quickly to one of deep pride. "Decommissioned, of course. It's French."

"I didn't even know you could own a decommissioned attack helicopter."

"Well, *technically* you can't," he smirked. "But it's all part of our contract."

I shook my head in awe. Not just at everything around me, but at all the incredible things they'd told me so far. In truth, it had been quite a morning. Starting with me being woken up for a fourth or maybe even a fifth round of lovemaking, depending upon how you counted it.

"This is turning out to be *some* contract," I said, as I finished my eggs. "I'm gonna need to hear more about it."

The guys glanced at each other, then back at me.

"Sorry, no can do."

I chuckled. "Really?"

"Seriously," Maverick confirmed. "You already know more than anyone else. If we told you any more, we'd have to —"

"Kill me and bury me in the desert?"

I smiled at my own joke, while pointing outside with my fork. Through the window, past the outer wall of their apparently militarized compound, the desert stretched endlessly to the distant horizon.

"I was going to say get you drunk enough to forget everything we told you," said Maverick. "Much less messy, plus we don't have to dig."

"Oh you boys can *dig*," I said, and I wasn't exactly talking about shovels. "Believe me."

"Have you *tried* digging out there?" Gage griped. "It's not pure sand like in the movies, it's solid calcium carbonite. You'll break your wrists."

He pushed his plate away and leaned back, folding his long arms behind his blond head. They were the same powerful arms that had held me weightless, while his friend drilled me to a life-changing climax. The same arms that had wrapped around me in the wee hours of the morning, as I woke sleepily to the feel of him nudging his way between my legs, right before his rock-hard thickness glided inside me again.

"Anyway, we're often required to be on different bases

for various things," said Maverick. "So... attack helicopter."

"Plus that thing gets into town in twenty-four minutes, flat," added Gage. "Very useful for when we run out of milk."

"Sure," I chuckled. "If you want to spend eight-hundred dollars in fuel just to pick up milk."

Maverick nodded approvingly. "Actually you're not that far off."

I shifted sideways and crossed my legs. The pleasant soreness between them reminded me of a night well-spent.

"No, burying your cute little ass in the desert is completely off the table," said Gage, sliding out from his seat. Circling behind me, he leaned down and kissed my neck, just below my ear. My entire body erupted in instant goosebumps.

"Besides," he whispered. "We can think of *much* better things to do with your body..."

# Eighteen

## JULIANA

"And I'm telling you, I've got it all under control. I'm ordering you to stay where you are and enjoy."

Aric's voice was stern and authoritative, even if it wasn't one-hundred percent convincing. Not that he could order me around, anyway. But it was amusing to hear him try.

"And what am I enjoying, exactly?" I asked.

I could envision Aric's smirk in my mind, even if I couldn't see it. "You know. Whatever his name happens to be."

Part of me wanted to growl into the phone. An even larger part, surprisingly enough, wanted to totally blow his mind by giving him two names instead of one.

With my silence, I did neither.

"When's the last time you took an actual vacation?" he demanded for the third time.

"This *isn't* a vacation," I protested again.

"I'm pretty sure it was that time you went to Vale," my assistant pressed. "You fought with what's-his-name and left after just two days. If I remember the expense logs correctly, you booked a three-thousand dollar flight home."

I frowned bitterly, remembering how angry I'd been. Brandon — the man-child I'd been dating at the time — had been a complete and total jealous asshole. Our trip to Colorado, which I'd been looking forward to for months, had been over before it even began.

"Look, you're obviously having fun," Aric pointed out. "I know you are. If you weren't, you'd already be home by now."

*Fun.* It wasn't exactly the word I'd use, but it was pretty damned close. Maverick and Gage had driven me back to The Renaissance the day after the storm, where they'd ravaged me again before leaving me a sopping wet mess in the center of my hotel bed. I'd lay there reeling for a while, enjoying the breathless thrill of being so thoroughly and doubly taken while staring up at the ceiling. Wondering whether or not I had time for a bite to eat before dropping off my rental on the way to the airport, for my trip back to New York.

Only I hadn't gone to the airport.

I hadn't dropped off the rental either.

Instead I'd extended my stay, added a few days to my rental car, then took the longest, hottest, most baptismal shower of my entire life. From there I ate dinner at the hotel, caught up on phone calls and emails, and generally tied up any loose ends back at the agency.

Finally, with nothing left to do, I'd driven all the way back out to the guys' house and knocked on their door again.

*Fuck yeah you did.*

It was shameless and I knew it was shameless, but Maverick and Gage had been thrilled to see me just the same. They'd welcomed me back with open arms, and I'd taken them into their respective bedrooms and done everything in the world to show them just how happy I was to be there.

That was four *days* ago. And here I still was.

"Juliana?"

Aric's deep, baritone voice snapped me back to reality. I'd spent the better part of a sex-soaked week in a haze of euphoria, running half-naked around this beautiful house in the desert, being passed back and forth between two sizzling hot military men. They'd done me in just about every room, spreading me over almost every surface. And I'd been brazen about taking them, too. I'd been every bit as depraved and audacious in my own wants, needs, and desires...

"Day after tomorrow," I blurted finally. "I'll be home the day after tomorrow."

I heard the familiar sound of Aric's glasses as they clattered to the surface of his glass desk. It was eleven o'clock in New York, and he was still at the office. I could visualize him rubbing his tired eyes.

"That's fine," he said eventually. "But seriously, take as much time as you like."

"Why, so you can take over my company while I'm gone?" I chided him.

"Maybe," he allowed. "Although that might take a little more than a single week."

"You do the math on that already?"

Two and half thousand miles away, my assistant chuckled evilly.

Just then Gage walked in, striding through an archway off to my left. He was gloriously shirtless. His whole body glistened with the sweat of his afternoon workout, and now it gleamed in the afternoon sun.

He saw me bent casually over one of the little tables in the foyer, pen and paper in hand, and grinned.

"Aric, listen," I said into the phone. "Stay on top of things. And when I get back there—"

Two hands went to my hips. They hooked themselves through the waistband of my shorts and shimmied them downward.

"I— uhh..."

My body shuddered excitedly as Gage folded around me from behind. He took his own shorts down, and a moment later I felt something warm, thick, and extremely familiar pressed against my ass.

"I'm pretty sure I... well... I..."

I bit my lip with a gentle huff, as my G-string was pulled to one side. There was a satisfying SNAP as Gage stretched it out over my left cheek and let go of it like a rubber band.

"You'll what?" Aric asked, confused.

My lover spread my rear end apart with one big

hand, while using the other to drag himself up and down through my now dripping furrow. I was wet all the time strutting around this place. And with good reason.

"Never mind," I answered, still biting my lip in anticipation of the first thrust. "I guess I really just wanted to say... thanks."

"You're thanking me?" Aric chuckled. "Seriously?"

"Yes, why?"

"Because I can count on one hand the number of times you've thanked me, completely unprovoked, just for doing my—"

Aric's voice faded into obscurity, as Gage pushed his raging hard-on slowly into my pussy. My eyelids went suddenly heavy. My knees went weak. The familiar pleasure was so overwhelming, I found myself gripping the table for support.

"Aric..."

"Yes my captain?"

"I—I have to go."

I pressed the red button to hang up twice, then double-checked it anyway. When I was satisfied my assistant wouldn't be getting an impromptu speakerphone sex show, I turned to look over my shoulder.

"You're bad, you know that?" I scolded Gage. "Really bad."

"Oh yeah?" he replied, amused. He bored down harder, impaling me with long, deep strokes. "Well your hips are telling me a different story."

"But I *just* showered," I lamented, albeit halfheartedly.

"I can tell. Your hair smells like strawberries."

His hands went to my breasts, his fingers swirling gratifyingly beneath my shirt. I arched my back as he pulled me into him, fucking me in a near standing-up position that gave him full, unfettered control.

"*Seriously?*"

We both whirled to find Maverick standing in the opposite doorway. He had a dish towel in his hands. I could see red sauce splattered across it.

"I thought we were waiting until after dinner?"

I shrugged helplessly, while still screwing back against his friend. Gage just laughed.

"You *do* know she just showered, right?" said Maverick.

"Yeah, well she's gonna have to shower again, that's all," said Gage. "So why don't you put dinner on hold and help out?"

Maverick faked a frown while pursing his lips. His lust-fueled eyes though, were still locked on my churning, writhing body. He was getting off on watching. More so each time we'd done this.

And we'd done it a *lot*.

Eventually he walked over, gingerly taking my face in his hands. The kiss he bent to deliver was slow and hot. Thunderously beautiful. Staring deep into my eyes, just the touch of his fingertips against my cheek brought every one of my senses to stark, tingling life.

"Fine then," he sighed, slinging the towel over one big shoulder. He nodded in the direction of the living area. "If we're going to make a big mess of her right now, at least bring her over to the couch."

# Nineteen

## JULIANA

The building, the elevator, the glass-walled offices were all exactly the same. It was like I'd never left. Like I'd gone down to the street for coffee, or a hot truffle cheddar pretzel from Sigmund's Pretzel Cart, instead of a week-long vacation at a sexual amusement park with two *very* giving hosts.

In other ways though, it was like I'd been gone forever.

"Welcome back boss."

One of my new graphic artists nodded cheerfully as he passed — Jonathan, I think his name was. With the recent explosion of hiring it was difficult to remember. I was greeted by a half dozen more employees on the way to my office, but before arriving there I located Aric through the glass-walled maze. I detoured to intercept him, feeling like a hamster making its way through a Habitrail. God, these walls were a blessing and a curse.

"Well take a look at you!"

Aric loosened his tie as he stared down through his glasses, sizing me up from head to toe. He must've liked what he saw, because his eyebrows stayed up and his smile widened.

"Damn girl, you got some serious sun."

"Yeah," I agreed. "The desert tends to do that to you."

He offered me a water bottle from one of the mini-fridges located throughout the office. "The desert, huh?"

"Mmm-hmm."

"You wanna tell me whereabouts in the desert you went?" he smirked. "Or were you on some mystery vision quest to discover your true self that you can't speak about?"

I took a long pull of ice-cold water, then screwed the cap back on the bottle.

"No mystery. No vision quest."

"A sweat tent then?"

"Ugh."

"Stargazing?"

I shook my head in awe and agreement. "No shit. The desert has some *serious* stars."

"Yeah well there's no light pollution," Aric went on. "I went to a wedding once, outside of Sedona. Dune buggies out to the middle of a dry lake bed in the desert. After the ceremony the sun went down, and the sky exploded with like a billion stars." He let out a long, wistful sigh. "Second most beautiful thing I've ever seen."

"Oh yeah?" I challenged. "What's the first?"

Aric's whole smile changed. "Wouldn't *you* like to know."

I let him have his secrets as we walked back to my office together. God knew I sure as hell had mine. Aric didn't press for more details of my trip, and I didn't offer any. Since arriving home yesterday I'd dropped my bags to the floor, fallen into my bed, and slept like the dead for a good ten or eleven hours straight.

It was strange, coming home to an empty apartment. For the first time in a week I was utterly and completely alone. There was no chance of being walked in on, swept up by a pair of strong arms, or made love to. There were no friendly voices in the kitchen. No one cooking me breakfast in the morning, or sliding me a cup of coffee.

Even more bizarre, my place in the hustling, bustling city no longer felt like home. I'd become too accustomed to the solitude of being in the middle of nowhere. Too spoiled by the idea of being bent over, spread open, and pleasured over every warm, welcoming surface of the cozy desert house.

"M—Ms. Emerson?"

Aric's assistant stepped in front of us, temporarily blocking our way. She was a nervous little intern with pixie-cut blonde hair and a slight underbite that made her look exotically cute.

"There's a visitor here, looking for you," she told me. "He wanted to wait in your office, but I obviously couldn't do that, so—"

"So you put him in mine?" Aric asked, peering through the glass.

The intern's expression went from nervous to outright terrified. She nodded anyway.

"I—I didn't know what to do!" she cried. "He seemed pretty insistent that—"

"It's alright Jenny," Aric smiled. "No big deal. We got it."

From this distance the glass distorted the oversized man pacing back and forth through Aric's office. It wasn't until we doubled back and stepped inside that I could see who it was.

When I did, my heart leapt straight into my throat.

"Hello Juliana."

Devyn was dressed impeccably in a full white Navy uniform, complete with gold-gilted buttons, stripes, and ribbons. The sheer number of colorful bars that dominated the left side of his chest was more than distracting.

"Uhhh... hi!"

I embraced him immediately, wrapping my arms around his thick, hard body. As I did I could feel him staring over my shoulder, directly at Aric.

"When did you get back?" I blurted. "And how are you in New York of all places?

"Aren't you going to introduce me?"

I stepped back, watching the two men face off in the center of the glass office. Aric was nearly as tall as the big SEAL, but with a much sleeker, more refined build. They were both staring back at each other with equal intensity.

"Aric, this is Devyn. Devyn, Aric."

A white-sleeved hand shot out, hovering in the air between them. Eventually Aric shook it.

"Pleased to meet you."

For the first time I noticed the series of fresh scratches on Devyn's stubbled, darkened face. There were at least eight or nine of them, of various lengths, streaked across in a rough diagonal from chin to forehead.

"Oh my God!"

I reached out to touch them, drawing back at the last second when I realized running my fingers over them would probably hurt. Devyn didn't even flinch. He only stared down his handsome nose at me, his brilliant blue eyes made even more beautiful reflected against his pristine, snow-white dress uniform.

"It's nothing," he finally said. "Couple of scratches."

"But what *happened?*"

He glanced at Aric, then back at me. "Long story. Take a walk with me and I'll tell you."

Still incredulous, I couldn't help but choke back my own excitement. Eventually I nodded. "Meet me at the elevator. I'll be there in a minute."

Devyn nodded curtly at Aric again, spun on his heel, and exited my assistant's office. When the door had swung shut and he was a safe distance away, my assistant let out a long, held-in breath.

"Is that *him?*" he hissed, with a hint of awe.

"Who?"

"The guy you spent the last week with!"

I shook my head quickly, before even thinking. "No, it's not."

"Bullshit," Aric spat.

"Seriously. He's not—"

"Juliana, just *look* at him!" Aric swore, his eyes laser-focused through several layers of glass. "A *soldier?* And a Navy officer, at that?"

"He's a SEAL, actually."

My assistant practically choked. "And you came back after *only* a week?"

"Aric—"

"I wouldn't blame you if you'd been gone for a whole year!"

I folded my arms across my chest with a resigned sigh. Aric had his mind made up though, and apparently nothing I could say would convince him otherwise. Not that I had a believable story to tell him anyway.

"Well?" he said finally, shooing me out of his office.

"Well what?"

"Go!"

I rolled my eyes. He rolled his own, right back.

"Juliana trust me, guys like *that*" he pointed dramatically "don't come around very often. When they do, you need to take full advantage of them."

"I'm not taking advantage of anyone," I protested. "It's just that-"

"Then you're batshit crazy," Aric winked.

# Twenty

## JULIANA

There were few places cooler than walking through Central Park, especially during the spring and summer. With all the leaves on the trees and the lush green lawns, you could almost forget you were in the City. If you went deep enough, you couldn't even see the buildings anymore. It was like suddenly being transported to another world where the traffic noise faded and everything slowed down.

On a day like today it was picture perfect; not too hot, not too cool. As we passed through Cedar Hill and down in the direction of the Great Lawn, the sky opened above us like a big blue marble. I marveled at how tranquil it was, swirling with puffy white clouds that made me forget all about work, my apartment, or the even City.

"So... shrapnel."

Devyn nodded again as we walked side-by-side. I learned his assignment had been a quick one, and that rather than fly home to the west he'd jumped on a C-130 that was headed for New York instead. He hadn't told me too many details, but whatever his mission was it had been short and violent.

"I thought you did deep-sea rescue," I said.

"I do," he confirmed. "But it's not *all* I do."

His hand accidentally brushed mine. As I was debating whether to loop my arm through his – I could've blamed it on the little hill we were currently climbing – Devyn slid our palms together and interlaced his fingers with mine.

"Let's just say I helped some people on the other side of the world," the SEAL said. "Good people."

My gaze traced the series of wounds on his face. My voice dropped an octave.

"But people hurt you," I said sorrowfully.

"Yes."

"Bad people?"

He nodded solemnly. "It's okay. I hurt them back."

Devyn squeezed my hand gently, guiding me along the path. I kept assuming I knew the City better than he did. In retrospect, that line of thinking was probably untrue.

"Is everyone else okay?" I asked, sweeping my hair back. "I mean... from your group–"

"UDT Team."

I could see his blue eyes scanning the park, side to side. His mind was elsewhere, though.

"And what's that?"

"Underwater Demol—"

He stopped walking abruptly, then turned to look at me. There was an inner conflict in his eyes, but also a deep, infinite patience.

"Everyone from my team is fine," he said finally. "More or less."

A pair of tricycle carts went by, towing tourists along the paved path on big aluminum-rimmed tires. As usual I tried to avoid them. They were always stopping abruptly to point out historic sights or features, all throughout the park.

"You never really got to tell me about you," I said to Devyn. "When the chopper picked you up, it cut our time short."

"Yeah, guess so."

"I wanted to know how you ended up in the desert," I told him. "I wanted to hear about your life, your family, your upbringing here in New York."

Beneath the collar of his uniform, I could see the bulge of the dog-tag he always wore. I reached out and touched it gingerly.

"I also wanted to know about *this.*"

Without a word the big SEAL pulled me with him, past a dozen or so people seated on benches, feeding the pigeons. Together we stepped off the path, climbing upward along a slow rise until we reached a flat spot at the top of a small hill.

It was there we sat down together, sprawling across the cool, bladed grass. Devyn undid his collar and opened it, revealing the serrated form the blackened dog-tag just beneath.

"This belonged to my father," he said solemnly. "He served too, a long time ago."

"Oh."

Devyn's eyes unfocused. His gaze seemed to settle upon something very far away.

"He died when I was very young. Got killed in an ambush while on a black-ops mission, somewhere in Bosnia."

Though we were sitting side-by-side with our knees bent, our hands were still touching. I closed mine over his, comfortingly.

"The worst part was he got betrayed by someone within his own cell," he went on. "Someone who got captured, and gave up his own brothers-in-arms."

Devyn winced, or maybe squinted into the sun. I realized at that moment he was telling the story to himself as much as me.

"One of the men in the cell ended up killing the traitor," he finished, "and eventually told me about it when I was old enough." He tapped the dog-tag. "He gave me this, taken directly from my father's neck."

The silence around us seemed abruptly serene. The trees didn't rustle, the wind didn't blow — even the sound of the birds was gone.

"Devyn, I'm so sorry."

"It's alright," he said, forcing a smile. "Happened a long time ago."

He leaned back on his arms, and I noticed a circle of pink skin at the very base of his neck. The dog-tag was so twisted, so jagged from whatever had happened to his father, it apparently had been digging into his flesh for a long, long time.

*Oh wow.*

Devyn wasn't bleeding however. He'd built up enough scar tissue there that it no longer mattered. I could only imagine how many years he'd been wearing it.

"I know what you're thinking," he said solemnly. "But I could never bring myself to file it down or bend it back into shape." He reached up to touch the relic. "I accepted it exactly as it is. I took the pain and blood as a constant reminder of my father, and what he fought for."

In the end, he shrugged. "After all these years, it doesn't even hurt anymore."

# Twenty-One

## JULIANA

I shifted closer to Devyn, as three kids began playing with a frisbee nearby. We watched them in silence for a little bit, before I turned back to face him.

"I completely understand you following in your father's footsteps," I said, "even if your family must not have been too happy about it. Especially you being a SEAL and all."

"You'd be surprised," he answered quickly. "My mother was actually very understanding when I told her I wanted to enlist. She drove me straight to the recruiter herself."

I let out a low whistle. "Now *that's* a strong woman."

Devyn nodded. "I was raised by strong women," he agreed. "Between her and my two older sisters, I actually had a very happy childhood."

I tried to envision him running around the streets of South Brooklyn, living the life of any ordinary child as the years of adolescence went by. Though his story was sad, there was no melancholy about him. He seemed as happy and well-adjusted as anyone else I knew, maybe even more so.

"The trick's not to live in the past," he said, as if reading my mind. "Trouble is, most people can't do that. They're too busy looking back to enjoy what's ahead."

He inhaled deeply for a moment, then stood up and pulled me to my feet. Face to face, his hands remained on mine as our eyes finally locked.

"I... I have to tell you something," I mumbled.

Beneath the cuts on his face, Devyn's expression remained wholly unchanged. I got the impression he was staring through my eyes and past my soul. Maybe even into that small, secret place I'd let very few people.

"I just got back to New York yesterday," I admitted. "I spent the whole week out in the desert... with Gage and Maverick."

There was no shock, no surprise. No anger or disappointment, either.

"I know."

My mouth dropped open. "You *do?*"

"Of course," he sniffed casually. "They tell me everything."

I hesitated, but only for a second. "*Everything?*"

Slowly, definitively, Devyn nodded.

For a brief moment my stomach dropped away, like an elevator taking off abruptly. The longer I stared at him however, the more I realized it didn't matter. At least not to him.

"I was hoping you'd be back," I said truthfully. "Although the guys said you probably wouldn't. At least not for a month or more."

"That's generally the case, yeah."

"And there was this raging desert storm," I told him. "A really bad one. We got stuck inside, but that was the first night," I admitted, "and then the storm passed. And after that, well, I don't know. I just... stayed."

He was still staring, still looking back at me impassively, and thankfully without judgment. But was that the hint of a *smile* I saw now, at the corners of his mouth?

"I needed the time away," I said, as if that explained things. "I didn't realize it until I'd left, but getting out of the city really... well it really—"

Devyn's hands slipped to my waist, pulling me in. Engulfing my body with his two strong arms, as he pinned me against his chest.

And then suddenly he was *kissing* me.

It happened fast but I responded even faster, inhaling his sweet tongue into my mouth and swirling it with my own. I'd dreamt of this moment so many times. I'd brought pleasure to myself just imagining what kissing this perfect specimen of a man might be like, and now it was actually happening, in the middle of Central Park with the whole world looking on.

I let my fingers roam hungrily through his long dark hair, being careful not to brush the tips against the sides of his shrapnel-scratched face. But I wanted to kiss those wounds, too. I wanted very badly to make them better for him, and to take whatever suffering he went through on myself, if for no other reason than to ease his discomfort.

But it was only the kissing that mattered now. The crushing of Devyn's lips against mine, as our bodies continued undulating warmly against each other. Yet as much pent-up passion and emotion was coming from my end, I could sense the same feelings from him as well. The dark-haired SEAL had certainly thought about this. In fact he'd probably even waited patiently for it, while dutifully completing whatever mission had taken him so quickly and rudely away.

We kissed like lovers for a full minute before breaking away. When we finally did, I must've looked like a deer caught in a pair of headlights.

"I've been wanting to do that since the day you showed up at my door," Devyn murmured.

We were still standing face to face, heads together. Shyly I looked up at him, and returned his now obvious smile.

"I've wanted to do that for even longer," I admitted to him. "So much longer."

I was dying for him to kiss me again. I could think of nothing else but the fullness of his lips, the enormous strength of his arms. The slow, steady rhythm of his heart beating against mine.

He didn't kiss me though. Instead, he tilted his head.

"Do you still want a baby by me?"

I swallowed hard, then nodded fervently. My whole body felt like it was on fire. "More than anything."

Devyn slipped something into my hand. Something thin and familiar.

When I looked down, I could see it was a hotel key.

"I'm here tonight only," he murmured, his lips just a few tantalizing inches from mine. "The Bowery. Room 503."

His cornflower eyes flared wildly. His stubbled face — crossed with scratches — twitched once, before he turned away.

"Come early enough, maybe we'll have dinner."

# Twenty-Two

## JULIANA

The rest of my 'workday' was nothing like it should've been. It was too full of distractions, too dominated by thoughts of Devyn and what would happen between us later that night.

I was thrilled, but nervous. Relieved he'd returned safe and relatively unharmed from whatever dangerous mission I'd seen him whisked away on, and also a little turned on by the sheer badassery of who he was, and what he'd presumably done.

Okay fine. A *lot* turned on.

On top of all that he was absolutely *delicious*, in all the ways that his photos had promised. I'd been hellbent on the idea of having a child with him for nearly a year, but it was only recently that I'd actually fallen for the man behind the sperm sample.

For all these reasons I knocked off early, went home, and took a long hot shower. I primped. I preened. I took a cab to East 3rd street, and walked the final block on firm, confident legs. By the time I arrived at The Bowery, I was more than ready for anything.

*You sure you want this?*

The question was rhetorical, as I exited the elevator and stepped onto the fifth floor. Hell yes I wanted it. I wanted it doubly too, in the sense that I wanted both Devyn *and* the biological necessity he'd provide me when it came to having a child.

There was no need to knock because he'd already given me the key. I knocked anyway, then inserted the key into the lock and pushed down on the handle.

The room was dim, but not dark. I'd intentionally waited until after the sun had gone down, which already made it fairly late. Coming early and having to sit through dinner was the last thing in the world I'd wanted. Plus, I never did like doing what someone told me to do.

"I was wondering if you'd even show."

Devyn's suite was one of the fancier ones. Right now he was standing at the bar between the kitchenette and living area, pouring a deep amber liquid into a crystal glass.

"Whatever that is I'll have some," I told him. "Please."

He nodded curtly. "Whiskey it is then."

The door closed behind me as I hung my bag on the back of the nearest chair. I'd worn a form-fitting black dress that was tight but comfortable, one that accented my curves and turned guys' heads yet could still be perfect for going out to dinner if Devyn insisted.

By the way he was dressed however, I knew that probably wouldn't be the case.

"On ice?" he asked, hovering a pair of tongs over a second glass.

"No, thank you."

He paused, obviously impressed. "Good girl."

I moved closer, giving my eyes permission to wander if they wanted to. And boy did they want to. Devyn wore a white button-down dress shirt that was entirely open in front. Down below, he wore nothing but a pair of tight red boxer briefs.

"Sorry," he said, catching my stare. "You caught me in the middle of something."

He nodded left, to where the rest of his uniform was stretched out over a hotel ironing board. His pants were already done, and draped over the bottom half of a hanger. The creases were perfect.

But it was Devyn's bare legs that had me drooling, all perfect and muscular and ending at that red-stitched hem. Those legs looked extremely dangerous. Coiled with power.

"Here."

He handed me my glass, just as my eyes bounced over the significant bulge in the front of his boxer shorts. I should've looked away, but I didn't care to. Besides, he'd looked me over on more than one occasion, entirely without apology.

"To making the most beautiful kid in the world," he smiled, suddenly raising his glass my way. Caught off guard,

I hesitated for a moment. Eventually I clinked it, toasting him nervously.

We drank, and it was a hell of a thing to drink to. Especially with the innocuous-looking amber liquid now burning a hole in my stomach, having traveled down the full length of my throat.

"What's wrong?"

The burning subsided slowly, and the flavor profile began. I could taste the sweetness of honey, the muskiness of peat. The liquid was pungent and smoky, yet surprisingly good.

"Nothing at all," I told him. "I guess I just feel... overdressed."

Locking me away in his sapphire eyes, Devyn took a long pull from his drink before setting it down. He was so handsome it was intimidating. So dominating and gorgeous, it left me breathless.

"Maybe we should fix that."

He moved closer, and with each step I could feel my heart beating faster. I felt uncharacteristically helpless all of a sudden. After a lifetime of being the predator, I actually felt like the prey.

"Here, let me help."

His arms folded around me, unzipping the top of my dress. He brought it down to mid-back, then stopped and pulled the arms downward, laying my shoulders bare.

"You're *ridiculously* beautiful," he murmured, planting a soft, brief kiss on one side of my exposed neck.

"You know that?"

There was no time to agree or disagree. A moment later his hands slid under my ass, his two big arms flexing like hydraulic pistons. They lifted me high into the air, easily depositing me right on the surface of the bar itself.

Our faces were so close our noses were touching. Devyn nuzzled me like that for a moment, enjoying the intimacy. I was dying to kiss him. Desperate to feel my tongue against his, but somehow, in some way, I was able to hold back.

And then my mouth surged into his, and I wasn't holding back at all.

*YESSS.*

I went at him frantically, planting my hands on both sides of his face. Sitting on the bar I kissed him like there was no tomorrow. Like the entire world was coming to a fiery, tumultuous ending, and the only thing that somehow mattered was to keep my soul as close as humanly possible to his.

I wanted my dress off. I wanted his boxers down around his ankles. Most of all I wanted the substantial knot of Devyn's growing manhood buried completely inside of me, as my hands wrapped around him to claw his perfect ass forward and into me.

Instead of all that, Devyn stepped back. His eyes found mine again, his expression strangely calm considering the gravity of our impending union.

"Listen," he said softly. "I want you to know we don't have to do this. Not if you don't want to."

I was emotionally and physically stunned. *Don't want to?!* Was he kidding me?

"You want my baby?" he repeated. "I'll give it you. I made all the arrangements already."

My head was still spinning. Numbly I managed: "Arrangements?"

Devyn nodded. "I contacted the clinic, and they've re-activated my profile. Tomorrow morning I'm going down to provide a new sample. You can use it to conceive."

I hadn't even been thinking about that. I'd been too preoccupied with other, more exciting ways to get his sperm.

"That's sweet of you," I said finally. "Devyn, thank you."

His hand grazed my face again. This time it moved so gingerly, so lovingly, it melted my heart.

"If anyone should have my child it's you," he smiled. "You're so driven, Juliana. So strong and intelligent and—"

I kissed him hard, obliterating the rest of his argument. My mouth was hungry. My body too.

"I want your child," I told him firmly. "I can't wait to feel it growing inside me."

My hand wandered lower. It settled over the warm, firm package straining hard against his boxer-briefs.

"But that doesn't preclude me wanting *this.*"

The bulge surged powerfully beneath my touch, moving like it had a mind of its own. I squeezed gently, trying not to gasp at the sheer size of the warm mass beneath my palm. I didn't know how he managed to keep it all in there, but I knew one thing for sure:

It was going to make me very, *very* happy.

As Devyn stood frozen I took another sip of whiskey. Maybe for courage. Maybe because the taste reminded me of the inside of his sweet, beautiful mouth.

"You're absolutely sure?" he whispered. "You really want this?"

In answer I set my drink down and kissed him again; hotly, wetly, letting my hair cascade forward on either side of us. Our churning mouths became one. The fingertips of my free hand traced the back of his neck, as my jaw rotated slowly and sensuously against his.

Then I hopped from the bar and dropped straight to my knees.

"Talk is cheap," I said, looking up his magnificent body and into his eyes. "In a situation this intense, talk is meaningless."

My hands found the elastic waistband of his ever-tightening boxers. Deftly, my fingers rolled the warm fabric down his magnificent thighs.

"Let me *show* you."

# Twenty-Three

**DEVYN**

The room spun dizzily as Juliana went down on me, my mind soaring through warmth and pleasure and space. I let my body relax as my head lolled back, my fingers wandering aimlessly through tons of soft, fragrant hair.

*Finally...*

It had taken a week to get home. A whole week and forever. I should've been laser-focused on the mission, totally dedicated to the task at hand. For once though, that hadn't been the case. For the first time ever, the distractions of home had made me careless. Quite possibly even leading to the wounds on my face.

And that's because the entire time, I'd been thinking about *her.*

*No,* I assured myself silently. *The charges going off prematurely had nothing to do with her.*

The Bayandor-class corvette hadn't sunk, but in the end that wasn't the goal. I'd blown a big enough hole in the hull to distract the entire harbor, and the resulting raid at the Bandar-e Abbas safehouse had been wildly successful. All six HVT's had been rescued without incident or injury. Minus the scratches on my face of course, or my Chief Warrant Officer's blown-out eardrums.

Thankfully Langston was healing nicely, and the scratches I received wouldn't even leave scars. I was on my way home before I knew it, and learning via sat-phone of the *very* interesting week my roommates had had.

"Mmmmm..."

Right now Juliana's mouth felt nothing short of amazing, as she dragged her beautiful lips up and down the full length of my shaft. She looked incredibly sexy on her knees. The mess of hair I kept pulling back so I could watch her pretty face felt like spun silk in my eager hands.

But yes, I'd been jealous of the week she'd spent with Maverick and Gage. Not jealous that they'd slept with her, because under the circumstances how could I possibly blame them?

No, I was more jealous that it hadn't been *me.*

The more I learned of Juliana the more I loved about her. And yes, my roommates had told me a good many things. She was intelligent and passionate; fiercely competitive almost to a fault. But she was sweet, too. Caring and affectionate and family-focused.

And beautiful. Oh my *God*, she was so very, very beautiful.

To be honest I'd made my decision even before I'd taken her out to lunch: that yes, of course I would help her conceive a child. We had too many things in common, too many like-minded goals. My past donation to the sperm bank wasn't something I'd thought about or even considered, but right now I was wholly and completely on board with giving this woman the baby she wanted.

I'd just wanted to spend a little more time with her, that was all.

And now here she was, finally in my arms. Rolling my balls expertly in the palm of her hot little hand, while taking me past those kissable lips and deep down her lovely throat.

I let her go on for a while, enjoying the fruits of her talented mouth. Tattooing the memory of this beautiful woman — the one who'd dropped so eagerly to her knees — on the surface of my brain.

Eventually I lifted her into my arms and cradled her against my chest. Her mouth was wet, her lips swollen with her efforts. I kissed those lips tenderly as I walked her across the suite and over to the bed, then spread her out across the sheets.

*Damn.*

Juliana rolled onto her stomach so I could remove her dress. When she rolled back again, her black bra and matching thong panties made my saliva-coated dick throb all on its own.

*She's perfect.*

She was really, in just about every way. Her only flaw was that she was here in New York, several thousand miles to the east. But the bigger flaw of course was on my end, and that was the sheer impossibility of bringing someone like this — someone with schedule and structure (and soon enough, a child) — into a chaotic, unpredictable world like mine.

For those reasons this would be our only night together. Our one incredible, unforgettable rendezvous. I'd decided it should be memorable, so that years later if she were ever to think about the biological father of her child, she'd have something special to reflect on. Something that we shared together, right here, right now.

No matter what, I wanted to make it as beautiful as possible.

Clearing my mind, I let my hands slide up along her naked flanks, where they glided over a delicately scripted tattoo in the form of a poem or saying on her ribcage. I didn't have the patience to read it. I was too busy positioning my body over hers. Too immersed in pulling her arms overhead and pinning her wrists to the bed with a soft, almost inaudible sigh.

Then I kissed my way down her tan, smooth stomach and buried my face in her pussy.

"Ohhhhhh!"

She was more than just wet, she was absolutely drenched. Her black thong, even more so. I pulled it aside to make room for my tongue, alternating between thrusting it in and out and eagerly lapping up her sweet, honeyed nectar.

Juliana wasn't just enjoying this, she was going absolutely insane. Her hands rolled into my hair, her fingers pulling me deeper and harder and even faster against her writhing body. Soon she was rolling her hips in perfect rhythm with my mouth, using the flat of my tongue to completely bathe her hot, swollen folds. Her hands tensed, her fingernails digging in when she wanted me to dive deeper. They relaxed too, when the area became so sensitive she wanted me to let up.

I ate her until she exploded like a bomb, clamping my face tightly between her two lusciously perfect thighs. But I never stopped. I never let up until the trembling subsided and her toes uncurled and her body went limp against the softness of the bed. Only then, my face still covered in her sweet, sticky sex, did I glide upward to kiss her over and over again. All while teasing the head of my cock up and down through her now-sopping entrance, until she was moaning and begging for what came next.

"*Fuck* me..."

They were the magic words — the only words my entire universe had needed to hear. With one surge forward I clenched my cheeks and buried the head inside her. It was so tight, so snug, I saw her mouth drop open and her eyes glaze over with the intensity of the pleasure, but also something entirely unexpected.

Something that looked like love.

# Twenty-Four

## JULIANA

He entered me slowly, which was good because it was the only way this was going to work. Flesh to flesh, inch by inch, the man I'd dreamt about for so long was finally piercing me to my core.

*Holy—*

I clenched the sheets in one hand, his ass in the other. Part of me wanted to scream, but I was too busy kissing him as I drew him in. Devyn was big, maybe even enormous, but he knew exactly what he was doing. He gave me just enough control that I was able to relax and accept him into my body, and I was so excited by now there was nothing stopping him from bottoming out in my warm, wet channel.

*FUCK!*

God, it felt so good! But it also felt precarious. If he were to start fucking me with any measure of speed or ferocity I wasn't sure I could take it, but in the back of my mind I craved it anyway. The whole thing felt dangerous, like playing with fireworks. Thrilling with an edge of peril, rapture walking the tightrope between pleasure and pain.

His body sank into mine, and all rational thought went out the window. My legs spread of their own accord, as my body surrendered to his. He'd take me and I'd enjoy the ride. There was something in his eyes that told me to trust him, and I had no reason not to.

"Hey..."

Devyn pulled back at the sound of my voice, just enough to look at me with those stunning blue eyes. I saw myself reflected there, in the light from the windows.

"I've wanted this for a long time."

His expression was full of respect, even admiration. He nodded once.

"So have I."

I gasped as he gently withdrew, then glided slowly back into my body. Once, twice, three times he did it, and each time was successively more amazing.

Buried inside me, with my legs wrapped around him, he kissed my forehead.

"I've thought about you all week, Juliana. Halfway across the world. No matter what I was doing..." he shook his head. "I just couldn't get you out of my mind."

He thrust into me again and again, still moving with rhythmic slowness. I could feel his glutes coiling and uncoiling beneath my trembling hand. Like some sleepy beast, flexing and unflexing as it shifted position.

"Are you... upset that..."

"No," he said immediately, shaking his head. "Gage, Maverick... these men are my *brothers*. There's nothing in the world that could ever come between us." He paused for a moment, considering. "And there's nothing in the world we wouldn't *share*."

With that he kissed me again, his tongue dancing hotly alongside mine as his hips rammed forward. He went so deep I gasped, accidentally biting his lip. But Devyn just smiled and kissed me some more, his incredible ass clenching and unclenching as he continued pumping away. His long, thick shaft stretching me wonderfully as it pumped in and out of me, while his hard, corded body surged forward and back.

*Share.*

The word sent a bolt of exhilaration through me, head to toe. It was such a simple word, a short word. But a word that held such complex meaning.

*Nothing in the world we wouldn't share.*

That Gage and Maverick had shared me, there was zero doubt. But now Devyn wanted me too. Apparently he wanted me in ways that had silently tormented him over the past week, especially having learned that his roommates and brothers-in-arms had already taken me in his stead.

But it hadn't changed anything for him. If anything, maybe he wanted me even more. Maybe knowing I'd been so free with his comrades had given him license to stop in New York and pursue me like this. Or maybe he'd sensed upon meeting me just how much I'd been obsessed with having him, and because of this he'd wanted it too.

I kissed him even harder, more hungrily, as I ran these things through my mind. Being shared by these men was utterly thrilling, in the most edgy of ways. It was societally forbidden. Expressly taboo. It was hot and sexy and oh so *very* fucking naughty, and it made my stomach do hot little backflips whenever I thought about the near endless possibilities.

But fuck... I wanted it anyway.

Bucking my hips I pushed Devyn upward and then onto his back, where I mounted him by slinging one warm leg over his waist. With a slight lift of my body I sank down on him. The feel of him parting me from within was exquisite, but it was nothing compared to when my ass met his abdomen and he was fully, completely inside me.

*MMMMMmmmm...*

I wanted to stay like that forever. To remain perched there over his ridiculously-hard body, letting him marinate inside me. I spread my hands over his perfect abdomen, giving my fingertips free rein to explore every ridge of his hard, well-earned six-pack. Then, locking eyes with him again, I began rocking forward and back.

Our movements became slow and dreamy. Soaked with euphoria. There was no hurry, no rush. No frenzied coming together of our bodies that would eventually build to a violent climax. Instead we rocked together, grinding deeply against each other. It felt like our souls were connected. And there was a warmth and comfort — a familiarity even — as we became lost in each other's eyes.

I don't know how long we went on like that. All I know is that we screwed slowly, comfortably, eventually holding hands and interlacing our fingers for leverage as each of us drew closer to the edge of oblivion. There was a lot of touching, a lot of kissing. And then suddenly Devyn was stiffening beneath me, his starfire blue eyes posing a question that only I could answer.

*"Come..."*

I smiled the word down at him, just before he let loose. It was all he'd been waiting for. All he needed to finally let go.

And then he was flooding me, filling me from within. Surging and pumping and throbbing inside me, until I could feel the warm splash of his hot seed so very far up near the deepest part of my essence.

*Yessssss!*

Devyn grunted and groaned, his body suddenly turning hard as a granite statue. I rode him to my own climax, which was slow and tremendous. It triggered while he was still draining himself inside me, and somehow I was coherent enough to reach back and give his balls a gentle, rolling squeeze.

Our bodies kept writhing for a long time afterward, until the aftershocks of our pleasure finally subsided. When they did I was leaning back against Devyn's thighs, a look of total satisfaction painted across my face.

"We're doing that again," I breathed wickedly, adding a wink. "And again after that."

My lover smiled. "There's going to be nothing left for tomorrow," he complained. "You're going to drain me completely."

"So?"

"So... remember?" he urged. "I'm supposed to make a deposit?"

Pushing off, I bent all the way forward until my body was molded against his. I giggled into his mouth, kissing him playfully.

"If you can't produce, you can't produce," I teased with a shrug. "Just one more reason for you to come back to New York."

# Twenty-Five

## JULIANA

"And you found him?" Addison pressed. "You actually met up with this guy?"

I used the plastic tongs to put a spring roll on my plate, then passed them to my friend. But Addison's plate was already full. She could barely fit another piece of food on it, so right now she was merely following me around the buffet.

"I found him," I said finally. "I met him."

"By *yourself?*"

I licked my finger and nodded.

"Damn, Juliana," she admonished. "That's dangerous."

"Why?"

"Because that address I gave you was in the middle of nowhere!" my friend cried. "You could've been killed. You could've been stuffed in the trunk of a car, or buried there out in the desert!"

"Turns out it's not so easy to bury someone out in the desert," I told her. "It's solid calcium carbonate."

"Depends on the desert," Addison shot back. "And it's *carbonite*, not carbonate."

I sighed and rolled my eyes simultaneously.

"And you should be on *Jeopardy* with all the fun facts you've got stuffed in that pretty blonde head," I countered. "And thanks for always correcting me. I fucking love it."

My friend grunted dismissively. It felt like the usual grunt of a someone trying to move on from something.

"Anyway, I'm just looking out for you," she finally said. "I didn't mean—"

"No, it's me who's being the asshole," I admitted. "Sorry. I'm just a little... on edge."

We continued down the line of delicacies and hot dishes, where I added even more to my second plate. Because yes, I was juggling two plates at once. What the hell else were you supposed to do at the best Chinese buffet in the City?

"So what happened?" Addison was asking. "You know, with Bishop."

"Devyn."

"Whatever."

We reached the end, and I grabbed another pair of napkins just because. After making our way back to our table, we sat down across from each other and began to pick.

"Basically I found him right where you said he'd be," I told her, "and so I knocked on his door. He looked just like he did in the photos, Addison. Maybe a little more mature, but the years suited him nicely."

I felt bad, telling her all this over a month after it happened. She'd been asking for weeks, but we'd both been too busy to get together. I could've pinned it all on my end, because minutes after leaving Devyn that next morning I'd driven straight back into work. But Addison had been working crazy amounts of overtime, too. The streets of New York had never been so restless.

"And you just *asked* him?" my friend demanded incredulously. "Did you hand him a specimen cup or—"

"No, no," I shook my head. "Nothing like that."

"Well did you have to convince him?"

Thinking back, I shrugged. "I did and I didn't. I mean, he was more than happy to provide another sample. But there was this... I don't know..."

Addison's eyebrows knitted together. "Don't know what?"

"There was this *connection* between us, too. I know it sounds silly, but I could feel it, Addison. And I knew he felt it too."

My friend paused, still unraveling the wrapper from her chopsticks. She was taking it off in a long paper ribbon, while staring back at me confused.

"Are you saying—"

"No, I'm not saying anything like that," I cut her off.

"I'm just saying it was a beautiful moment. And he was sweet, too. Even sweeter than he seemed in his profile."

"He was practically a teenager in his profile," my friend reminded me.

"I know."

She began pouring tea from a steaming teapot, which wasn't exactly my thing. I usually drank the tea anyway, because of her. Also maybe to expand my horizons.

Today though, the thought of drinking the tea made me sick to my stomach.

"So you got what you wanted," my friend eventually shrugged. "You tracked him down – thanks to me, you're welcome very much – and he gave the clinic another donation."

I nodded, picking up my chicken skewer. I twirled the wooden stick between my thumb and forefinger, staring blankly as it rotated.

"So when will you do the deed?"

I blinked. It was like coming out of hypnosis.

"What?"

"When do you plan on trying?" Addison went on. "Are you going to wait a few months, try for a summer baby, or are you looking to get started right away?"

It was a fair question. So far I hadn't even called the place. I knew Devyn had done his thing, because they sent me three separate messages telling me so. And Devyn himself had also called, not long after landing in Phoenix.

*Arizona...*

I'd spoken to the guys twice over the past month, and not for their lack of trying. Maverick had sent me a few very sweet messages, and Gage had sent three times as many funny ones. As much as I wanted to engage them, the nagging voice in the back of my mind told me it probably wasn't a good idea.

But shit, I didn't even know why.

Instead I'd gone back to immersing myself at the office, which had always been my one true sanctuary for clearing my head. Shameless Marketing needed to be streamlined, especially with all the recent hires. I had to promote the good people. Trim away the bad. Between Aric and I, we'd have the place running lean and mean going into the fall and winter months. From there I could revisit the idea of implantation and conception.

"My God Juliana, you can't focus on *anything!*"

I looked across from me, where Addison was busy eating her pot-stickers. I still hadn't separated my wooden chopsticks. She was right though. I'd been unreasonably distracted.

"You really *do* want this, don't you?"

Numbly I nodded. It might not have seemed convincing, however.

"Look, I know it's a lot," said Addison. "I've got three of my own, remember? Raising kids is a shit-ton of work, and it's a twenty-four seven job. At times, you'll be ready to pull your own hair out."

"Not exactly the pep-talk I was hoping for," I smirked.

Reaching out, my friend closed her hand over mine. Her smile was warm and genuine.

"You know what though?" she pressed. "When they're looking up at you with those bright, beautiful eyes? And they close their little hand around your finger?"

My friend settled back into her chair and sighed happily.

"That's when you realize it's the most rewarding, amazing thing in the whole world."

# Twenty-Six

## MAVERICK

"Yeah, I agree," I said solemnly, looking down at the series of photos. "This right here... this would be the big one."

I tapped the third photo in particular, as blurry as it was. The man was behind a wall. Only part of his head was visible, but there were enough pixels to make out exactly who he was.

Especially since we'd been hunting him the better part of the last decade.

"When exactly was this taken?" asked Gage.

"Two days ago," Ramos grunted. He pointed at a time stamp. "Fifty-one hours, to be precise."

The Rear Admiral scratched at his salt-and-pepper beard, which had a lot more salt in it than the last time I saw him. He looked tired. I guess at a certain point we all got tired. It just takes some of us longer to get there than others.

"So when are we getting him?" demanded Devyn, anxiously. "We should leave right now."

Ramos shook his head. "No one's getting anyone," he said. "Not just yet, anyway."

Maverick threw up his hands. "And why the fuck not?"

"Because there's *procedure*, that's why," Ramos snapped. "There's rules to follow. Yes, we have confirmation that Bashir's back in Somalia. But that's all we have right now, until the rest of the intel comes in."

The room was too hot, too small, too plain for my liking. I could never understand the mindset when it came to shit like this. We'd flown all the way to Point Loma for an emergency briefing, only to be stuffed into a closet the size of a bathroom.

"He could be halfway across Africa by the time the intel comes in," said Devyn, in what we always called his 'diplomatic' voice. "Do you really think it's wise to wait?"

"It's a lot smarter than rushing in and finding a bunch of candy bar wrappers and empty water jugs," snarled Ramos, "then getting rained on by mortar fire." The Admiral's expression went dark. "Do I have to remind you about Damascus? That was a goddamn mess! A total clusterfuck if ever I saw one!"

Damascus. Of course he'd bring it up again. Never one of the other two-dozen successful missions we'd run for him. No. Always Damascus.

"You know how many months I spent explaining what the hell happened," Ramos shouted, "to half the fucking command? And all because we didn't wait. We dropped you in there guns blazing, dicks in your hot little hands, only to have—"

"Alright, alright," Gage assuaged. "Let it go."

Ramos laughed manically. "Let it *go?*"

"We get it," I reiterated. "Trust us."

"No, you *don't* get it!" Ramos countered loudly. "Because if you got it, you wouldn't be asking. You wouldn't be pressing for—"

"Damascus was a longshot right from the beginning," Devyn jumped in. "A desperate fantasy based on bad intelligence, pushed by some higher-ups hellbent on making a name for themselves."

The Rear Admiral's mouth twisted to one side. He couldn't argue. That much I knew.

"He's right," I said calmly. "Things got rushed all around."

Ramos had been pacing the room ever since we showed up. Only now did he finally stop.

"Look, we're all on the same side," he eventually relented. "We all want to nail this asshole."

"Then let's nail him."

"We will," the Admiral assured us. "But it's not just a matter of locking down his whereabouts, it's also confirming he's accessible."

Gage hissed and folded his arms. "You mean making sure he's not hiding out in the back of an orphanage, or camping at some children's hospital."

"Unfortunately, yes."

Bashir was slippery, but mostly because of his dirty tactics. The man had spent his whole life surrounding himself with innocents and incidental targets. We'd watched helplessly as he planted mines and IED's along roads leading into whatever city he'd hole up in next, then move on without caring about the havoc and collateral damage caused afterward.

In short, we'd cleaned up too many of his messes already.

"We need to get him sooner rather than later," Maverick advised. "His army never shrinks, it only grows."

Ramos' mouth curled in bitter agreement. "That's the problem. He's recruited enough children from nearby villages over the past decade to create a whole second army."

"And then used that army to get rich off the taking of hostages," I added.

I glanced down at the file spread out over the desk again. The place he'd been photographed could've been a safehouse, or even a base of operations. Or it could've been nothing — merely a place he slept that night, while transitioning somewhere deeper into Africa.

*Shit.*

The problem was, it was a big fucking continent. The last thing we wanted was to lose our shot.

"Sorry to bring you down here for what amounts to a tease," said Ramos, "but I needed to loop you in. I wanted all three of you to know we could be moving on this very soon."

"How soon?"

"Could be days maybe," he shrugged, "or it could be weeks or months."

"Or it could be not at all," Gage frowned.

The Rear Admiral nodded solemnly. "That's a possibility too."

There was a quick rap at the door, followed by an ensign poking his head in. The rush of cooler air was like heaven. The man mumbled something, and the Rear Admiral headed for the exit.

"Take all the time you want here," Ramos said, pointing down at the file. "After that, consider yourself relieved."

The door closed, and the room went back to the stifling closet it actually was. Gage shook his head.

"There's too much red tape," he spat. "Way more than when we first started."

He wasn't wrong. It seemed like a thousand years had passed since BUDS school, and the soldiers we'd come up with were all but gone. I barely recognized anyone these days, and that included the brass above us. Old crows like Ramos were a welcome sight, but they were few and far between.

"Let's get this over with," said Maverick, pulling up a chair. "So we can get home."

"Why not stay in San Diego for a day or two?" I asked. "Change of scenery."

"Change of scenery?" Gage laughed. "Really?"

"Yeah. Home's lonely."

They looked at me, and as always I knew what they were thinking. Home hadn't always been lonely, at least not a month ago, when *she* was around. We hadn't heard from her in weeks though, and for that they blamed me. My impromptu trip to New York had apparently given Juliana exactly what she wanted.

Gage and Maverick however, had rather I'd returned home so she'd have to come get it in person.

"Look, I don't want to hear it," I said preemptively. "You both had your time with her. Don't begrudge me for having mine."

"But—"

"No buts," I cut Gage off. "Look, maybe she'll call. Maybe she won't. In the end, what's done is done. It is what it is."

"It is what it is?" Maverick repeated mockingly. He pushed a map of Mogadishu to one side of the table and smirked. "Got any other wise sayings or nuggets of wisdom?"

"Sure, I've got one right here."

With that, I fished into my pocket for a few seconds and returned him the middle finger.

# Twenty-Seven

## JULIANA

The decision to have a child didn't come on all at once, but it definitely came on strong. It was ratified every time I visited my many nieces and nephews. Cemented as something I desperately wanted, after having spent time with Addison, Evan, and their three adorable little rugrats.

Turning thirty soon would hit hard, but that was really only the catalyst. Because the true motivating factor was simply being alone. Coming back to an empty apartment each night, with nothing to show for all my hard work but a big laundry list of material things.

Don't get me wrong: the material things were fun, too. But as the youngest of five, I always had the sense of just missing out. I had memories of fun times and holidays and even a few vacations with my older brothers and sisters. But they were always tighter, their bonds stronger. Five years behind them, it always felt like I'd missed out on so much. There were too many stories only they could share. Too many inside jokes and wordless laughter that, unfortunately for me,

I'd missed by being born too late.

Family. It was extremely important to me growing up. And yet I'd sacrificed the scant blood relationships I had by coming to New York and setting up shop here. Sure I went home sometimes, and I was always welcomed with open arms. But it was during those times I really saw what I was missing. It was during those trips when I'd fawn over little Abby falling adorably asleep in my brother Patrick's arms, or I'd watch Colin look up at my sister Jessica and give her a 3-year old smile so bright and beautiful it could shatter the world.

There were Andrew's gorgeous twins, Zach and Kaitlyn. The three little boys my sister Mariah gave birth to in rapid succession; Jonah, Louis, and Randall. I had so many nieces and nephews I practically needed a secretary to keep track of all the birthday and holiday cards and gifts.

And yet every time I went home, my apartment was dark and silent.

I didn't want to wait five years, and end up with a child too young to play with his many cousins. But it was more than just that. There was an invisible call that tugged at me in the dead of the night, staring up at my ceiling. A piece of my heart that had always been missing, whether I wanted to admit it or not.

I wanted *motherhood*.

All these thoughts and more swirled through my head, as I wandered the carpeted halls of the clinic again. I knew what I wanted, now. I'd already gone for the bloodwork and was ready for the series of prenatal vitamins and necessary injections. I'd read all about the procedure of follicle stimulation and extraction. Of embryo creation and implantation.

At times it seemed coldly formulaic and planned, but then again I was always a planner. I realized this suited me. If all went well, I could conceive in two to three months. I would be carrying a child. Growing it inside me...

*Devyn's child.*

Biologically yes, but that would be the extent of it. And not just Devyn's though.

*My child.*

The thought made me warm inside. On deeper levels than even I'd anticipated.

"Ah, Ms. Emerson!"

The director was standing just outside his office, behind the receptionist's shoulder. He ushered me in, pointing with the tip of his wire-rimmed glasses.

"Please. Come sit."

His office was exactly the same, the books on the shelves entirely untouched. For some reason that part seemed sad. I wondered how many old, obsolete books at the New York Public Library had been sitting on the same shelves, decade after decade. Untouched, unopened. Wholly forgotten.

"So your bloodwork came back," the director began, tapping a folder on his desk. "And I have some good news and some bad news for you."

My stomach rolled, making me abruptly nauseous. It had been doing a lot of that lately.

"Alright," I sighed. "Give me the bad."

The man looked me over very carefully, then folded his hands on his desk.

"I'm afraid we're not going to be able to help you conceive," he said flatly. "At least not right now."

Anger seethed through me. My upper lip curled back on its own.

"Why?" I demanded. "Did you lose Mr. Bishop's specimen *again?*"

Slowly, wordlessly, the director shook his head. "No. Not at all."

"My bloodwork then?" I tilted my head.

"Is all well within normal ranges," the man assured me. He pulled a piece of paper from my file. "Good liver function. Low cholesterol. In fact, you're quite healthy."

Healthy. Healthy was good, wasn't it?

"I don't understa—"

"You'd actually be a prime candidate for IVF," the director said merrily. "Except for one small, but disqualifying thing."

My mouth was still open as he rotated the lab report one-hundred eighty degrees and then slid it my way.

"You're already pregnant."

# Twenty-Eight

## JULIANA

The journey was so much longer this time, so much less pleasant. There was a layover in Philadelphia. A delay on the tarmac. It turned out the rental car company had lost my reservation, so I spent an extra hour at Sky Harbor airport waiting to be shoehorned into a compact car.

It didn't matter. I'd be returning the thing in a matter of hours.

The ride into the desert was bleak and cold, my tired eyes fixed on the long line of perfectly straight asphalt that stretched into the darkness. Two hours later I was standing before the house. All the same lights were on, but it looked so much less warm and inviting than it had the last time I was here.

The giant iron knocker felt cold and heavy as I took it in my hand. As I slammed it against the teak door, my whole body felt fifty pounds heavier.

"Holy SHIT! Jules!"

Gage's smile was so genuine, so wholesome, it nearly broke me. He swept me into the biggest, most amazing bear-hug of my life, practically spinning me around the foyer as the others came rushing in from the back of the house.

Devyn went next, crushing me against his chest as I forced a smile. But my smile didn't last long. It faded throughout the rest of the greeting, until Maverick had finished hugging me and was finally putting me back down on my feet.

"I can't believe you're here!" said Maverick. "I never would've imagined you'd surprise us like—"

"I'm pregnant."

The words obliterated all smiles, all happiness and merriment. Not because they weren't still happy or anything, but because all three men were stunned into complete and utter silence.

For a long moment, the only sound was the desert wind outside. It howled through the open atrium, like some strange but haunting song.

"P—Pregnant?" said Devyn.

"Yes."

"You're sure?"

I cocked my head and made a face.

"Okay, sorry," he said apologetically. "Of course you're sure." His expression of shock turned into one of awkward hospitality. "Come in! Come in, please."

I didn't want to come in. I didn't want to go anywhere. I only wanted what I'd come for, and what I'd come for would take all of three minutes.

"Listen, it's not like I didn't want this," I began. "And I'm very happy about it. Trust me. The only, uh... small detail is—"

They were already halfway to the kitchen, herding me down the hallway as they had last time. I went reluctantly, and by the time I arrived Gage was already reaching for the wine glasses. Maverick shot him a dirty look, and he quickly offered me a bottle of water instead.

I waved the water away. Devyn pulled out a chair for me, and I refused that too.

"I need something from you," I said, trying to be brave. "All of you."

Gage glanced downward, his gaze settling upon my belly. "Seems like you already got something from us," he smirked.

I ignored the joke. From my jacket pocket I pulled three long swabs in plastic tubes. Each was labeled with a different name.

The kitchen went even more silent than the foyer had.

"You need to know who the father is," said Maverick plainly. "That's why you're here."

I nodded, slowly. Their expressions went blank.

"It's probably one of them," Devyn said, jerking his chin at the others. "You spent a week here with them. You and I only spent a single night together."

"Maybe," I allowed. "But the night you and I got

together was closer to my ovulation date. Roughly, anyway. So it could conceivably be any one of you."

"Conceivably," Gage spoke, but for once the joke was mirthless.

"Sorry. Poor choice of words."

The men stood there for a long time, staring curiously at the swabs. I held them out, spread in three directions, pointing at each of them. But no one moved.

"Look, I know how stupidly formal this is," I said, "but I need to be sure. We didn't go through a fertility clinic or anything, obviously. Still, I'm willing to take on one-hundred percent responsibility insofar as custody, financials, and such. Once paternity is establish, I'll have my lawyers draw up a petition to surrender parental righ—"

"You're kidding, right?" Maverick interrupted. "*That's* why you're here?"

"What?"

"You want our DNA? You came all the way out here for that?"

I was confused, tired, disorientated. Taken aback, I shrugged.

"So you didn't come here to see or talk to us," Gage squinted. "You came here for cheek swabs... and that's *it?*"

My mouth went as dry as the desert outside. All of sudden I wished I'd taken the water.

"I... I just wanted—"

"You wanted what?" said Maverick. "A baby? Well seems like you got one. But you don't want a father, do you?

No, not that. You just want a donor. A donor who walks away."

"But it's always been that way," I shot back. "Nothing's changed. This is always what I wanted."

"Yeah?" Gage offered. "And what about what *we* want?"

I hated seeing Gage like this. He'd always been the one to make me smile, make me laugh. Right now though, he looked confused. Hurt. Even angry.

*Fuck.*

Gathering myself, I tried to examine it logically. I still didn't understand their reactions at all. They knew why I'd come here the first time, they knew what I'd been seeking. Devyn had even offered it, but Devyn was being uncharacteristically silent.

I stood half in the archway, still refusing to enter the room. The guys took turns staring at each other in silence. For a very long time, no one spoke.

"Well... I guess congratulations, then."

Devyn had finally spoken, from the other side of the kitchen. Leaning against the counter with his arms crossed, his face was stoic. His expression entirely unreadable.

"Do what she wants."

He took the lead, plucking his swab from my hand. Locking eyes with me, he opened his mouth and dragged the cotton tip through the inside of one cheek, twisting it in both directions. I wondered how many times he'd done this for the military. More than once, it looked like.

By the time he'd reinserted the swab into the protective tube, the others were doing the same.

"There," Maverick said when everything was finished. He was the last to hand me his swab. "You got what you wanted."

I tried to swallow but I couldn't. I could only nod. "T–Thank you."

"Is there a hotel we could drop you off at?" he asked.

His words were cold. Clinical. Gone was the warmth, the levity, the affection.

"No. I have a car."

"Good then," he said turning away. "Drive safe."

One by one they left the room, with Devyn exiting last. He shot me one final look — something that looked like understanding maybe, but laced with sorrow.

Then he was gone.

The walk back through the foyer seemed to take a thousand steps, but I made it alone. I closed the door, started the car, and choked back tears as I turned out of the driveway.

# Twenty-Nine

## JULIANA

There was feeling bad, and there was feeling like utter and complete shit. Both sucked, but the third option – the feeling like utter and complete shit tinged with uncontrollable, irrational anger – that was the absolute worst.

The ride home was a nightmare montage of being angry, falling asleep, then waking up and feeling terrible all over again. I knew I'd handled the whole situation poorly. I'd broken the news to the guys in a way that was cold and clinical, at a time when they were all so happy to see me.

Then again, I needed to break ties. The longer I delayed cutting things off, the harder it would be for all of us. I obviously had to tell them, and I needed to know my child's biological father. But beyond that, I didn't need anyone else in my life. There would barely be time for the baby. And the baby, I knew, would require my full and total attention.

For the next week or more I remained numb, immersing myself in my work. I would stay at the office for as long as possible, before coming home exhausted and flopping into bed.

I eventually made appointments with a well-recommended obstetrician. I was given a clean bill of health and a regimen of prenatal vitamins and strict orders to avoid stress, caffeine, and a whole host of other things. From there I tried to focus on the joy of finally being pregnant. I even put together the baby's nursery piece by piece, lovingly decorating everything I could without yet knowing the baby's sex.

But no matter what I did, there was no joy. There was no happiness to the whole thing, knowing how I'd left it with the guys.

*Shit.*

So far they'd given me my space and hadn't contacted me. Probably because it's what they imagined I wanted. And it *was* what I wanted... to an extent. At least it was what I told myself I wanted, for a good twenty-three hours of the day.

But it was always that last hour, right before sleep, that the doubts crept in. Those final delirious moments before sleep took me, where the loneliness was thickest and my heart felt heavy and the memories of being with all three of them would flood my tired, weary mind.

It was during one such night, right before midnight, that I picked up my phone on a whim. I punched in all three of their phone numbers and sent a single, two-word text message, making sure to hit the SEND button before something inside me cause me to change my mind:

# I'm sorry.

I thought it might make me feel better. It didn't make me feel anything. Maybe because, as Gage had pointed out, I was still only thinking about myself. I was only trying to rationalize things within my own brain and assuage my own guilt. I still wasn't thinking about *their* needs, *their* wants, *their* desires.

In short, I sucked.

The guys still hadn't responded to my text, nor did I really expect them to. I could only hope they believed the sincerity of the statement.

Their swabs still rested in the pencil-holder on the corner of my apartment's desk. Three plastic tubes. Three names. Three amazingly brave, fantastic men who would be the envy of any woman in the world. Men who would each make an incredible biological father, no matter which of them it might be.

And yet I still didn't know.

Pre-birth paternity tests were so simple now, and non-invasive. Nothing like the potentially risky amniocentesis tests of old. It required DNA swabs from the potential fathers, and a small sample of the mother's blood, taken right from the arm. It was quick. Easy. Definitive. And it could be done as early as the fifth week of pregnancy, which I was well past.

*So how come you still haven't done it?*

That was the million-dollar question. There was something stopping me, some unknown reason preventing me from going forward and finding out whether my baby would be Maverick's, or Gage's, or Devyn's. I'd thought hard about all three of them. I could even admit I loved each of them in their own special way, and would be thrilled no matter who ended up fathering my child.

No, the guys were definitely not the problem.

The issue was with me.

I was waist-deep in the usual bullshit of the day when Aric came bursting into my office, moving at least fifty-percent quicker through the glass hallways than usual. His Clark Kent face was drawn with something that looked like worry. And worry wasn't something that suited him.

"We might have a problem."

I stopped sifting through the artist proofs for Bagel Maniac, which I'd promised to make the premiere bagel outlet in all five boroughs. The campaign would be fun, funny, and aggressive. I was actually looking forward to it.

"I just heard from Robert Valentine," said Aric. "Really strange phone call. I got the sense he *might* be giving us the brush-off."

"*Valentine?*" I laughed. "C'mon. You're being paranoid."

"Maybe," Aric allowed. "But could you give him a shout to put my mind at ease? Or would you rather we be caught with our pants down?"

Robert Valentine was our oldest client. Our biggest client. He was the CEO and lead designer over at Legendary Gaming — the company I'd "made" with my viral zombie ad campaign.

We'd done every single piece of work for LG since its inception. All concept art, all promotion. Every last ounce of their marketing, from real-world campaigns to running every branch of their social media.

"What did he say exactly?"

"It's not what he said," Aric replied. "It's what he *didn't* say. He seemed nervous as hell, and he didn't ask about anything. There were no deadline adjustments, no changes to concept. No progress reports he wanted to talk about. It was the shortest weekly phone call we ever had with him. By the time he hung up, the entire conference room was left looking at each other, baffled."

Aric still looked worried. That concerned me.

"Alright. I'll feel him out."

"Thanks boss."

I watched him go, exiting my office stiffly and without his usual, casual gait. He was definitely rattled. Eventually I would have to tell him I was pregnant, and that time would have to be sooner rather than later. Aric was the one person I trusted, and it wouldn't do to keep it from him for too long. Plus, I was sort of looking forward to it. So far, keeping my pregnancy to myself had made it seem almost surreal. Like it wasn't really happening.

Picking up my phone, I dialed Robert Valentine's direct number. Maybe I couldn't spill the beans about the child I was carrying just yet, but at the very least I could put my assistant at ease.

# Thirty

**GAGE**

The dune buggy's engine sputtered as I killed the power, coughing out one last misfire that echoed through the garage. It definitely needed service. Especially considering how hard we all rode it.

But sometimes, you just have to get way out in the desert to think things through.

It had been one of those epic sunset rides. The kind where you drive to the most remote place you can find and just sit there, absorbing the silence. I'd watched the sky turn yellow, then orange, then a crazy, beautiful red. I stayed there for the blues and purples, too, just thinking about everything.

And that's when I'd made the decision to call her.

It was going against the others, and I hated that part. But in the end, I couldn't get Juliana out of my mind. Not just because she might be carrying my child, although that was definitely a part of it. But mostly because in the short time we'd spent together, I'd felt closer to her than any other woman in my entire life.

I killed the lights and made my way through the courtyard, passing beneath the double arch that guided me back into the main part of the house. Music blared from the direction of the gym: AC/DC by the sound of it, which meant it was Devyn. Maverick would've gone with something ridiculous like Mozart or Beethoven, which I could never understand. How you could bench-press anything to the sounds of someone hammering away on a piano would always be a mystery to me.

I crept upstairs, feeling almost like I was doing something wrong. At this point though, I didn't care. It felt even more wrong *not* reconnecting with this woman who'd been dropped into our life like an atomic bomb. I for one was tired of living in the radioactive ruins of our bitter silence.

"Look, we're obeying her wishes," Devyn had assured us, several times already. "Trust me, she wants it this way."

I wasn't a hundred-percent sure of that, but I'd respected it anyway. Still, the 'I'm sorry' message she sent a few days prior was a good indication that she was at least *thinking* about us. That we weren't entirely in her rear-view mirror, at least in her heart, if not her mind.

Devyn's door was closed, and the television was on. I chuckled, remembering how pissed he'd been upon learning we'd first bedded Juliana in his own bed. Maverick and I hadn't planned it that way, his just happened to be the first room at the top of the stairs. The earliest place we could finally get at her.

Pushing into my own room, thoughts of that night

ran wild through my head. I could remember the raw intensity of our threeway connection. How wet and eager Juliana had been to have us between those warm, beautiful thighs. Maverick and I had done so many wonderful things to her over the course of that week, both together and alone. Sharing her over and over again, until her whole body trembled.

I could still recall her sneaking into my room in the dead of night, after having screwed Maverick to sleep. I could remember the softness of her lips. The feel of her warm, naked body — still flush with sex — gliding deliciously alongside mine.

It was during such lovemaking in the dead of night, staring deep into each other's eyes, that the two of us truly bonded. That our most personal attachments were formed.

Even while buried inside her I loved making her laugh. Her smile became the world. Her laughter was the medicine that healed my soul. It all seemed stupidly sentimental, looking back on it in the morning. And yet now, sitting alone in this empty bedroom, I realized there was nothing stupid about it at all.

Letting her go back to New York was bittersweet, but as far as I was concerned there was always the chance of something more. There was no way the three of us could've had *that* much fun and not want to repeat it again, especially since we parted on such amazing terms.

But now, thanks to one of us at least, she'd gotten exactly what she wanted. And now that she had it...

*Fuck this.*

I picked up the phone, crossed the room, and locked

the door. Then, settling down into the very bed we'd shared together, I dialed her number...

... and hoped she'd have the courage to pick up.

# Thirty-One

**JULIANA**

"Mmmpph... Gage?"

It was well past midnight, and yet somehow I'd just closed my eyes. I wasn't necessarily asleep yet. But I wasn't entirely awake, either.

The name that appeared on my phone's screen however...

"Yeah, hi. It's me."

I sat upright, positioning the pillow behind me. Pinning my hair back over both ears, I pressed the speakerphone button.

"Sorry for calling so late," he apologized. "I know you're a couple hours ahead of us, but—"

"No, no," I cut him off. "It's all good."

"You *were* asleep though?" he ventured.

"Not sure you could really call it that," I sighed, "but okay."

There was a moment of silence, as the two of us waited for the other to speak. If he was calling me this late he probably had something important to tell me.

Then again it was Gage we were talking about here.

"So how's our kid?"

"*Our* kid?"

"Yes."

I couldn't help but laugh. "And what makes you so sure it's yours?"

"Because I know I went farther than the others," he said proudly. "I shot deeper, too."

"Really?" I challenged. "And how do you know that?"

"Because I just do."

I chuckled. "You sound pretty sure of yourself."

"Wouldn't you be, if you were me?"

I could envision his smile, at the other end of the phone. Bright. Mirthful. Damn, I missed that smile.

"So how are you feeling?" he asked.

"Pretty good," I replied. "I think I'm past the morning sickness. No more nausea, at least."

"Sounds promising."

"Yeah."

"You've still got lots more to look forward to though," he added cheerfully. "Heartburn, fatigue, swollen feet. Going to the bathroom all the time."

"Great," I chuckled.

"Insomnia."

"Got that one locked down," I groaned.

"Restless leg syndrome. Migraines—"

"Migraines?" I winced. "Really?"

"I think so," Gage offered. "I remember reading *something* about them."

I shifted back into bed, pulling the blankets around me. They felt warm. Comfortable.

"So you've been reading about pregnancy?" I asked.

There was a short pause at the other end of the phone. Then: "A little, yeah."

"That's cute, Gage."

"Cute?"

"Very."

It had been so long since I'd heard his voice, I'd almost forgotten what it was like. The memories came flooding back now, all at once. Along with some *other* memories, whether I wanted them or not.

"I just got done riding through the desert," he said. "Did a lot of thinking. A lot of reflecting."

"Reflecting on what?"

"All kinds of things," Gage murmured.

Riding through the desert. Blazing through long stretches of sand, in the middle of nowhere. It sounded amazing right about now.

"So where are you now?" I asked him.

"In my bed," said Gage. He paused again. "You remember my bed, right?"

A knot was forming, somewhere deep in my belly. A warm knot.

"Umm-hmm."

"My bed misses you," said Gage. "It doesn't smell like you anymore."

I opened my mouth to speak, then eventually closed it. I just didn't know what to say.

"Other select parts of me miss you too," he added.

"Yeah," I smirked. "I'll bet."

Static crackled over the phone's speaker, as he exhaled a long, close sigh.

"Jules?"

"What?"

"*I* miss you."

The knot tightened. The warmth in my belly spread.

"I... I miss you too."

There. It was out there now. The words had traveled two-thousand miles in the span of a second, and I couldn't take them back.

"I miss all three of you actually," I added, with the thought it might dilute the impact of my previous statement. In retrospect, it probably did the opposite. "I hate how I left you guys. That whole thing... I handled it wrong."

Was that the other half of an apology? If so, it was very uncharacteristic of me. I couldn't stand being wrong, and I hated eating crow. Still, uttering just these few words felt cathartic. Like lifting a weight from my already tense shoulders.

"It was a difficult situation," said Gage. "I guess there was no easy way to put something like that."

"But—"

"Look, you're a direct person, Jules. It's one of the things we admire about you. Never apologize for telling things how they are."

He stretched, grunting softly into phone. It sounded manly. Sexy.

"Yeah, well there are better ways for sure," I admitted. "I didn't take any of your feelings into account, and that was wrong."

My comforter felt heavy and secure now, warming me to a new level of relaxation. For a second I imagined Gage was behind me, pressing into me from behind. His long, beautiful arms wrapped tightly around me instead of the blanket.

"Everything else okay?" he asked.

I inhaled slowly, deeply, then let it out as a sigh. "Pretty much. Just some work stuff I have to sort through. Nothing I can't handle."

He chuckled gruffly. "I know *that.*"

"How about you guys?" I asked. "How's Maverick? Still dangerous?"

"Dangerous as ever," he said in his Iceman voice. "I won't fly anywhere near him."

My smile widened. "And Devyn?"

"Devyn's Devyn" he said simply. "He's a little quieter than normal, maybe. Which is fine by Maverick and I, believe me."

Images floated back, mental pictures of the house, the guys, and everything we'd done in it. I wanted to focus on the good ones. But I kept seeing the helicopter, taking off. The three of them slowly exiting the kitchen, turning away from me after handing over their swabs.

"Do the others know you're calling me?" I asked abruptly.

"No," Gage admitted. "But they will tomorrow."

"Because you tell each other everything."

"Always, yes."

I nodded into the phone. The longing was there again, the feelings growing stronger, more dangerous. Like Maverick buzzing the tower, in Top Gun.

"I gotta get some sleep," I told Gage.

"Cool. No worries."

"I have an early meeting tomorrow. It's sort of important."

"Kick its ass, then," he said. "That's an order."

I sighed again, more sleepily this time.

"Goodnight Gage," I breathed.

"Goodnight Jules."

"Oh, and one more thing..."

I paused, but only for a moment.

"You can call me again," I said. "You know... if you want to."

Without even closing my eyes, I could already visualize his white-toothed grin.

"You can count on it," he said, and hung up.

# Thirty-Two

## JULIANA

I hadn't seen Robert Valentine in almost half a year, except on Zoom calls. And I hadn't been to Legendary Gaming in almost twice as long, ever since Aric took over the everyday aspects of dealing with our most important client.

The building was the same, although they'd taken over many more floors. Legendary had acquired a few fledgling game companies and had recently swallowed a pretty big rival. They were expanding fast into the realm of virtual reality, and had built a cutting-edge rendering engine that would apparently "blow the doors off" anything else out there, if they could ever get it released. The problem was the project kept getting knocked back. The specifications kept changing with the invention of newer technologies, and at times it seemed the whole thing would never get done.

I didn't envy Robert *that* seemingly unending problem, nor did I begrudge him for being unusually short on the phone with me the other day. But going over things for a second or third time and replaying our call in my mind,

I had to agree with Aric's simple but vague assessment:

Something was definitely wrong.

The elevator deposited me into their same old lobby, where I encountered their new front desk and all new receptionist. Everything was bigger and more impressive, except for the short, pale man behind the desk who didn't seem fit at all.

"Good morning miss, how can I help you?"

Even the man's voice was thin and tinny. The enormous desk seemed to swallow him whole, making him seem small and out of place. Like a little boy trying on his father's shoes.

"I'm here to see Mr. Valentine."

His eyes went wide. A moment later, after scanning something on the desk in front of him, he shook his head.

"I don't have any visitors, for—"

"Never mind. I can find him myself."

I pushed past him, moving in the direction of the steel-framed door off to one side. Before the man behind the desk could protest, I reached out and pressed the button I knew would buzz me in. The desk was new, but the button was still the same... and located in the same spot.

"M–Ma'am!" he stammered. "You can't just—"

Whatever other protests the receptionist had were cut off as the door swung closed behind me. I made my way swiftly through the maze of initial corridors, then out into the project management floor.

"Damn."

In the past, this had been the lifeblood of Legendary Gaming – the brainstorm area for all creative hired talent. In the past it had been full of mismatched desks and tables, even a few couches here and there. People discussed things in the wild. They drank coffee together, and huddled over laptops while shuffling through flowcharts, proposals, and concept artwork.

But not anymore.

Gone were the couches, the tables, the homegrown, grassroots feel. The haphazard placement of desks had been replaced by long rows and columns of prefabricated walls and whitewashed partitions. The whole thing was a giant cube farm now, filled with evenly-spaced people sitting in standard office chairs all working on identical terminals.

*Like good little plants, growing in their little square pots.*

It was a phrase Aric had once said, when we were pitching a campaign within a similar style office. I had been sad, then. It made me even sadder now.

"Juliana! Hi!"

The dark-haired, middle-aged woman who came rushing up beside me swept me into a semi-formal hug. Tori was one of Legendary's first six employees, and had been with the company long enough to be calling me by my first name. Which really said something.

"Oh my God, it's been *forever!*" she gasped. "How in the world are you?"

*Very pregnant,* I wanted to say. But that cat wasn't out of the bag just yet.

"Better than average," I smiled instead, hugging her back. "And you?"

"Pretty damn good," she declared, "except for the three different college tuitions kicking our ass at once right now."

"College!" I smiled. "Already?"

"Already," she groaned, rolling her eyes. "Then again it was David's idea to have the kids so close together, so this is all on him. If it were up to me, I would've spaced them out a little. Given my poor body a break, you know?"

I stood there for a moment, trying to remember her children's names and coming up totally empty. Luckily, Tori put me out of my misery.

"You're looking for Robert?"

"Yes please."

"He's all over the place these days," Tori groaned, "especially with all the new stuff going on. But come with me. I know where to find him."

Through a half dozen doors we went, and up two flights of glass-walled stairs. The offices on the higher floors stretched around the outside of the building, giving everyone a window view. In the shape of a U, they looked down over the project area as well.

I found Robert Valentine in the ass end of a small, executive break room, stirring synthetic sugar into a steaming mug of very black coffee. When he saw me, his eyes went wide as billiard balls.

"Juliana!" he cried. "What a great surprise!"

It took less than a quarter second for the fear to leave his face, replaced immediately by a warmth so genuine it was almost convincing. He gave me the obligatory hug, then ushered me quickly into what amounted to his new office. Which, I noted, was smaller than his old one.

"I had no idea we had a meeting today," he began. "I didn't think we—"

"C'mon," I cut him off, with a quick glance that said everything. "It's *me*."

Robert stopped talking while I paced his new office, taking it all in. His desk was the same one he'd always had, but in this room it was too large. There were no more plants. Half his little aviation tchotchkes were missing too.

*Ahhhh, shit.*

Something was most definitely wrong. Something big enough that not even Robert could get a handle on it.

"Wanna tell me what's going on?" I asked.

Robert's usually cheerful face was criss-crossed with sleep and stress lines. The worry in his expression was gone now, though. At the moment, he wore the relieved resignation of someone tired of running. Someone eager to finally make a full confession.

"I'm sorry Juliana," he said, his voice sounding hollow and defeated. Raising one weary arm, he pointed to an empty chair.

"Sit down and I'll tell you everything."

# Thirty-Three

## JULIANA

"God*dammit* Robert!" I shouted again. "Just like that? After all this time!?"

The news was shocking, and yet a bigger part of me could totally believe it. I'd become blindly complacent. Unreasonably comfortable. I'd taken my biggest, oldest client completely for granted, and now it was finally coming around to bite me right in the ass.

Legendary Gaming was signing on with someone else.

"Who?" I demanded. "Who could possibly—"

"We're going with Skyline." Robert said flatly.

It was the worst thing he could've possibly said. I would've rather he just stabbed me in the stomach.

"*Those* vultures?" I grunted. "Seriously?"

"Juliana, it's not my decision," he reiterated.

"You're the CEO!" I blurted. "The owner! The founder! The—"

"We went public, and we have shareholders now," Robert pointed out. "There are a whole new level of higher ups. Higher even than me."

I shook my spinning head, still trying to understand what happened. Our biggest client. Even worse, our biggest revenue source. Ripped right out from under us.

"I'm sorry," Robert said for the hundredth time. "I fought like hell for you, believe me. It's not like you haven't done right by us, but there other factors."

"Other factors?" I laughed bitterly. "Like what?"

"Connectivity," Robert said simply. "Skyline has west coast offices as well as the one here in New York. When it comes to audience they cast a wider net. They have much longer reach."

"So?" I challenged. "They have double the overhead. And you're the one paying for it."

"It's so much more than that, though," said Robert. "They have the finger on the pulse of—"

The tag-line was so lame I actually broke out laughing before he could finish. Long and hard I laughed, but inwardly I was more saddened that Robert was actually buying into this bullshit.

"I hear they're not even organic," I practically spat. "Multiple times they've been caught buying followers. They use click-farms to bump up their numbers, and make client's campaigns seem much more successful than they actually are."

Robert steepled his fingers together. He appeared to be thinking.

"I've heard those rumors too," he said at last. "But the whole thing's practically done, and the decision's been made." He shifted uncomfortably in his chair. "We'll finish out all current contracts with you, of course. Anything we're doing with Shameless right now will be seen through to the end, no matter what."

I let out a short, sardonic laugh. "How magnanimous of you."

"Juliana—"

"Remember the beginning, Robert?" I jumped in. "When it was just you and me? When you came to me with half a game concept and zero budget and I still took you on and risked everything I had?"

His chin lowered as he looked down at his desk. "I remember."

"We forged our companies that day," I said proudly. "From the fires of creativity. You had *balls* back then, Robert! We both did. Balls so big we weren't afraid to take them out of our pants and wave them around."

At that he laughed. "Now *there's* a visual, huh?"

His attempt at levity fell on deaf ears, though.

"Goodbye, Robert."

I whirled, spinning on my heel and launching in the direction of the door. He called after me, but I could tell his heart wasn't in it. Maybe, I realized, his heart hadn't been in anything since his company had gone public.

*Remember this moment.*

My friend had finally sold out, so to speak. But was

he really the wrong one? At least he'd lined his pockets before giving up the mantle of power. Maybe, between the two of us, *I* was the asshole.

Right now at least, I definitely felt like one.

# Thirty-Four

## JULIANA

The next few weeks were a whirlwind of work and stress, made a thousand times worse by the fact I could only drink decaf. I had to dump out the coffee Aric brought me some mornings, and sneak in my own. I also had to stop our Friday afternoon sushi meetings, by pretending to crave Mexican, or Thai.

Aric and I spent all day every day trying to book new clients, while our teams stepped up to keep the clients we had happy. We sat down with our accountants. Ran the numbers every which way. In the end though, there were no two ways about it: the loss of Legendary Gaming would radically change our business, in ways I shuddered to even think about.

*Damn.*

I laid one-hundred percent of the blame on myself of course, for putting all my eggs in one basket. I'd just always thought that basket would be there. I was also to blame for not paying more attention to Skyline, and their rapid encroachment on the marketing industry. Their business had exploded so quickly, and in so many directions, I should've been wary of something like this.

It wasn't all bad, though.

For one, the guys had taken to calling me every other day. They did it one at a time, taking turns making nighttime calls so they wouldn't 'overwhelm' me. Gage had of course told them we'd spoken. In that respect, he reopened Pandora's Box.

At this point I welcomed it though.

Still keeping things secret until the second trimester, I had no one to talk to about my pregnancy, not even my family. But with Devyn, Maverick and Gage, I had a whole trio to run my woes by. They got to hear all about my aches and pains, my mood swings and cravings. And it was good just being able to talk to them again. Their advice, as strange or funny as it was sometimes, was always welcome.

Another thing that happened: Gage started sending me gifts for the baby. They started small; adorable camouflage onesies, or bibs with funny sayings on them. They progressed to teething rings and toddler toys and even books, some of which I didn't have the heart to tell him were years away from being read. Eventually the gifts got even bigger: activity jumpers and baby swings, even a really expensive-looking glider that would take me a good two hours to put together. Worst of all he sent these things to the office address, where they always arrived wrapped in plain brown paper.

I began piling the gifts in the back corner of my office, behind a large Ficus tree and a high-backed chair. But there were too many of them. So many I even stopped opening them. Eventually Aric came in and closed the door behind him, and the face he made was full of sarcastic excitement.

"You *know* all the walls in here are glass, right?"

I thought of two to three lies, in the span of five quick seconds. The lies all sucked though.

"Is it?" my assistant's face lit up. "*Are* you?"

He saw in my eyes before I even said it. For the first time in a while, I allowed myself a genuine smile.

"Yes. I am."

Squealing with joy Aric rushed forward, engulfing me in those big, long arms. It felt wonderful, being enveloped by him. Squeezing him back, I let a single tear flow down my happy cheek.

"Juliana! CONGRATULA—"

And then the floodgates opened all the way, and I was crying openly into his chest.

It felt amazing, all around. The warmth. The comfort. The physical closeness of someone I knew and respected and even loved, holding me so tightly while I let out weeks worth of pent-up emotion and strain. For a full minute I just stayed there, crying but not sobbing. Not even caring that all the walls were glass, and the entirety of the company could be witnessing my apparent breakdown.

"This is amazing," Aric was saying. "Better than amazing! Have you told your family? Is that where all these gifts are coming from?"

I shook my head. Aric put on his pondering face.

"Oh! I see!" He squeezed my shoulders. "They're from *him*." He examined my expression, trying to read me. "Is that a good thing or a bad thing?"

"A good one," I croaked.

"Then I'm thrilled for you," he said wholeheartedly. "I know how much you've wanted this, Juliana. I know how many hoops you've jumped through to get here."

He looked down at me in a brotherly way and touched my cheek. His grin was so wide it was infectious.

"I can't believe it! You're going to have a baby!"

"I sure am."

"Holy shit. Holy fucking shit!"

"I know," I chuckled. "It still hasn't hit me yet."

"Wait until this poor kid sees what he's up against!" Aric declared. "His mother's a ruthless tyrant!" He paused for a moment, rubbing his chin in consideration. "Or maybe he or she will rule *you*," he theorized.

"I doubt it," I smirked.

"Oh no, I think that's it," Aric teased. "An adorable little boy is going to steal your heart. And if it's a girl..." he shook his head slowly. "She's going to be a mini version of yourself. She'll give you such a run for your money you'll be coming in here crying each morning, begging me for help."

I laughed, and the laughter felt so good I couldn't stop. We both ended up laughing long enough for me to dry my tears, although the front of Aric's shirt was still wet with them.

Eventually we fell silent, just staring at each other.

Through his dark-framed glasses, Aric's eyes seized mine.

"You know we're going to get through all this," he said softly. He twirled one long finger in a circle. "That Shameless is going to be totally alright?"

I sniffed. I nodded.

"Good. Because I need you focused," said Aric. "I need you *mean*. I need the old, merciless Juliana — the one who won't take no for an answer. The one who kicks ass without even taking names, because taking names is for losers."

My eyes went glassy. In this moment, I never admired him more.

"You've got her," I said sternly. "I promise."

He stared at me for another long second or two, then nodded firmly. When he finally let go of me, he pointed to the pile of gifts in the corner.

"Might want to get someone to take this stuff out of here," my assistant grinned. "Before everyone thinks we're opening a baby nursery."

# Thirty-Five

## JULIANA

I woke the next morning refreshed and re-energized, and ready to take on the world. And for the next twelve hours I *did* take on the world, which left me breathless and happy and somewhat exhausted, at least mentally, by the time I'd finally returned home.

It was Friday, and I usually rewarded myself with a few drinks at the bar on the corner of my block. Since that wasn't currently an option, I'd let my recent Fridays be motivated by food, instead.

My indecision had me stopping before my building, in the middle of the sidewalk. I was so famished I could eat right now. I could head north, to the Greek place along third avenue. Or one block west, to Lexington, where they had the most delicious—

"Hey beautiful."

I whirled, ready to serve up my most sarcastic retort. But instead of a stranger, I was staring into the face of familiarity.

"Oh my GOD!"

I rushed forward, throwing my arms around Maverick so quickly it didn't even matter how he got there. I was just so happy to see him. Surprise and shock and explanation — all those things could be figured out later. Right now the only thing that mattered was the feel of his two incredible arms wrapped tightly around me.

"You're *here*..." I breathed.

"Sure am."

He wasn't wearing a uniform, or his fatigues, or anything remotely military. He wore jeans and black boots. A forest green shirt with a black leather jacket.

"You coming back from somewhere?" I asked. "Like Devyn was, or—"

"No," said Maverick. "I came here for you."

I swallowed the lump in my throat, then realized he'd been camping out in front of my building. I don't know how long he'd been standing here, waiting for me. I just knew I was happy and grateful.

"You hungry?" I asked.

"Sure."

I slipped my hand into his. "Let's go. I know a place."

For the next two blocks we walked in happy silence, holding hands like a couple. It felt good. Beyond good, really. The further we walked, the more excited I got.

"Italian?" I asked, pointing up at the awning.

"You're the boss," Maverick smiled.

I intentionally ushered him in first, so I could enjoy how incredible his ass looked in those tight blue jeans. Maverick was every bit as delicious as I remembered him. Probably even more so, since my pregnancy had made me three times hornier than normal.

The place wasn't packed but it wasn't empty, and there was still plenty of seating in the back. We took a darkened booth in the far corner. One that was curved, so we could slide in next to each other.

"You have no idea how good it is to see you," said Maverick. His eyes dropped to my stomach. "So how are you—"

I leaned back, exposing the slight rise that had finally developed in my lower belly. I didn't have very much of a baby bump yet, but there was definitely something there.

"Can I?"

I chuckled happily. "Are you kidding? Of course!"

His hand slid gently, lovingly over my abdomen. I watched it go up and down, his big palm rolling in slow circles just below my navel.

"So is it mine?" he asked, flat out.

I tore off a piece of bread from the basket at the center of the table and shrugged. He looked confused.

"Gage's or Devyn's, then?"

"I actually don't know," I told him. "Those swabs are still sitting on my desk, untouched."

Maverick cocked his head curiously but said nothing.

"It's weird," I told him. "It's like I want to know, but I also don't. I mean, I know I *need* to know, eventually anyway. But it's like... like I want it to be..."

"All of ours?"

Relief flooded through me. They were just the words I was struggling to find.

"Yes. Exactly." I glanced down at my plate. "Does that sound strange to you?"

"No actually," said Maverick. "Not at all."

The waitress arrived and we ordered food and drinks. But the longer I looked at Maverick, the more I found myself suddenly uninterested in eating.

"So you came here for me, huh?" I asked, when we were alone again.

"Yes."

"Why?"

He lifted one sculpted arm and slid it past my shoulders. Pulling me closer, those hazel eyes found mine.

"I was hoping you'd come home with me," he said. "Or rather, *we* were hoping."

"We?"

"Yes."

The warmth was back in my stomach. This time it was hotter than ever.

"Home?" I murmured. "To Arizona?"

Maverick shrugged one beautiful shoulder.

"We talk about you all day, every day," he said. "Juliana, we're *obsessed*."

"With me?"

"Of course with you!" Maverick smiled. "You showed up out of the blue and rocked our world. And now you're having our *child*. But you're here in New York, all alone, and that part drives us crazy."

I shook my head in confusion. "Why?"

"Because we want to take *care* of you," he breathed. "And not just you, but the child inside you. You're facing this whole thing alone, going to doctors visits and sonograms without anyone there to support you."

His eyes glimmered with compassion, with love. I'd been bullshitted by the best of them, and I could dish out a good amount of it myself. But right here, right now, I could tell Maverick meant every single word.

"Gage, Devyn and I... we want to feed you, take care of you, rub your feet at night," he went on. "We want to *be* there for those things with you. We want to hear the sound of the baby's heart beating."

He studied me for a reaction, but I was too shocked to even move. Too surprised to give him one.

"I know it sounds stupid," he began. "Even silly–"

"It's not silly," I cut him off. "It's not stupid."

I reached out and placed my palm against the sharp, masculine curve of his stubbled jaw.

"It's sweet."

I wanted to kiss him so very badly. Kiss him long, kiss him hard. But I wanted *more,* too.

So much more.

"I'll come."

The words tumbled from my mouth, totally unexpectedly. I didn't regret them.

"For a few days at least," I said. "But yes. I'll come. Let's go."

Maverick's face was so lit up it was actually adorable. But I'm not sure he was a hundred-percent convinced.

"Do you mean it?" he asked hopefully. "Because there are flights out of here tonight. We can—"

Now I *did* kiss him, my hungry, churning mouth devouring his. There was no awkwardness, no hesitation.

*Mmmmmmm....*

I sighed in submission as his tongue sought mine, rolling hotly through my mouth with the impact of a thunderclap. In that one instant we were lovers again. Like no time had passed at all.

"We can eat first of course," he smiled, when we finally broke apart. "Before we—"

"Or you could follow me in there and bend me over," I pointed to a nearby door. "Pull my panties to the side and fuck me from behind."

I didn't even wait for an answer. I slid from the bench seat, walked halfway down the hall at the back of the restaurant, then slipped through the door I'd mentioned.

My pulse quickened as it swung closed to the sound of footsteps behind me.

# Thirty-Six

## JULIANA

The unisex bathroom was clean and pretty — a well-kept, single-use version of the other two flanking it. I'd knew this already, because I'd been in here before. But never like this.

The light was off. The door lock clicked.

"C'mere."

It was the only word he said. The only thing Maverick uttered before grabbing me by the hips, spinning me around, and shoving me forward with his strong right hand.

*Yes!*

My skirt came up. As the cooler air kissed the skin of my warm bottom, I heard the jangle of a belt buckle and the sound of a fast zipper.

A second later, deft, nimble fingers were stretching my thong to one side.

*Fuck yes.*

I gripped the cold porcelain of the sink in my hands, thrusting my ass backward as Maverick's palm slipped between my thighs. He rubbed three fingers up and down, getting them slick with my wetness, then used that wetness to coat himself as well.

By the time he pushed snugly against my opening, my legs were shaking with anticipation.

"Oooohhhhhhh..."

I couldn't contain my excitement as he filled me from within. Buried inside me, his warm body curving against mine, Maverick clapped one stern hand over my mouth.

"*Shhhh,*" he breathed, into my ear. "You can't make noise."

With that he pulled back and shoved himself inside, stifling my moans with his thick, meaty palm. Harder and harder he went, picking up speed, fucking me in the darkness with raw, savage abandon. One hand gripped my hip so hard it almost hurt. The other covered my mouth.

*OhmyGod OhmyGod Ohmyfucking–*

My moans slowly turned to whimpers, then breathless sighs. Cautiously Maverick removed his hand, sliding it down to my other hip so he could gain more leverage...

Then he began fucking my brains out.

My body was his. My surging ass felt like it belonged in his strong, capable hands. Eventually my eyes adjusted to the darkness, and with the light seeping in through the door-cracks I could watch myself in the mirror, bouncing backwards to meet his thrusts.  It was so fucking hot, seeing myself like this.  Watching myself get utterly taken, totally owned.

*Fuuuuck!*

My hair bounced wildly.  My mouth hung open, locked in an 'O' of pure ecstasy.  Our bodies crashed together again and again, the pleasure building, the pent-up excitement of finally being filled again washing over me and obliterating everything else in my world.

*Oh my GOD I needed this.*

I did, and I hadn't realized how much until now.  I'd gone from a week of incredible two-on-one sex any time I wanted it to a passionate night with a third lover who'd taken me over and over.  And then... nothing.

For the past few months I'd been hornier than ever, replaying all these sexual encounters in my mind.  And on top of that, I was pregnant.  Whatever crazy hormones were surging through my body kept me constantly excited, always wet.  At first I was alarmed by how incredibly turned on I was, but eventually I learned to suppress it.  There was too much else to do.  Too many other things to worry about.

But now...

Now, at least for the upcoming weekend, I'd decided I was giving myself the gift of 'what the fuck.'  I'd happily surrendered to the touch of this hot Navy SEAL hellbent on fucking the life out of me, and right after that I'd fly across the country and fuck his friends, too.

And I knew I'd love every dripping second of it.

"Juliana..." I heard Maverick growl in warning. His voice was terse, like he was holding something back. Something tremendous.

"Go for it," I breathed, already soaring over the edge.

We came quickly and explosively, one right after the other. Our grunts were low, our hisses through clenched teeth as we climaxed silently in the warmth and darkness. Maverick's hands flexed powerfully into the curve of my hips as we screwed our bodies against each other, so tightly and with such force we'd surely have bruises tomorrow.

The whole encounter took three, maybe four minutes, tops. Which was absolutely *perfect*.

My lover withdrew with an animalistic grunt, then pulled my thong back over my swollen, come-filled pussy. Patting it twice for good measure, he pulled my skirt down as well.

"*Now* I'm hungry."

# Thirty-Seven

## JULIANA

Flying back was so much better with a companion. So much more relaxing with Maverick at my side, cuddled together as we stared out the tiny oval window at the clouds and sky.

It had taken me five minutes to pack. Two minutes to call Aric and tell him I was escaping New York for the next few days, and my assistant happily assured me he had 'had things' while I was gone.

By the time we landed in Sky Harbor it still seemed like Friday, which it almost really was. Maverick's hand guided the steering wheel as we sped away from the lights of Phoenix, slipping into the darkness of the desert only to be swallowed by the nighttime sky.

I was exhausted, mentally and physically, but my excitement built again as the house faded into view. I relished the warm, orange and yellow glow of the many windows. Craved the warmth and camaraderie that I knew awaited within.

Devyn and Gage weren't just awake at this late hour, they were thrilled to see me. They burst through the front door and raced right down the driveway, hugging and spinning me around happily but still gently, each of them staring at my belly and wondering how much I could take.

"Don't worry," I grinned back at them. "I'm far from fragile."

They swept me quickly from the cold night and into the house, where the warmth and coziness enveloped me like a favorite blanket, straight out of the dryer. The kisses came next, first fast and then slow. I stood there in the center of their little circle, kissing them back and squeezing all the various parts of their hard, beautiful bodies that I remembered most.

But it was late. Very late. The wee hours of the morning.

Luckily the guys had that covered, too.

"Come on," said Devyn, slipping an arm around my waist. "You've had a long trip."

He led me into the living room, where the gas fireplace was already providing its soothing warmth. The windows were shuttered throughout, all the way down to the floor. The lights were off. Everything was dark and warm.

In the dim light I could make out a vast pile of blankets and pillows, spread out across the floor. The guys led me in that direction, then took turns removing my clothing. They stripped me down to my underwear, each taking a moment to glide a slow hand over the slight swell of my pregnant belly. It was cute, watching how tentatively they did this. Maybe the most adorable thing in the world.

Then they were taking their clothes off too, and my eyes were busy crawling over every glorious stretch of firelit muscle.

Eventually they pulled me down into the nest of pillows and comforters, and curled up on either side of me. I was spooned and cuddled. Enveloped by warm arms, kissed by soft lips. They shifted their hard bodies against mine, covering every inch of my exposed skin with the warmth of their own. All while the fireplace crackled in the background.

*Mmmmmmm...*

It was total heaven. Pure nirvana. Best of all it was the polar opposite of loneliness, as I now had three amazing men surrounding me, holding me, shielding me from the world. Three men that I somehow knew would attend to my every need.

In time the kisses grew sleepier, the touching lazy and slow. Somewhere in the warm shadows of the flickering firelight, my eyelids grew so heavy it became impossible to keep them open.

And so I didn't.

The last thing I remembered as sleep took me was Devyn wrapped around me from behind, his face resting lightly against my cheek. He whispered softly, sweetly, his breath hot and electric against the outer rim of my ear.

"You're *home* now."

# Thirty-Eight

## JULIANA

I dreamt, and in my dream I was swimming naked through a beautiful, tranquil lake with an island in the middle. The water was warm and soothing. Crystal clear. It enveloped me with a wonderful heat as I swam along, leaving me sleepy and contented.

After swimming for a long time I reached the island, and emerged beneath a breathtaking star-filled sky. I had no clothes, no towel, but I wasn't cold. The moon cast a strange, blanketing warmth over everything, almost like the sun but somehow different.

At the island's center stood a house, glowing warmly from within. I entered the house without knocking, and found myself in a hall with many doors. All of them were open. Soft golden light spilled from each one.

I traversed the hall and found each room was filled with people, laughing and drinking and having fun. They ignored me, largely. Almost like they couldn't see or hear me. Yet one person from each room *could* see me, and that person stopped what they were doing to reach out and pluck something from me. Only I had nothing. I carried nothing, I wore nothing.

Looking down, I realized they were taking *pieces* of me away.

For some reason this didn't alarm me, although it should've. I kept walking, kept stopping at the doorways. And people kept taking from me. Removing small pieces of my arms, my legs, my torso. It didn't hurt. It didn't affect me or stop me from going on. In fact, I sort of *liked* it.

The dream went on, with me sharing pieces of myself until there was almost nothing left. And then I was outside, slipping into the lake again. Surrendering to the warmth of the water, and its soothing tranquil heat.

Little by little, I allowed myself to dissolve away into nothing. But I did it willingly. Happily. I just floated there beneath the star-flung sky, until darkness crept in and a comforting sleep I knew would be utterly endless finally took me...

"Whoa. She lives!"

I sat up abruptly in the sea of blankets and pillows, running both hands through my tangled hair. The room was still dark, but only because the shutters were still down. Through the windows' edges, I could see sunlight fighting to stream in.

"H—How long did I sleep?"

Gage and Devyn were standing in the archway that led into the game room, each with a set of darts in one hand. They were showered. Dressed. They looked ready for anything.

"Probably about eleven hours," Gage reasoned. "Give or take."

"ELEVEN hours!"

I sprang to my feet, and the blankets fell away. I realized — and simultaneously remembered — that I was only wearing a thong.

"Seemed like you really needed the sleep," shrugged Devyn, struggling hard to keep his eyes on mine.

"But—"

"And you were sleeping so soundly and peacefully too," added Gage. "Like an angel. But sexier."

"*Much* sexier," Devyn grinned.

Now they *did* look, and for some reason I didn't bother to cover up. I scratched my head, got my bearings, and turned in the direction of the bathroom.

"An angel with a great ass by the way," said Gage.

I shook that ass for them on a whim, then began gathering my clothes. Though I'd just woken, I didn't feel the slightest bit sleepy. I actually felt pretty fucking fantastic.

"Your stuff's upstairs," said Devyn, "in your room."

*My room.* So I had a room.

"Where's Maverick?"

"Sitting in his Tomcat," joked Gage. "Playing with his joystick."

"Actually he's out back, packing the chopper," Devyn

offered. "Getting us all ready for lunch."

"Lunch?"

"Yeah it's already late for lunch," Devyn went on, "so it's more of an early dinner. But we figured you gotta be hungry, so—"

"I *am* hungry," I told him, realizing just how much as I said it. "Actually, I'm ravenous."

"Good," he smiled back. "Shower, change, and dress for a desert picnic."

"A desert picnic?" I laughed. "And what exactly does a girl wear to a desert picnic?"

Both men looked at each other for a moment, then back at me. Arms crossed, their eyes crawling my practically naked body, the two of them laughed.

"Does it really matter?" Gage winked.

# Thirty-Nine

**DEVYN**

The Gazelle swung in low, cutting through the dry desert air smoothly and efficiently as we hurtled through the canyon. I had to hand it to the French. The thing was a well-oiled piece of engineering, built for speed and maneuverability. Its engine roared with strength. Screamed with power.

But for most of the trip, my eyes were on *her.*

Juliana sat beside me in the back of the chopper, marveling at the sheer beauty of the spectacular scenery. The red-walled canyons of the Tonto Basin raced by. Up ahead, the looming mesas southeast of Sedona jutted upward, the flat-topped plateaus gently kissing the blue and yellow sky.

All I focus on however, was the smooth, warm thigh butted up against mine.

At first I thought it was a miracle that Maverick had talked her into coming back to us. That maybe he had a slicker tongue than both Gage and I originally thought. The more I looked at her however, the more I realized she needed to be here. Whatever was happening back in New York was taking a toll on her. I could tell she was looking to escape from it — at least temporarily — every bit as much as she'd come here for us.

And God, I was hoping that part was true too.

An updraft pushed us another fifty feet in the air, and Juliana's hand clenched my own leg a little tighter. It was cute, watching her push down her nervousness. Her curiosity was infectious, and her childlike wonderment over the landscape was something I actually envied.

Up and up we went, until the object of our quest came into view. Maverick swung us over the flat-topped mesa with casual grace, and a few seconds later we were touching down onto the hard rock surface.

"Oh my God!"

It wasn't the third or fourth or even fifth time she'd uttered the words. I honestly couldn't blame her. The ride had been fast and furious, and the view up here was absolutely staggering.

"Everybody out," Gage said, hopping down. "Lots to unpack."

The whine of the Gazelle's engines wound slowly down, giving way to wind-whipped silence. I helped Juliana from the chopper, guiding her toward the middle area of the rocky platform we were most familiar with. A rough circle of blackened stones served as our fire-pit, made with rocks we'd taken up here from our own property.

"So you've been here before?" she asked, looking

down.

"Lots of times," I told her. "But you're our first and only guest."

She spun in a slow circle, taking in the breathtaking view that came with being three-thousand feet above the canyon floor. Her hair floated in the wind behind her perfect face. Her eyes were glassy and gorgeous.

"Unreal," was all she said.

I kissed her plump, full lips, unable to help myself any longer. It was like drinking from a fountain of liquid rapture.

"Be with you in a minute."

Maverick was already tying the bird down to the series of metal anchors we'd driven into the rock years ago. Gage and I set about unpacking the cargo hold, which was stuffed with everything from blankets and food to bundles of firewood. We'd spent half the morning gathering ironwood while our angel slept, and we had more than enough to make things warm and cozy.

Eventually we spread out in our usual spot, but this time with an array of picnic blankets and a few pillows to make thing softer. It was a little bit of an adjustment, having a woman around. We weren't used to accounting for feminine comforts, but I think all three of us quickly learned that we loved providing them just the same.

Gage got the fire going, and between the wind and the dry desert wood it was blazing hotly in no time. Maverick unpacked the food itself — a bunch of fruit and cheese and other stuff we never would've brought here except for her — while I spun the cap off the first thermos of hot chocolate.

"I can't believe we're on top of a *mesa*," Juliana breathed.

"And we didn't even have to climb," Gage smiled.

I chuckled my agreement. "Climbing's for suckers."

"Suckers and non-pilots," Maverick said, raising his mug.

We toasted by clinking our mugs together and downing the milky, chocolaty deliciousness that Maverick had prepared.

"Well this is amazing," Juliana declared, still staring around in wonder. For dozens of miles in every direction, there was nothing but rock and sky. "Best of all, it's the exact opposite of New York City."

"I still don't see how you live there," said Gage, shaking his head.

"Well look at that," Maverick laughed. "The Oklahoma kid can't figure out the big city. Who would've thought?"

Gage threw a seedless grape at him. He ducked, deftly, but the second shot bounced off the side of his head.

"Maybe it is a little bit like the City," I offered, pointing. "Those other mesas could be fellow skyscrapers. All the wolves and mountain lions running around down there could be the people."

"Diamondbacks too," said Gage. "Slithering through the alleys of the canyons."

If Juliana heard us, there was no indication. She was still staring into the sky, her eyes lost somewhere on the distant horizon. In that one frozen moment she looked heartbreakingly beautiful, and I found myself wondering what she was thinking about. Secretly, I hoped it was something good.

"Hey... here."

Gage nudged me while she wasn't looking, and when I glanced down he was holding a small flask of rum with the cap already off. I poured some into my mug, nodding appreciatively.

"Who's hungry?"

Maverick passed out sandwiches, and we ate while talking and laughing and feeding the fire. Juliana didn't speak much about work, and we didn't inquire about it. She asked plenty about what we'd been up to lately, and while we had to skirt around certain details, we talked a little about our trip to California.

"We're sort of on standby for something," I eventually offered.

Gage nodded as he laid another piece of ironwood across the fire. "Something big."

Eventually the sun came down to kiss the horizon, painting the sky a spectacular array of colors that changed minute by minute. Just before darkness fell, Maverick shot me a knowing glance and I nodded.

"Would you like to stay the night up here?" I asked, shifting my gaze to Juliana. "We can, you know."

Her expression was one of skeptical disbelief. She

searched around, as if suddenly the mesa had grown a house or something.

"Here?" she asked. "How in the—"

"We have a tent. A big one, actually."

Her eyes grew wide. A smile I'd never seen crossed her pretty face. "Really?"

"Yes, really. But only if you'd like—"

"I'd like."

Gage grinned with a childlike wonderment, scooping her into his arms and kissing her long and deep. I felt a flash of jealousy, but it was jealousy laced with a strange new heat. One that whirled like a turbine, spinning fast, somewhere deep in my core.

*It's hot, just watching them.*

I swallowed hard.

*Watching* her...

The realization was stark but undeniable. The longer I looked, the more turned on I was. Gage and Maverick had tried explaining it to me; how they'd felt the same way over the course of the week I'd been gone. I hadn't really understood it though, until now.

Maverick was already at the chopper, nodding me over to help him unload the large canvas tent. There wasn't much in the way of daylight left. We still had to set it up and lock it down.

"Word of warning," I called over, to where Juliana stood flush with excitement. "With the wind and the chill and the altitude... it can get a little cold up here at night."

The others nodded in unison. "Very cold."

But our girl seemed entirely unfazed. Moving to stand between us, she set both hands on her shapely hips.

"I'm not too worried," she said slyly. "I'm pretty sure I'll find *something* to keep me warm."

# Forty

## JULIANA

We retreated to the comfort of the tent as the wind picked up, whipping the fire in so many different directions there was no way of telling where it came from. By then it was dark, and we'd eaten and drank our fill. We'd talked about anything and everything, except the one topic I really needed clarified: why they'd brought me all the way back out here in the first place.

Other than the obvious reason, of course.

"So tell me about you guys being obsessed."

I sank down into the pile of sleeping bags, which were laid over some pillows for extra cushion. The tent was spacious and sturdy, and tall enough that two out of the three of them could stand without bending. The portable electric heater they'd plugged into a battery kept it warm and toasty inside, but just touching my palm against the cold canvas walls reminded me of how fast the desert temperatures could drop at night.

"Obsessed?" Devyn asked, raising an eyebrow.

"Uh huh," I replied glibly, nodding toward Maverick. "That's the word *he* used, anyway."

One by one they sat down around me, their great muscles bending and flexing as they dropped to the floor. Gage rested casually back on his palms. Devyn sat with his arms locked around his legs, his hands fastened in front of his shins.

*Damn, they're gorgeous.*

They really were. All three men sported model good looks, chiseled jaw-lines, and smoldering eyes. They had shoulders to die for, and arms for days. Even so, none of them knew what say.

"I came here because I needed to get away," I said, in the absence of any other conversation. "Work sucks right now. New York's finally getting to me, and that frightens me because I always loved it, even during the times when I didn't." I cocked my head and laughed. "Does that even make sense?"

"Yes," said Gage. "More than you know."

I nodded, considering the thoughtfulness of their expressions. All three of them were looking at me, eyeing me over. But not in the usual way.

"Juliana," Devyn began slowly, "we need to tell you something. A few things, actually."

"Oh boy." My smile curled into a smirk. "Here we go."

"They're good things," Maverick added quickly.

"Important things."

I wasn't used to beating around the bush, and neither were they. These weren't men who spoke hollow words or made empty promises. These were the kind of men who said exactly what they meant.

"We *want* this child," said Devyn, calmly. "We'd like to be a part of its life. We want to father it. Nurture it. Even help raise it... but only if that's what you want too."

A piece of canvas flapped outside, whipping rhythmically in the most recent gust of wind. It was the perfect metaphor for my heart, which was skipping wildly within my chest.

"There's only one problem," Devyn went on. "And it's kind of a big one."

My lips went tight as the other shoe was about to drop. "What?"

"We can't have children," said Gage.

I lowered my chin to look downward, then rubbed my stomach. "I have a swollen belly here that says very differently."

"It's not that we *can't* have them," Maverick corrected his friend. "Obviously we can."

"Obviously," I shot back.

"But it's in our contract," Devyn explained. "No wives. No children. No distractions. Nothing to tie us down or keep us from duty."

I stared at him for a few seconds, studying his handsome face. Wondering what kind of contract could decree something that specific, that bizarre.

That *lonely*.

"We're to be ready to leave at any time," Gage continued. "Go anywhere, for any reason, at a moment's notice."

I thought about the helicopter that picked up Devyn. About them betting to see which one of them it was actually for.

"I see."

"Up until now this hasn't been a problem," said Devyn. "We've never wanted anything *but* this kind of arrangement. But now..."

"When does your contract expire?"

"It's been up several times already," said Maverick. "And we've always renewed it."

I let out a small shrug. "Then your choice is obvious," I told them. "You love what you do. You do what you love."

"Or," Gage countered carefully, "we just haven't found a reason to get out yet. We haven't encountered anything compelling enough that we'd end our service."

Maverick nodded. "We always assumed it would be something that would be ours. That we could share together, all three of us, like everything else we've done in our lives."

"A business venture?" I offered. "Or maybe–"

"No," said Devyn. "Something like *you*."

His eyes were still fixed on the swell of my belly. All

at once, the full realization of what he was saying dawned on me.

"Me."

"Yes."

"Share *me?*"

"That's right."

"I'm not a pizza," I frowned instinctively. "Or an ice-cream cone. Or—"

"Hey. Jules."

I stopped everything and looked up into Gage's blue-grey eyes. For once they were dead serious.

"You *know* it's not like that."

His expression held me, keeping me from looking away. Forcing me to understand what he was saying, even if I couldn't fully believe it.

"We've never met a woman like you before," Devyn went on. "You're tough. Fierce. Powerful in your convictions."

"You're driven and ambitious," added Maverick. "Take this as a compliment, but you're a fucking shark."

"And yet you're also sweet," Gage jumped in. "You have a soft side. A sensitive, loving side." He shrugged one big shoulder. "On top of all that you're drop dead gorgeous. Sexually insatiable."

The others nodded as their friend finished.

"You drive us wild."

For another long moment no one said anything. Then Devyn took my hand.

"So yes, we're obsessed with you," he said, his blue eyes blazing. "We want the child in your belly, but we want *you* even more. Juliana the warrior. The lover. The soon-to-be-mother."

"We want to *share* you," Maverick reiterated. "You and our child. And we want the both of you to share our lives, too."

*Our child.* Those two words had never before been put together. Up until now it had always been nothing but me.

"W—We don't even know whose child this is," I breathed, touching my stomach.

"And we don't care," said Devyn firmly. "As far we're concerned it's all of ours."

I gulped, trying to get past the lump in my throat. They were all so genuine, so understanding. Between all three of them, there wasn't a hint of anything but truthfulness.

"One day it might become obvious who the biological father is," Devyn went on, "but that still won't change anything. If you stay with us — if you're willing to become o*urs* — that child is going to have three fathers instead of just one."

"Three very *kickass* fathers," Gage smiled gently. "Let's not undersell that part."

*Become ours.*

The words startled me, frightened me, even made me

dizzy. But they also struck me with a bolt of pure, unbridled excitement.

*Three men, three fathers. Three boyfriends...*

Holy fucking shit.

They shifted closer, surrounding me on three sides. Maverick's mouth was very close to my ear as his voice dropped into an almost-whisper.

"You don't have to answer us immediately," he murmured softly. "Right now, you don't even have to think about it."

The warmth of the tent, the comfort of being surrounded by them... all of it was giving me the tingles. It felt strangely amazing, being this isolated, this remote. This far out in the middle of the cold and wind and untamed elements, yet so safe and relaxed at the same time.

"For tonight, just enjoy being here," Gage whispered from behind me.

His body wrapped comfortingly around mine, as his two strong hands found their way around my midsection. A nose sifted its way through my hair, and then I was sighing softly as his lips settled over my bare neck.

"Tonight," said Devyn, "just enjoy *us.*"

His mouth slowly probed mine, eliciting the hottest, most beautiful open-mouth kiss. I sucked in a quick breath as more hands began roaming my body, warming me from the outside to match the heat already rising from within. The kisses became moans, followed by shivers of pleasure. The three of them passed my mouth back and forth, drinking deeply from my lips. Breathing my every hot breath, as their hands wandered eagerly yet gently into much more forbidden places.

*Holy...*

In the end I surrendered happily, falling backward against Gage's broad, sculpted chest. Still kissing, still touching, they lowered me into the softness of the thick down sleeping bags, as they began stripping the clothes from their ripped, beautiful bodies.

And then they did mine.

# Forty-One

## JULIANA

The floor of the tent was a warm, wonderful playground, all smooth and soft. A perfectly supple nest that gave in just the right places, especially when one or more of my playmates wanted to roll me over and position me according to their wishes.

And trust me, they had plenty of positions.

And many, *many* wishes.

*Mmmmmmm...*

Over and over I prostrated myself across the satin surface, arching my back or spreading my legs for my three ripped, sun-bronzed lovers. And they took me again and again, together and alone. Flipping me onto my stomach to drill me from behind, or stretching me out between them so they could enjoy my body and mouth from both ends.

*Three guys.*

I honestly couldn't believe it. Even after the last

time, with two, it just seemed over the top.

*Three fucking guys, Juliana!*

The whole thing was naughty. Dirty. Filthy and wrong. And the more I thought about each of those words, the more I absolutely fucking *loved* it.

Throughout the early course of the night I made sure I took what I wanted, screwing each of my lovers greedily, fiercely, and to my complete and utter satisfaction. I rode Gage like a stallion until I exploded hard, surging around him, then bent over his lap so Devyn could drill me deep from behind. I slid my thighs around Maverick's sexy waist and clawed at his ass while he pounded me breathless, then hooked my feet behind his back to lock him inside me, just as he finally came.

Spent and delirious I eventually gave myself over, happily succumbing to the guys' every whim. I surrendered my body fully to these three steel-armed warriors, who proceeded to flip me and flop me and hold me down. They took turns locking me in place, with arms overhead or behind my back. Each of them pinning me against their own warm flesh while the others fucked the life out of me, until the cheeks on both sides of my face were glistening with tears of joy.

Best of all, I'd arrived at some kind of golden zone: a warm, wonderful place between two and three mugs of hot chocolate. The sugar kept me wide awake enough to savor every glorious thing these men were doing to my body, both together and one-on-one. But the warmth of the milk also relaxed me enough that every depraved, sensuous act drove me that much closer to heaven. Every shiver of pleasure was heightened by my comfortably coco-drunk state.

One by one I screwed them to sleep, first Maverick, and then ultimately, Devyn. I rode them hard and milked them dry as they unloaded inside me, filling me with so much of their warm cream that the entire tent totally reeked of sex.

And my God, I loved that too.

I kissed their faces and foreheads and lips, until their eyes fluttered closed and their breathing became regular. But I kissed other parts of their body, too. Parts like their broad, beautiful chests or rippled, washboard stomachs.

Parts that while they slumbered, were only for me.

In the end it was only Gage and myself, screwing like bunnies. Kissing and fucking and grinding our hips into one another, until he flipped me over and lay his entire body over mine, from behind.

"Jules..."

He murmured the word dreamily into my sweat-soaked hair. The desert beyond the canvas was wind-swept and freezing, but inside the tent must've been close to eighty degrees.

"I *love* you."

At first I wasn't sure I'd heard him correctly. But somewhere deep in my heart, I knew that I had.

"I love you too."

The words came naturally, without hesitation. There was no questioning them. No second-guessing they were the absolute truth.

*I love him.*

With that I bucked back against him one last time, driving my soft cheeks against his hard, shredded abs. It was all he needed. The final trigger.

*I love all of them.*

Gage shuddered as he exploded into me, his cock twitching and jumping as it throbbed deep in my swollen channel. His grunts were primal. The feel of him splashing against my pregnant womb sent me into a magnificent climax, howling against the wind outside.

*Hoooooly FUCK!*

Over and over he surged into me, draining himself to completion. His strong arms held me tightly, firmly. His hot mouth whispered breathlessly into my ear.

"My *God,* I love you..."

I smiled, reaching back to pull him close. Leaving him inside me as we collapsed sideways, back into the warmth of the sleeping bag.

Physically I was in heaven. Emotionally though, I should've been frightened. Such an admission would've scared the hell out of me in the past. My own realization that I loved all three of these men, even more so.

Instead I was merely content to turn my head and kiss Gage goodnight, as one big hand slid down over my lower stomach. I closed my hand over his. It was comforting. Even beautiful.

Cradling the baby together, sharing the feel of the silky, satin fabric against our naked skin, we finally drifted off into sleep.

# Forty-Two

## MAVERICK

Juliana's weekend away turned into a week, and then that week turned into ten days. I wasn't sure when she'd go back, or if she'd go back, or what would ultimately happen between us.

All I knew was that we absolutely loved having her here.

It was obvious she was burnt out, and desperately needed this time away. Whatever was happening in New York had stressed her completely. She still hadn't opened up about it, but she spent a good amount of time on the phone with her assistant, who was apparently taking care of things while she was gone.

As each day went by however, her smile widened a little more. With each night that she spent cuddled between us or taking turns in our beds, we could feel her body releasing more of that coiled up tension.

We took her out into the desert often, and this

seemed to clear her head more than anything. We knew this because it had worked for us. Juliana loved driving the dune buggies out into the middle of nowhere, and soaking up the solitude. She drove fearlessly, even recklessly at times, worrying us so much that we had to sometimes take the wheel from her hands.

One day we surprised her with a trip to Phoenix, where we'd set up an appointment for a sonogram. We did this because we knew she'd missed an appointment back home, but there were ulterior motives as well. Reasons that were entirely selfish on our part:

We all wanted to hear the baby's heartbeat.

It was thrilling, listening to the machine's speaker crackle with that strange, rhythmic sound. But even more amazing was staring into the monitor together, catching tiny glimpses of the human growing inside her. We could see hands, fingers, feet. The shape of the tiny arms and legs, attached to a body the size of a lemon, or lime.

Until then it hadn't seemed real, at least not all the way. But yes, we were bringing a baby into this world. One of us, anyway. Or all of us. It didn't matter really, who the father might've been. We'd done it together, as always. And in that respect, it was absolutely perfect.

It was on the eleventh day that I knew our time was coming to a close. Juliana had taken another call, this one more serious than the others. She looked actually angry this time, instead of worried. Somehow though, I think I liked the anger better.

"You're leaving, aren't you?"

I said the words as I came up behind her, leaning

alone over the railing of the upstairs balcony. Juliana was staring out into the desert. The wind sent her hair across her beautiful face.

"Yes," she answered. "I have to."

I moved to the railing beside her, leaning out over the horizon as well.

"How'd you know?"

"It's in your face. It's in your body language."

She considered my words for a moment as we stood together in silence. The sun was setting, and the sky was ridiculous. Eventually, she turned toward me.

"It's not that I don't want to be here," she said. "You know I do. These last two weeks have been the most amazing ones of my life, really."

There was no convincing her, so I didn't try. Besides, these weren't excuses, or brush offs, or even exaggerations. She was speaking from the heart.

"It's just, well... there's something I have to take care of," she explained. "Something Aric can't handle alone."

"I get it."

Her brown eyes softened. "You do?"

"Yes," I nodded. "We all get it, Juliana. Maybe it's a little different for us, but we've been there, too."

She pursed her beautiful lips, then turned her face back into the light of the dying sun. I was starting to see her as two people, now. The woman we'd somehow fallen madly in love with... and the child she was carrying so proudly inside her.

I'd admired her strength, her ambition, her fearless tenacity. In witnessing first-hand the life she'd carved out for herself, I'd admired everything she'd ever built.

But now, most of all, I admired her courage.

"The others are still going to take it hard, though," I told her. "And don't think they won't."

"Why?"

I shrugged and smiled. "Well Devyn's flat out obsessed with you, the same way you once were with his profile."

She seemed amused by that. "He is, huh?"

"Yes," I chuckled.

"And what about you?"

The question caught me somewhat off guard. I almost bit my tongue.

"I'm head over fucking heels," I responded quickly. "Can't you see that?"

I was joking but not joking. She saw through it all.

"Yes," she repeated. "I do."

Her eyes caught mine, and the way she peered into my soul made my heart race. It was crazy that one person could have so much power over me, much less a woman. But on another level, I didn't mind it at all.

"And then there's Gage..." I went on, changing the subject. "He's just as much in love with you as he is with the idea of having a baby with you."

"Love?" she said, turning again. "You really think

so?"

"Yes."

There was fire in her eyes now. An emotional warmth behind those pretty brown irises.

"Well the baby thing I agree with," she said. "And it's adorable. You don't know how many baby gifts he's already sent back to New York."

At that, I laughed long and loud.

"What?"

"You don't know the half of it," I told her, placing my hand over hers. "Come with me."

I led Juliana back into the warmth of the house, where the smell of marinara sauce wafted up from below. The garlic and onion and simmering spices smelled delicious; a far cry from the cooking Devyn or Gage were normally capable of. Absently, I realized they were pulling out all the stops.

"Where are we—"

"Just come."

Down the upstairs hall we went, straight past the two pairs of bedrooms. Juliana was very familiar with all four of them, of course. Yet another fun fact that excited me in ways I still wasn't used to yet.

"Here," I said, pointing to the last room at the end of the hall. "Open it."

She did, although a little apprehensively at first. By the time she'd stepped inside however, both hands moved to cover her mouth.

"Oh my *God!*"

The nursery was fully-decorated from top to bottom, with pastel blues and soft, beautiful whites. There was a wooden crib, decked out with baby blue bedding. A shaggy blue area rug, centered between a rocking chair and rocking horse. The walls were painted with murals of trees blossoming, and birds singing on the branches. Animals smiled from the grass, which had been painted just above the base moldings all around the entirety of the room.

"Gage *did* this?"

I folded my arms in satisfaction. "Well it was his brainchild, yes," I admitted, "but once he got started Devyn and I took over. He wasn't happy about it at first, but in the end I think the group effort made it better."

Juliana walked the room, running her hand over the smooth rails of the crib. Her eyes flitted from one baby blue thing to the next.

"And how do you all know it's even a boy?" she challenged, rubbing her stomach.

"We don't," Gage chuckled abruptly from the doorway. "But redecorating would be just as fun, and we figured we had a 50/50 shot."

Devyn materialized behind him, and together they entered the room. Juliana responded by walking over, smiling, and throwing her arms around each of us one by one. Starting with Gage, of course.

"This is incredible," she said, physically choked up. "I mean...

"We know you won't always be here," Gage said

quickly. "Or maybe you won't even bring the little guy here at all."

"Or little *girl*," Devyn cut in.

"Yeah. But—"

Juliana cut him off by kissing him, straight on the mouth. She kissed me next, excitedly smashing her soft lips against mine, and I was still reeling as she spun away and kissed Gage too.

"No one's ever done *anything* this sweet for me before," she said, in a strangled but happy voice. "Or this thoughtful. Or this... this..."

"Obsessive?" I joked, giving Gage the side-eye.

Juliana's eyes were wet. She choked back tears as she turned to face me.

"This isn't obsessive," she corrected me. "This is amazing. This whole *place* is amazing," she sniffed, looking around. "I– I'm really grateful for it."

For a moment we sat there, just letting her take it in. Eventually Devyn laid a hand on her shoulder.

"Yeah, well you deserve it," he said softly.

"The *baby* deserves it," Gage nodded.

Juliana's chin dipped in contemplation of everything that was going on. I could see the conflict behind her pretty eyes. She'd been so decisive, so sure of herself about everything. But maybe for the first time ever, I saw that she was torn.

"I have to go," she said, turning to face the others. "For now, anyway."

The others' expressions changed quickly. Devyn looked forlorn. Gage outright flinched.

"But not forever," Juliana added carefully.

Gage coughed, then cleared his throat. His own eyes were glassy.

"Promise?"

She paused, then nodded slowly. "I... I promise."

We closed around her again, this time in a hug. Her body was so incredibly warm. Her face was far too beautiful to be crying.

"We're here whenever you need us," I said, although I couldn't promise it would always be true. "This place is forever yours."

Gage smiled, rubbing her belly. "And *his*."

"Or hers," Devyn grinned.

Juliana sighed, sniffed, then used one sleeve to wipe her eyes. She glanced up at us, and I nodded.

"Let this be your getaway from the chaos of that city, if nothing else," I told her. "An oasis, for you and your baby."

She managed a cute little laugh. "My oasis in the desert."

I squeezed her tightly.

"Whenever you want it."

# Forty-Three

## JULIANA

"Go on," I boomed, loudly enough to be heard throughout the office. "Send him in."

John James of Skyline walked down the long L-shaped hallway that led to my office, before finally ducking inside. I could see him the whole way, of course. After all, the walls were glass.

"Ms. Emerson," he smiled, closing the door behind him. "Thanks so much for seeing–"

"Get to the point," I cut him off quickly. "There *is* a point to you being here, right?"

Peripherally, my eyes scanned his Brioni suit up and down, along with his Gucci belt and Balenciaga sharkskin shoes. The man was tall and thin and immaculately groomed, from his styled, gelled hair to his cuticle-less fingers. Right now those fingers were tapping the back of the chair in front of him.

"Shall I sit?" he asked politely.

"No need," I told him. "This isn't going to take long."

I knew what the man wanted, and I knew exactly why he was here. Aric had tried keeping me from even taking this meeting, but I'd never been one to shy away from a good confrontation.

Besides, after flying all the way home for nothing but bad news, I could really use a laugh.

"Very well then," said John James. "Let's start with the facts, shall we?"

*Shall.* Only an pretentious asshole or a stuffy librarian used such a word in real life. I'd only just met him and I couldn't stand the man already.

"Fact: your marketing company recently lost Legendary Gaming to ours."

The way he said it made him sound all smarmy and aloof. As much as I hated it though, it still didn't make the statement any less true.

"Fact: you'll most likely be okay until your current contracts run out, but after that you'll be hemorrhaging money."

My scowl deepened. I couldn't deny this one either, although his timeline was probably a little bit off.

"Fact: your company is quite competent. Extremely competitive. You have good people and great resources, overall."

Flattery. Maybe. Either that or he was finally about to get to the point.

"You just put too many of your eggs in one basket, that's all," the man said coolly. "You expanded too quickly, without diversifying your income sources." He shrugged theatrically. "And it bit you in the ass."

True or not, I hated him for using my own analogy against me. Rather than giving him the satisfaction of knowing that, I yawned and tried on my most bored expression.

"Are you done?"

The man slid forward instead of retreating. And now, against my wishes, he *did* take one of the chairs.

"Let me buy out your company," John James said excitedly. He leaned forward, his eyes going wild. "Let me take over Shameless!"

With that he pounded a fist on my desk. Instinctively my arm shot out and grabbed him by the wrist.

"What the—"

The door to my office flew open so fast it nearly shattered into a thousand pieces. Aric was on the man in a second, sliding one big arm just beneath his chin and wrapping it tight with the other.

"Aric, no!"

He flexed, and I saw John James' face turn bright purple. He was five seconds away from being squeezed unconscious. Maybe three, considering how angry Aric was.

"Let him go, Aric! Please."

My assistant relaxed his grip, although he didn't fully release his prisoner. John James let out a huge gasp of heated air, then looked around like he didn't immediately know where he was. Very slowly, the color began returning to his face.

"He was slamming things around," Aric insinuated. "I saw him raise his hand toward you, and—"

"It's okay," I cut my assistant off. "Our guest got a little too excited, that's all. But he's all good now. Right?"

Slowly, groggily, the man in the chair nodded. He didn't look much like the CEO of a major marketing firm, much less one that had stolen my biggest client. In fact, he looked like a 25-year old kid who'd just woken up with a really bad hangover.

"Could you get him some water?" I asked Aric.

My assistant was reluctant to leave. Eventually I shooed him away.

"Go on. I'll be fine."

Aric retreated slowly, this time leaving the door to my office open. When I was alone again with my guest, I turned to face him.

"Fact: your rich, real-estate mogul of a daddy gave you the money to start this company. At the rate you've been spending it, you'll be crawling back to him for more very shortly."

John James looked confused, then hurt, then infuriated by the accusation. But I wasn't done.

"Fact: your company uses click-farms and employs the use of bots to bump up the subscription counts of those you represent in social media. For that reason, you won't be able to deliver any actual results. The clients you *did* steal are going to abandon you quickly, as soon as they figure out they're paying for nothing."

The man seated across from me rubbed at the base of his neck. He opened and closed his mouth a few times, testing his jaw.

"Fact: you yourself know absolutely nothing about marketing," I told him. "Sure, maybe you've hired some halfway decent people, but they're nowhere near the caliber of people I have working for me. And do you know why that is?"

He coughed once, then shook his head. "No. Why?"

"Because I built this company from scratch," I said angrily. "I worked hard for it, I shed blood for it, and I've vetted every single one of the people that are here."

Aric returned just then with a bottle of water. It was one of the warm, room-temperature ones from the storage room, rather than a cold one from one of the mini-fridges.

*It's the little victories that tide you over*, Aric had once told me.

"Now you might've swayed Legendary with some flashy sales pitch," I went on, "and the promise of having a west-coast presence. But the second you can't produce for them they'll see right through your bullshit. They'll drop you just as fast as they dropped me, only they won't even fulfill their existing contracts because they owe you no loyalty." I leaned back and shrugged. "In fact, they might even sue you for misrepresentation, or at the very least take back any deposits they've already given you."

I don't know if it was apprehension I sensed, but there was definitely doubt creeping in. In just a minute or two, the man's whole demeanor had changed. The confidence and swagger he'd walked in here with had been utterly shattered.

"You're going to lose them," I finished, twisting the knife, "and there's nothing you can do about it. So be prepared."

John James finally stood up. Red-faced and practically shaking, he set the water bottle down on my desk and looked at me pointedly.

"So you think you're getting Legendary back?" he sneered. "Is that your master plan?"

Once again I delivered a shrug. "Maybe. Maybe not."

The man snorted, turned, then glared at Aric, who stood silently in the corner.

"If they come my way again, I'm sure I'll take them back," I reasoned. "But not at the old rates. Not at the 'we've been loyal partners forever' rates, because now I know their loyalty is fleeting."

My own anger began boiling up inside me. Not at John James, because now I could see the CEO of Skyline was nothing more than a kid playing grown-up with other people's lives.

No, I was more mad at Robert Valentine. Or more specifically, the people above him who actually thought they'd save money by letting this infant destroy their brand.

"We'll talk again soon," said my uninvited guest, on

the way out of my office. "Maybe sooner than you think, oh she-who-knows-everything."

He said the last part with such a sneer of contempt I couldn't help but laugh.

"Oh I don't know *everything*," I told him. "Not even close. But James?"

He slowed contemplatively, then eventually stopped to turn around in the glass hallway.

"One thing I do know is that you'll never, *ever* buy out my company."

# Forty-Four

**GAGE**

The call came at the worst possible time, as it almost always did. I was face-down, spread eagle in bed. Still woozy from all the alcohol of the previous night, as the three of us had gone out to cut loose for a little while.

Cut loose... and try to forget about *her.*

It wasn't that we wanted to forget about her either — just the opposite, in fact. It was more like we had to get her out of our minds for a while. Juliana had us preoccupied with all kinds of crazy thoughts, but in the few weeks since she'd gone back to New York, she still hadn't given us an answer.

*Was there really an answer to give?*

If you asked Maverick, we'd scared her away. Devyn wasn't so sure though, and neither was I. Yes, what we'd suggested had been radical, unbelievable, totally out there. Society-wise, maybe it was even groundbreakingly fucked up. In the end though, I didn't care. And that's because we'd been genuine. We'd told the truth.

"Get up."

I groaned, turning sideways toward the doorway. The shape of Maverick stood silhouetted against the light coming from the hall.

"They'll be here in eight minutes."

I noticed he was already putting his boots on. Which could only mean one thing.

"It's time?"

"Yes."

Somewhere in the wee hours of the morning we'd gotten a call. *The* call actually, as in the phone that never really rang except for one reason only.

"Alright," I grunted. "I'm up."

Rolling out, I shook my head and tried to forget Juliana for a while. I *needed* to forget her in fact, if we were to focus on the job the three of us had to do.

And not focusing on the job at hand could have deadly consequences.

Eventually I found my way to the bathroom, splashed cold water on my face, and stared into the mirror. I looked like hell. Hell, I felt like hell. But I knew in an hour or two I'd bounce right back.

"Don't forget to brush your teeth," Maverick called as he bounded away, satisfied I wasn't going back to bed. "I can smell your whiskey breath from here."

He disappeared down the stairs, leaving me

grumbling and reaching for whatever toothbrush was closest. I stood in front of the toilet for a full minute, killing two birds with one stone, then returned to my room and started pulling on clothes over my mostly naked body.

I found the others in the kitchen, greedily sucking down coffee. It was still pitch black outside. Already I could hear the chopper.

"You think this is it?" I asked, rubbing my eyes.

"I know it is," Devyn said firmly. "I've got a feeling."

I nodded my agreement. "Good. Me too."

Maverick handed me a mug, and I downed as much as I could before the rotor-wash began flinging sand against the kitchen windows. The rest I dumped in the sink.

"Do we tell her?"

The question came from Devyn. It echoed hollowly in the kitchen, even with the scream of the helicopter's engines outside.

"Might be best if we don't," said Maverick. "Go in with a clear head. Keep things strictly business."

We'd given Juliana even more space since she'd gone back, and she'd even taken some of it. But we were in touch. We were still talking. For those reasons, it didn't seem right to just fly off without telling her anything.

But more important than anything, I didn't want to worry her.

"She's pregnant, she's stressed, she doesn't need this," I said. "Agreed?"

The others nodded. Through the window, we

watched the chopper touch down.

"C'mon," I told them. "Let's get this party started already."

We left, locking the door behind us, wondering as always when we'd see the place again. Or if. With jobs like this there was always the 'if' factor. It was something you became more acutely aware of the longer you did this job, until one day the 'if' became a more sinister 'when.'

For some reason the chopper had touched down on the opposite side of the driveway than usual. Different pilot, maybe. By now the adrenaline was kicking in. It made me wide awake. Alive. Ready for anything.

"Bishop! Abraham!"

No one came out from the chopper this time to get us. Instead, a man was waving us in. In his flight suit, it took me a second to recognize him as Ramos.

Immediately, my smile widened.

"Gunarson!"

I ran to the chopper and leapt inside, just as it pulled from the ground and lifted off. Ramos gave me a nod. The nod said everything.

"Alright then," I grinned, saluting dutifully. "About time."

The Rear Admiral motioned to the pilot, who immediately nosed forward and pinned the throttle. That part made me laugh. Going fast was fantastic, but if we were headed where I *thought* we were, we had a hell of a long ride and quite a few stops ahead of us anyway. A ride with plenty of time to talk and plan and get briefed on the mission.

For now though at least, I could lay my head back and get some much-needed sleep.

# Forty-Five

## JULIANA

The trip was lonely as always, but this time it had an edge of excitement to it. I'd jumped a flight spur-of-the-moment. I'd left New York without telling anyone, even Aric, who I could always call in the morning.

And that's because I wanted to *really* surprise them.

The past few weeks had been like riding a freight train with no brakes. I'd been working nonstop. Taking meetings at all hours of the day or night, from one end of the City to the other. I'd been doing so much that Aric actually held a one-man intervention, locking me in my office and forcing me to sit on the couch and do nothing for a straight hour. It was the longest hour of my life. Like being held in solitary confinement, but with glass walls so I could watch everyone else do all the things I couldn't.

Aric had taken to coming with me to the obstetrician too, and he wouldn't take no for an answer. It was the sweetest thing, watching his eyes go wide at the sound of the fetal heartbeat. Observing his childlike awe as the baby moved and kicked, stretching its tiny arms and legs before us. After ten straight minutes of begging I even let the sonogram technician tell him the baby's sex, as long as he promised to keep it from me. It brought a tear to my eye, just seeing how moved he was by the whole thing. And it was in that moment I realized what a great father he'd someday make.

One day soon I'd have to tell my family I was pregnant, and the barrage of questions would begin. I'd have to explain the donor process, especially to my parents. I'd have to make up more than a few other things as well.

At least for now. At least until I knew for sure in which direction I was going.

I thought talking to the guys on only a semi-regular basis would allow me the clarity to possibly let go. Instead, it did just the opposite. Not hearing their voices made me miss them more than ever, and trying not to think about them only filled my head with even more conflicting thoughts.

And not having them in my bed…

God, I missed them *desperately!* Mentally, emotionally, but of course physically too. I missed the feel of their warm naked skin, sliding against mine. The delicious sinfulness of being spread open and filled by each of them, engorged and enormous and toe-curlingly magnificent.

My belly kept swelling, and so did my now unstoppable libido. In their quest to pleasure my body (and theirs), the boys had spoiled me, sexually. As a side effect of being hopelessly pregnant, I woke up more and more horny each day.

But my attachment to them went well beyond that, which was the reason I was actually here. I needed their strong arms, their firm lips, but I also needed the company. I needed the laughter and warmth and camaraderie. The three of them shared an indescribable bond that made being around them naturally fun and relaxed. And of course, I loved them. And they loved me.

*Damn right you do.*

The realization was more of an epiphany this time around, and less of a surrender. There was no reason to hold back. No reason to put up walls, when what I truly wanted was to tear down the ones I'd kept up all these years.

And so I flew to Phoenix, without saying a word. The people behind the rental car's counter were getting to know me on a first name basis, and within minutes I was driving through the desert, speeding in the direction I knew would provide warmth, happiness, and comfort.

If these men wanted to share me, I was willing to try. I'd already given myself over to each of them, mind, body and soul, and they'd done nothing but take the utmost care of me.

Now it was time to give them my heart as well.

The sun had set hours ago by the time I pulled through the open gates, and the house looked less warm and alive than usual. There were still lights on inside, but not many. It was almost like my sexy, personal SEAL team had gone to bed.

*All the easier to surprise them.*

I parked away from the windows, being careful to close the car door as silently as possible. Then I padded up the walkway and stood before the giant teak doors. There would be no knocking this time. The last time I was here, after talking about the place being my oasis in the desert, the guys had presented me with a large brass key.

Telling me I was welcome 'home' any time I wanted seemed like nothing more than a sweet gesture. But now, after careful thought...

My heart raced even faster as I inserted the key into the big iron lock. It turned with a click and I pushed inside, stepping into the shadows of the foyer. The house was quiet, the interior lit mostly by ambient lighting. There was a light on in the kitchen though. But there was always a light on in the kitchen.

*They're asleep.*

I smiled, thinking about what a surprise it would be for me to just climb the stairs, strip naked, and slide into bed with one of them.

*Which one though?*

I decided I'd pick the first door, which would be Devyn's. That way I couldn't be accused of favoritism. Besides, this whole thing started with Devyn. It seemed only fitting.

Not to mention, whichever bedroom I started in wouldn't necessarily be the same bedroom I finished.

I ducked through the archway and into kitchen to make sure it was empty. Maverick was prone to random bouts of insomnia, and Gage's appetite had him up sometimes, fixing all sorts of crazy midnight snacks. It made me happy, thinking about how well I was beginning to know them. But there was still so much to learn. So many things I had yet to share with them.

That's when I noticed the mugs in the sink. And the coffee pot sitting in the middle of the counter, still about a third full of rich black liquid.

Going to bed with the kitchen like this seemed strange to me, especially in light of Maverick's obsessive cleaning habits. But I crept up the stairs anyway, turned the knob, silently pushed on Devyn's door.

It swung open into an empty bedroom, and an unmade bed.

Frowning, I tried the others and found them exactly the same. All three rooms were empty. All three beds were unmade.

A cold feeling stole over me as I realized I was in the house alone, way out in the middle of the desert. I became hyper-aware of the darkness and shadows. Every little sound – the wind, the blown sand, the house settling – sent a chill down my spine.

That's when my phone rang, causing me to practically scream.

# Forty-Six

**JULIANA**

"Juliana?"

Devyn's voice barely registered over the high-pitched sound of some unknown background noise. He'd called from a strange number I didn't recognize. Even with my heart racing double-time, I was so grateful to hear his voice.

"Oh my God where are you!?" I gasped. "You're not here. I—I came out to the—"

"You came to the house," I heard him say. "Yes. We know."

My eyebrows knit together. "How do you know?"

"Silent alarm. Cameras." His next sentence was chopped up by static. "We... an alert... front door opened."

I was walking as I talked, flipping on every light I could find. The house felt so much more welcome with the lights on. So much warmer and safer than in the dark.

"Your trucks are here," I said. "The chopper too. I

thought maybe you'd be sleeping, but—"

"Juliana, we're on a mission right now," he cut me off. "Or at least we soon will be. We're thrilled you're there and we'd ask you to stay, but we have no idea how long we'll be gone. It could be weeks. Months, even."

My hammering heart dropped. "A—And you weren't going to tell me?"

There was a long pause at the other end of the phone. I thought for a moment we'd been disconnected.

"We didn't want to worry you," Devyn said sadly. "And where we're going—"

"Are you going to be okay?" I demanded, frightened. "Will you be *safe?*"

It was a stupid question and I knew it. These men weren't just soldiers, they were special forces. They ran the most dangerous operations in the world.

"We'll stay safe," Devyn assured me. "I promise."

His promise however, did nothing to assuage me. My heart had already sank into my stomach.

"I have to go," he said again, over the sound of some kind of alarm. "We— I—"

"Be safe!" I called into the phone. "Please, tell the others too. Watch over each other! And I—"

The noises stopped abruptly. The line went dead.

*FUCK!*

My hand was trembling as I slowly lowered the phone. Not only had I missed my chance to talk to the others, I'd spent the few moments we had trying to guilt-trip Devyn about not telling me they'd left. All while having shown up here totally at random, after a few weeks of barely calling them.

*Not cool, Jules.*

And now they'd been yanked away, sent on some dangerous mission to God knows where. Tasked with doing God knows what, and thrown into a situation so dangerous I might not see one or more of them ever again.

I tried convincing myself I was being dramatic. But in my heart, I knew the grim reality of the situation. And it hurt ten times more than I thought it ever could.

Looking around, I realized I'd be staying the night in an empty house. There was no way I was driving back to the airport, at least not until morning. I was simply too tired. Besides, right now I felt like total shit.

I went back to the kitchen, washed out the mugs, and cleaned up the coffee maker. Then I sank into the nearest chair, dropped my head into my hands, and got ready to cry.

*No. Fuck that.*

A voice in the back of my head broke up my inevitable pity party before it even got started. It was a strong voice. A frighteningly fierce voice that I hadn't heard in quite some time.

*GET UP.*

I rose. The hair on the back of my neck stood up, as my whole body started to tingle. This time it was a good tingle.

*Great. Now pull your shit together.*

Without hesitating I locked up the house, turned on the fireplace, and stood before it. There, staring into the yellow-blue flames, I relaxed my body and let my mind do what it always did best: think.

For the first minute or two, I could only think of my men. I envisioned their handsome faces, their hard bodies, their deep, powerful voices echoing through the now empty house. I reminded myself I loved them. I told myself that was totally okay. I convinced myself all three of them were going to be fine, and that they'd look out for each other, and that they'd come back to me whole and happy and filled with even more love for me than they'd left with.

Then I shoved my gorgeous Navy SEALs out of my mind, and I began thinking about everything *else*.

Ideas formed. Plans coalesced. I ran to the kitchen and found a pen and paper in one of the drawers, then sat on the couch to begin recording the incredible stream of creative consciousness that was telling me what to do, when to do it, and how best to get it all accomplished.

It reminded me sharply of the old days, of my old self. Of my first few weeks in New York, and how I'd chased my ambitions tirelessly and relentlessly. I'd accomplished everything with hard work, brainpower, and elbow grease. But most of all I'd done it by pushing all fear, negativity, and apprehension out of my fucking way.

By the time I was finished it was nearly two in the morning. My body had been exhausted for hours, but now my mind was finally drained. Thrilled and satisfied, I killed the fireplace and climbed the steps back to the bedrooms.

Once up there I didn't even change. I stripped down, climbed into Devyn's bed, and inhaled the musky, wonderful scent of him that permeated the bedsheets.

I fell asleep the very second my face hit the pillow.

# Forty-Seven

## DEVYN

Ramos flew with us all the way to the coast of Somalia, but the USS Nimitz is where our time together ended. We were inserted under the cover of darkness, crawling up along the white sand shores. Invisibly we skirted the various fishing boats that dotted the harbor, slipping noiselessly from the beach as we pressed onward.

Our squad circumvented Kismaayo entirely. We crept past the chaotic jumble of architecture that made up the ancient port, humping our gear across the sun-blasted landscape as we moved deeper west. Before dawn broke we'd melted into the lower Jubaan province, where the scrubby green canopy covered us completely.

Unfortunately it wasn't the only thing green.

Maverick and Gage notwithstanding, our squad consisted mainly of men we knew and trusted. There was Christian, who could track a grasshopper through sagebrush. Evans, with his TAC-50, could place a round center mass from thirty-five hundred meters away. Bringing up the rear we had Hyde, who'd earned the nickname because half the time he was irrationally angry, and Parker who'd never in fourteen missions let us be ambushed from behind.

But we also had three fresh-faced rookies who looked pulled straight out of BUDS school. Men so green, Gage joked their trident pins were so shiny he was going to make them rub dirt on them.

"Vaughan!"

The scout ahead of me halted and turned around.

"You're running point, not a marathon."

He squinted back at me, confused. Moving double-time, I caught up with him.

"If I lose sight of you, you're no good to us," I told him. "You got that?"

"Sorry chief. This is all just so... exciting."

He knew it was the wrong thing to say the moment it left his mouth. I saw it in his expression.

"Exciting?" I hissed.

The man lowered his eyes, but wisely said nothing. At least he knew that much.

"Your first blowjob is exciting," I told him sharply. "Scoring the winning touchdown in overtime, that's exciting. Do you need more examples?"

"No sir." After a moment's silence, he nodded. "I– I get it."

Maybe he got it, maybe he didn't. I sized him up anyway, trying to determine which. I'd seen experienced men die painfully of decompression sickness, from nothing more than a ten-second hypoxic lack of judgment. I'd watched another SEAL raise his arm overhead to prematurely high-five his comrade after a firefight, only to have a sniper turn his hand into a thin pink mist.

The point was, all people made mistakes — even professionals. Sometimes a mistake meant you were dead. Other times it could leave you with nothing more than a thumb for a right hand. I remember our commanding officer calling that particular soldier "Fonzie" after that, which was a reference I didn't understand. After looking it up and realizing how brutal it was, I felt even worse.

"Look, it doesn't help anyone if you sprint headlong into Bashir's men and we're too far back to even know it happened," I told Vaughan. "Right?"

He nodded curtly, then cleared his throat. "Won't happen again, sir"

I felt a sharp sting as the jagged edge of my father's dog-tag bit into the skin at the base of my neck. Which was weird, because it hadn't done that in years.

"Good," I said, now a bit distracted. "Now get back up there with Christian. He's going to pick something up soon, if he hasn't already."

I watched him go, trying to remember how I'd behaved during my first mission. Shit, it seemed a thousand years ago. A few veterans held the other end of my leash back then, and I remember rolling my eyes at them as they tried to rein me in. But now that I was on the opposite end of the equation, I finally understood.

"Did you tell him to slow the fuck down?"

Maverick had moved into step beside me during all this. His eyes were still on the horizon.

"Yeah. More or less."

"I thought I heard something about a blowjob?"

I laughed into my hand. "I promised you'd give him one if he found Bashir before Christian did."

Maverick grunted and shot me a dirty look. "That ain't gonna happen. Either way."

"I know. Christian's too good." I shrugged and smirked. "Sorry though, if you were looking forward to—"

A shrill whistle stopped us both, mid-insult. It could've been a bird, or some kind of insect. We both knew it was neither.

Up ahead, face-down along the next ridge, Christian made the hand-signal for everyone to stop. Our training took over. Wordlessly, soundlessly, we each blended into the nearest tree.

Our scout pointed, and I saw the same thing he did: a spiral of lazy white smoke, rising against the sky. It was high up on the next ridge, a good four clicks away.

"Get Travers up here," I muttered to Maverick. "He's got the Zeiss."

Not a minute later I was staring through the top-of-the-line range-finding binoculars, watching the anomaly Christian had previously spotted. The smoke wasn't an active fire, but the remains of one. A cooking fire, most likely.

"They're moving," I told the others. "Which means we are too."

Travers squinted up at cliff ahead of us, so young and green there wasn't a single line on his face. To his credit he looked entirely unfazed.

"Climbing gear?"

I nodded grimly. "It's the only way."

# Forty-Eight

## JULIANA

After a full week in the guys' house, I had to admit I was getting comfortable. By the second week however, I'd developed a full-blown daily routine. It involved waking in one of their beds, showering with their shampoo, and carefully shaving my legs with the same razors they used on their handsome faces. I worked out in their fully-stocked gym to clear my head, watched their television for entertainment, and enjoyed sitting out on their patio at night, staring up at the stars.

Wondering if they were looking at the same stars I was.

I also ate their food, drank their milk, and finished every box of cereal in the house — especially the sugary ones. Because while I never used my pregnancy as carte blanche to devour anything I wanted, I decided early on that indulging my sweet tooth was just going to happen.

Once every two or three days I went to Phoenix, where I signed documents, took meetings, and began hiring the crew of people I'd need to make certain things happen. And things *were* happening. At a much faster and even accelerate pace than I could've ever imagined.

And still, Aric knew nothing about it.

That part made me feel a bit guilty, but in the end it was for the best. Despite his assurances I knew my assistant would be too controlling, too involved. Besides, he'd find out soon enough. Just not until there wasn't anything he could do to dissuade me.

I also didn't feel guilty because this was my company, and therefore, my call. And if what I planned on doing would ultimately work out? Well, then Aric was getting the mother of all pleasant surprises anyway.

"Here you go, Ms. Emerson."

The local attorney I'd hired was a cold, shark of a man with zero interest in bullshit and not even the slightest hint of a smile. In short, the perfect lawyer.

"They signed off on the stipulations?"

He nodded firmly as he handed me the lease agreement. "All of them."

I was genuinely impressed. "Well done."

"Take the time to look them over," he urged. "Just be sure to get them to me by the end of the week."

"You'll have them tomorrow morning," I countered. "Early."

He nodded again, giving me the impression that *he* was impressed. If I didn't know any better, I would've assumed he was from New York.

"There's still the matter of the zoning board," he went on, "but the expediter assures me he'll have that buttoned up in a few days. After that, pending the wire transfers, we'll go to closing."

"And get the key."

The lawyer cleared his throat. "And get the key, yes."

He knew I was anxious, but for all my pushing he never wavered. I'd paid handsomely for speed, and I expected to have it. Every day that went by was an opportunity lost.

"Thanks again," I told him before turning away. "If there's anything else, don't hesitate to call. Doesn't matter what time it is."

"Oh I'm very aware," he said perfunctorily. "Good day Ms. Emerson."

With that we parted ways, traveling in opposite directions down the sidewalk. Maybe it was how much I was paying him, but he'd been good about meeting me anywhere I needed him to. And these past few days, I'd been staying in Phoenix more than I'd been staying at the house.

*What if they're home?*

The thought always crossed my mind: that the guys could come back at any time. I kept my phone glued to my side, always charged, always ready to answer any number no matter how strange or foreign it looked. So far I'd picked up three people trying to upgrade my phone service, another two asking if I'd be interested in home solar panels, and at least a half dozen "last chance" robo-calls telling me my car's warranty had expired.

But so far unfortunately, nothing from Devyn,

Maverick, or Gage.

The baby suddenly kicked, as if somehow it knew I was thinking about its father. Or fathers, depending upon how you looked at things.

*I can't wait to show them...*

The punching and kicking in my belly was a brand new development. I honestly thought it would weird me out, but I'd actually found it quite adorable. The more I grew accustomed to it, the more I started looking forward to the little signs of life that were now going on, deep in my womb.

*Gage is gonna flip out!*

I smiled, thinking about how cute all three of them would be once they saw me again. My baby bump was much rounder now, and lower too. The swell of my belly was noticeable no matter what I wore, so I stopped trying to hide it and picked up a few oversized T-shirts that stretched tightly and securely over my little bump.

Although I'd woken in Phoenix with the intention of exploring the city on a less business and more personal basis, my body decided to call it an early night. Into the hotel lobby I went, my stomach growling impatiently as I realized I'd skipped lunch. There was just too much to do. I'd already made so many contacts it was hard to keep track of them all. But the faster I did it, the quicker I could get back to the beautiful house in the desert.

And the faster I could wrap myself in the pillows and blankets that smelled like *them*.

# Forty-Nine

**MAVERICK**

The terrain was uniform enough to make every direction look exactly the same, but sparse enough to make following someone an even bigger pain in the ass. For that reason we hung back, and climbed to vantage points whenever we could. We were able to scout the groups ahead of us, which we determined to be three specific factions.

Hanging back however, wasn't something the others wanted to hear. So far Vaughan was still on his best behavior, but I could tell Travers and Langston were getting antsy. And when your *medic* gets antsy, that's saying something.

"Any word yet?"

I shook my head at Gage, who asked the same question at least five times a day. We'd been tracking all three groups for the better part of a week now. Not exactly ideal for a mission that was supposed to take two to three days, tops.

"Hyde's up at eighty percent" he said, lowering his

voice. "Maybe eighty-five."

The Hyde percentage was something we'd made up several operations ago. It was an indication of just how much of his personality had gone over to the darker, angrier side. Up until now, that percentage had never measured higher than seventy.

"Should we pick it up?"

I was asking them all now: Gage and Maverick both, along with Parker who'd come in from the rear. All three men looked at each other and nodded simultaneously.

"They've been pretty diligent," I added cautiously. "You don't think we'll spook them?"

"They're going to split up anyway, eventually," Maverick pointed out. "And we don't have the resources to track them halfway across the continent."

That point was only partially true. Even with supplies running low, there were always ways to keep going. The real question would be what shape we were in when we got to the end.

"Might be easier to handle them once they've broken up," I countered. "Wait for them to split off. Dictate things on our terms."

"Maybe," said Parker. "But then we might miss Bashir."

Asad Bashir was the worse kind of evil; a vicious warlord who seized any and all resources he came across while starving the native people into submission. If you wanted to eat, you joined his militia. Or he just showed up one day in your village and took whatever he wanted, and that included *whomever* he wanted, as well.

As a result his army constantly grew, which meant it had to keep moving to feed and supply itself. There were very few places Bashir settled down, and when he did it generally wasn't for long. The asshole was as paranoid as he was nomadic. And considering the number of enemies he'd made, with good reason.

Intelligence had put Bashir's core group of followers in this region. That, coupled with another pair of grainy photographs, had been enough to initiate our insertion. It would've been nice to fast-rope in from a Blackhawk, or even HALO jump past all this blasted terrain by the light of the quarter-moon. Both methods would've alerted Bashir though. Either one would've sent him scurrying back into the brush, like a rat through one of a million holes in the floorboards.

Two nights ago, Evans had made Bashir through the zoom-optics of his Schmidt and Bender sniper scope. If it were up to me, he would've taken the shot. But it wasn't up to me.

"If they follow the same pattern they'll camp early and leave before dawn," I said finally. "We'll keep our distance for now, but tonight, if everything looks good..."

Parker's eyes flared dangerously. I saw one corner of his mouth curl into a smirk.

".. at zero one-thirty we'll move in."

Gage nodded his immediate approval. Maverick, usually the cautious one, was on board too.

"By dusk I want everyone armored up, weapons

checked, ready to roll.  No snags.  No delays."

Decision finally made, I jerked my chin backward.

"And someone tell Hyde, before he kicks over a cactus."

# Fifty

## JULIANA

"Really?" I pressed, as the elevator doors closed. "You *still* don't know why I flew you all the way out here?"

The man next to me shook his head again, while sweating profusely. Not because he was nervous, but because Robert Valentine was way overdressed for Arizona.

"Not a clue," he admitted, tugging on his collar. "And for the record, you didn't fly me out here. I bought my own ticket."

I laughed. "And why's that?"

"Because you're cheap?"

"I prefer the term thrifty," I smirked, "but sure, money's tight right now. Why else, though?"

Robert shrugged meekly. "Because after what happened between us, I guess I owed you that much."

"You did," I confirmed, as the elevator jerked to an abrupt stop. "But you also came for another reason."

The doors opened. Like a game show hostess, I waved my arm grandly.

"You came because you trust me."

I urged Robert forward and out onto the landing, which looked out over a large, empty room just one floor below. A walkway with office doors encircled the second floor area, running all the way around the perimeter of the building in a rectangle.

"What's this?" asked Robert.

"Shameless West."

His shrewd eyes narrowed. "Wait, what?"

"You said the board wanted a marketing company with a west-coast presence, right?" I stepped up to the railing and gestured downward. "Well here you go. You're looking at one right now."

The man whose company I'd made — and who'd subsequently made mine — turned to stare back at me. He was still incredulous.

"You're opening another marketing company?" he breathed.

"Not another one, just an extension of the one I already have."

Robert Valentine cocked his head. "But..."

"But what?"

He stared down again at the empty floor. "There's nothing here."

"Not yet," I countered.

"No desks, no computers, no people…"

"What if I told you we'll be up and running in less than two weeks?"

He couldn't contain a laugh. I couldn't blame him.

"No, really. I've got everything coming at once. Contractors setting up partitions, segmenting the departments. Bringing in all the physical infrastructure to set up a kickass office…"

I pulled out my phone and pressed a few buttons. The speaker cracked with the sound of an outgoing email.

"There, I just sent you the mock-ups, the floor plan, and all the specs. Click on the link and you can even take a virtual tour."

Robert Valentine had always been a visionary, and I brought him to this unfinished space because I knew I could count on his creative mind. Judging by his expression now, I knew it was the right move. His eyes scanned the upper perimeter, where he could see the offices and conference rooms that would take shape. He saw the soon-to-be bustling floor, which would ultimately be the beating heart of this new branch of my company.

"Research department's over there," I pointed. "Sales and support in that corner. I've got Jennifer Akin coming on as the social media manager."

Robert's eyes went wide. "*The* Jennifer Akin?"

"Of course."

"Wow."

The admiration in his eyes was genuine, and it was

good to see. Especially since I'd promised Jennifer the moon, Jupiter, *its* moons, and various other parts of the solar system to get her down here.

"As for the design team, I'm bringing four people over from New York, plus another three locals. I'll have some floaters that will spend time at both offices, of course. Oh, and then of course there's Anthony McKenzie..."

Robert was still gazing absently over the empty office space, taking in my vision. At the mention of that last name however, he whirled on me so fast I thought his head might spin off.

"You're talking with *McKenzie?*"

"Talked to, not talking," I told him. "And yes, he's coming on."

My guest folded his arms and shook his head. "But he's with Skyline!"

"*Was* with Skyline," I corrected. "I hired him as of two days ago. In fact, he's landing tomorrow."

"But—"

"In fact, I poached three others from Skyline too. All of them really good people," I added proudly. "The cream of the crop, actually."

"Surely they're bound by a no-compete clause?" he theorized.

I shook my head. "James was too stupid to make them sign one."

"Holy shit."

"Yeah."

For the first time in forever, I saw a glimmer of the old, savvy software developer. The one I'd met in that grungy New York coffee shop, a whole decade ago.

"Who'd you take?" he grinned devilishly.

"You'll know the names, Robert. Trust me."

He looked back at the empty room again, perhaps seeing the same vision I did. A Phoenix office was a perfect location, too. I had the Midwest, a good portion of the south, and from Sky Harbor airport it was a quick hop to Los Angeles or San Francisco. Coupled with what I'd already established in New York, it opened all new doors to all new things.

Hell, I probably should've even done it sooner.

"You're nefarious," Robert sighed finally. "You know that right?"

"Am I really?" I laughed. "Because the way I see it, if John James can steal my number one client, I can certainly skim off the best people he has working for him. Which of course leaves him nothing but a bunch of unimaginative, inexperienced college graduates."

I saw his shoulders slump. Not sorrowfully, but in resignation.

"The ones with really lame advertising ideas," I piled on.

We walked the entirety of second floor catwalk, past the sweeping, contemporary-style staircases that flanked either side of the main floor. By the time we'd returned to the elevator, I knew my old ally was fully on board.

"What do you need me to do?"

"You already know."

"Go to the top brass?" he sighed. "Tell them what a mistake we made?"

"By now the first campaigns should be coming in," I shrugged. "You don't even have to tell them how bad Skyline is. You could just show them."

"That shouldn't be hard actually," he acknowledged.

I patted him on the shoulder. "And when you're done, show them this place. Tell them we're happy to go back to the way things were, but we're gonna need a little more of a solid commitment this time around."

He cleared his throat. "A new, less escapable contract I'm assuming?"

I pulled out my phone again, punched a few new buttons, and hovered my thumb over the send button.

"Believe it or not, I've got that too," I grinned.

# Fifty-One

**GAGE**

The first half of the mission unfolded silently, wordlessly, and with the utmost precision. Night fell. Our targets camped. We waited long enough for all but the perimeter guards to be fast asleep, then we crept up on them like the slow-moving shadow of death we truly were.

It took three whole hours to move just one-hundred yards, crawling along on our bellies, moving only when the lookouts had their heads turned or their attention drawn elsewhere. For those three long hours, it felt like some messed up life-or-death game of Red Light, Green Light.

But the second half of the mission took only three minutes.

On our orders, Evans dropped the guards from his position on the southwest ridge. His TAC-50 made no sound; only the brief whir of a supersonic bullet shattering the stillness of the night, followed by the noise of dropping bodies.

From there we converged on the camp from all directions, the beams of our laser sights sweeping like deadly lines, moving from target to target. Those beams were invisible to all but us, illuminated only by our night-vision optics. Our goggles lit up the encampment as if it were the middle of the day, while the groggy soldiers of Bashir's army woke only to shadows, darkness, and ultimately, oblivion.

The hierarchy of the camp was something we'd made out long before we moved in, and here luck proved to be on our side. Bashir's closest lieutenants and long-standing men made up the inner circle of the encampment, while the younger, recent recruits made up the outer rings. For this reason we started in the middle, eliminating the more dangerous element of the army before driving the newer, greener soldiers backwards and into the brush. Our goal here was to save lives, wherever possible.

Devyn, Maverick, Travers, and Langston each took a quadrant. They were tasked with clearing any potential threats so fiercely and loudly that most of the young, unarmed soldiers would flee, confused and screaming, into the night. The plan worked flawlessly, with just a few exceptions. Three or four young men had enough wits to take up arms against us, but were immediately neutralized by the butt of a rifle, or in one case, being tackled and zip-tied by an overly-anxious Hyde.

The whole thing happened so fast we almost didn't notice the two men that burst forth from one of the bigger tents, firing AK-47's as they retreated. I heard Parker cry out in pain, followed by the scream of another .50 cal bullet that caught one of the men in the upper torso. In a fraction of a second the arm that had been holding his weapon disintegrated, turning him a spinning, blood-splattered top.

"BASHIR!"

I was rushing toward Parker when Christian's voice spun my attention in the opposite direction. There, outlined perfectly in my panoramic night-vision goggles, our unmistakably gangly target was making a beeline for the thickest part of the foliage.

"I got him!"

I hurdled two men who'd already surrendered, then kicked my feet into high gear. Bashir was shockingly fast, probably due to his long legs. He also wasn't carrying sixty pounds of armor, weapons, and equipment.

Distantly I heard Evans over my ear-piece, telling us he no longer had a shot. My target was gaining ground. He was almost to the treeline.

I didn't want to shoot, but I might have to. Our orders were to capture and not kill unless necessary. But was this necessary? Bashir was the highest value target on the continent right now. If he somehow managed to slip away...

*Fuck.*

I hated making these calls. I usually left them to Devyn or Maverick or–

I tripped. It happened so fast my legs didn't know it until my chin was scraping the hard, dust-choked ground. It was a hard fall too. One that I really should've felt, if not for the adrenaline. Cursing and grumbling, I rolled back to my feet and shrugged off my pack. By my eyes...

My eyes were greeted only by darkness.

Raising my hands to my helmet, I realized my goggles were gone. They'd been torn away from the fall or they were shoved so far backward I couldn't feel them anymore. There was no time to fix them anyway. Bashir had already disappeared into the brush.

"GAGE!"

The shouts from behind me sounded like warnings rather than encouragement. I was either being ordered to halt at the edge of the clearing or my pursuit completely waved off.

It's a good thing my ear-piece had popped out during the fall, because there was no way in hell I was obeying.

Into the brush I went, holding one arm forward to protect against sticks and branches and God knew what else. And then I felt it — a booted foot coming down hard on the back of my knee. My leg flew out from under me and I fell sideways, swinging my rifle around as I went...

Then something struck my rifle, and that was gone too.

"Fuck you!"

The words were spat with such venom, such hatred, I actually recoiled from the sound. I looked up to find Asad Bashir standing over me, leveling an evil-looking pistol at my face. His mouth was a horrendous snarl. His eyes were wild and filled with bloodlust.

I put one hand up to shield my face, while bringing the other behind me to grab my own sidearm. Abruptly, a pair of shots rang out. I thought for sure I was dead, until—

"ARRGHH!"

The full weight of a pistol clattered against my helmet. Screaming in pain, my assailant doubled over and fell down on me, clutching his stomach.

"Chief!"

By the time my savior arrived I was already on top of Bashir and yanking his arms violently behind him. I whipped my head left, to see Vaughan bounding over.

"You alright?"

I noticed a curl of smoke drifting up from the barrel of his rifle. Still fighting away the battle-hysteria that came with the usual adrenaline overload, I nodded.

"I think I hit him," Vaughan breathed.

Securing his wrists, I flipped our quarry over. Blood was already seeping through his shirt, just below his navel.

"He's gut-shot," I confirmed. "Twice."

Vaughan's expression suddenly changed. He looked legitimately worried. "That good or bad?"

"Bad for him," I shrugged, watching the pain contort Bashir's face. "Good for Somalia."

I stood up, retrieved my rifle, and fixed my optics. Then I punched Vaughan in the chest and hugged him, all in the span of the same two seconds.

"Parker?" I asked quickly.

"He's fine," Vaughan assured me. "Took one in the left shin. Looks like it hurts like hell, but it passed right through."

I let out a relieved laugh. "That's the third time he's

gotten shot in that same leg. Maybe we should start pinning the purple hearts right onto his knee."

Vaughan laughed too, until another sound drew our attention. Down at our feet, Bashir's groans were growing louder.

I took a moment to decide something — a very long moment, actually — before finally shaking my head.

"Get Langston," I spat, wiping my mouth. "As enjoyable as it would be to watch this piece of dogshit bleed out, I'd rather see him rot in a six-by-eight cell for the rest of his miserable life."

# Fifty-Two

## JULIANA

I was just stepping out of the most amazing shower of my life when I heard the sound: a muffled bang from outside, followed quickly by a second one. Neither noise sounded ominous, really. But they didn't sound natural either.

And this far from civilization, anything unnatural was concerning to say the least.

Wrapping the towel around my dripping body, I crossed into Maverick's bedroom. Sliding my hand between the two mattresses, I retrieved the thick black handgun I'd found the first time I'd changed the bedsheets.

I knew now that the weapon was an HK45C, with a slimline grip and an underside-mounted crimson trace laser sighting. I'd learned these things over the course of several lessons at Caswell's shooting range, taken only because I felt safer knowing how to fire the thing rather than use it as a club.

Pistol in hand, I crept smoothly down the staircase to get a view through the lower floor's front windows. A pair of taillights grew distant, glowed bright red for a moment, then passed through the gates before turning onto the highway.

Just then the door opened, and two large figures stepped through. I raised the gun. Crouching down on the staircase, I pulled my arms in tight to make myself a smaller target...

"Oh my GOD!"

A second later I'd dropped the weapon altogether and was flinging myself down the lower steps and into Devyn and Gage's open arms.

"What the hell!?"

The guys were overjoyed to see me, but even more shocked and surprised than I was! They kept kissing and hugging and squeezing me tightly, tearing me bodily in and out of each other's arms so many times that my towel fell to the floor.

"You're... wet!" Devyn laughed, taking a step back.

"And naked!" Gage noted.

I'd forgotten those inconsequential things entirely, until I saw their gazes both drop to my swollen belly. After that they began handling me more slowly and gingerly, touching my stomach as if it were the surface of a hot stove.

"I won't break, you know," I giggled.

Even so they moved with extra care, totally dumbfounded at how much bigger I'd gotten while they were away. Eventually the kissing started all over again, this time coupled with a few naked pinches and grabs that they just couldn't help.

"You're really *home?*" I asked, worried about the answer.

"More than you know," said Gage.

My gaze swept to the door, which they'd shut behind them. My mouth dropped abruptly open, my eyes going wide.

"M—Maverick???"

"He's fine," Devyn assured me quickly. "He's in San Diego, a day behind us. Still debriefing."

Warm, blessed relief crashed over me in a giant wave. I hugged them again, twisting back and forth to look at each of them.

"And you're all good?" I asked, gingerly touching Gage's face. He had what looked to be wicked road-rash just beneath his chin. "You're all okay?"

"Better than ever," declared Devyn. "Especially now that *you're* here."

"Speaking of which," Gage grinned happily, "what *are* you doing here?"

"Lots of things," I said proudly. "Lots of awesome, amazing things."

The house was dim, warm, and welcoming — especially with the fireplace lit, which I kept going every night. It looked almost as if I were expecting them. Prepping the house, to welcome them home.

"Ummm... one more thing," said Devyn.

I kissed him on the cheek, happily. "Shoot."

"Was that a *gun* you were pointing at us?"

I shrugged, trying my best to look innocent. "What answer are you looking for here?"

"The right one."

"Okay, then yes," I winced.

Blushing a little, I explained everything. From how I'd shown up trying to surprise them a few weeks back, to sticking around a bit, to staying at their place all the way up until now. I talked about finding Maverick's gun, and learning how to use it. I even explained how I'd upgraded their coffee maker and watered their plants.

But I never said a word about Phoenix.

"So we walk into what should've been a cold, lonely house," said Devyn, "and instead *you're* here. The heat's on. The fireplace is lit. And you're naked. Naked and wet."

"Naked and wet and carrying a pistol," Gage added. "Which needless to say is even hotter."

My nakedness hadn't even occurred to me, I was just too happy to see them. I was so effortlessly comfortable around them, my dropped towel was an afterthought.

"We need to talk," I said, scooping the towel up from the floor. I wrapped it around my still-wet hair, and tucked it into a bun. "But not until all three of you are together."

The smile on my face told them the talk would be a good, not bad one. It raised their spirits. Caused their hands to begin wandering again, this time to other parts of my naked body besides my pregnant belly.

"Maverick lands tomorrow," said Gage. "We're supposed to pick him up in Phoenix."

"Phoenix!" My eyes glowed. "Perfect."

One powerful hand kneaded my ass, as another cupped my breasts from behind. Devyn dropped his wet mouth against my bare shoulder. He kissed me and squeezed, sending electric shivers all over my body.

"So what do we do until then?" he murmured into my ear.

Reaching downward and back, I closed my hands excitedly over a pair of very familiar crotches.

"I'm sure we'll think of something."

# Fifty-Three

## JULIANA

The arrival gate at Sky Harbor airport was abuzz with life, as we stood there waiting for Maverick to come home. Wanting to surprise him, we stood tightly together with me in the back. This left me totally eclipsed by the two big SEALs in front of me, at least until the very last moment.

I should've been sore after last night. I should've welcomed both men home with long hours of vigorous, passionate lovemaking that made *them* sore too.

Instead I'd led them by their hands and taken them up to bed, where I took them on one at a time. I spread my legs for Devyn while soul-kissing Gage, clutching his tightly-pistoning ass and grinding him slowly and deliberately to a monster orgasm. Then I'd pushed Gage backwards and carefully mounted him, this time kissing Devyn while riding his friend's thick, beautiful shaft to a climax of my own.

By the time he was bucking his hips and draining himself inside me, it was already late. Dreamy and contented, the three of us fell fast asleep with both men cradling me in a fetal position between their hot, naked bodies.

Lucky me.

Up ahead people began disembarking from the latest flight. Devyn and Gage sidled closer together for a few moments, then abruptly stepped away from each other to reveal me.

I couldn't even yell out the word 'surprise.' I was too busy flinging myself into Maverick's arms, and drinking in the expression of pure joy that crossed his face the moment he realized I was actually there.

We hugged and kissed and shared the moment, which came with a thousand questions. But such questions would have to wait until later.

"Okay, now come with me."

I led them outside, where we ultimately packed everything into Gage's truck and took off. I guided them along. Fifteen minutes later we stood before the building, the guys still extremely perplexed. And five minutes after that...

"Voila."

The elevator doors slid open, as they'd opened for Robert Valentine days before. A lot of things had changed since then. And thanks to the work crews they were still changing, even as we stood there.

"You didn't..." Devyn swore, after a brief moment of confusion.

"I did."

Devyn's expression went from bewilderment to total elation. His smile said everything.

*"Really?"*

I met him mid-hug, squeezing him back. His grin was infectious.

"Really," I breathed. "Yes!"

I sprinted ahead, thrilled to show them everything, practically dragging them along. For the next several minutes I never stopped talking, telling them everything I planned on doing, showing them every hallway, every office, every corner of the vast, beautiful space that would soon become an extension of the company I'd proudly built from such humble beginnings.

Eventually we arrived at what would soon be my office — a large corner unit whose only glass consisted of two converging windows that looked out over the bustling city. After all these weeks, Phoenix didn't look so foreign anymore. In fact, it was getting to feel a lot like home.

"Close the door," I nodded, when they were all inside.

Devyn was the last one through. The heavy oaken door clicked shut behind him, divorcing us from the noise of the nail-guns and chop-saws just outside.

"Last time we were all together I stupidly left," I told them. "I pushed you away, because as always I was too concerned with doing everything on my own. And that's because I *could* do everything on my own."

Slowly I walked toward them, moving into 'my spot' between their strong, hulking bodies. The guys converged around me, moving into their own positions without uttering a single word.

"But then I realized something," I went on. "I don't *want* to do it on my own. Especially since I'm not going to be on my own very much longer."

With that I reached down, running a hand lovingly over my belly. The tiny child inside me rolled a little, almost on cue.

"I love you," I said simply. "All of you. Each of you. At first I tried to convince myself that wasn't possible. That I was deluding myself to think you'd love me back..."

I glanced down for a moment, searching for the words. A slow hand touched my cheek, lifting my gaze back their way.

"You're deluding yourself in thinking we don't," Maverick said gently.

The others nodded. There was adoration in their eyes. I could say in that very moment that I finally *knew*. But in all honesty, I'd known long ago.

"When I finally realized it, it frightened me," I told them. "This child was supposed to be mine. Not because I wanted it that way, but because that's just the way it was with me. It's just the way it's always been."

Gage looked hopeful. He raised an eyebrow. "But?"

"But now I'm tired of fighting it," I sighed. "I can't live without you! I went back to New York and I was utterly miserable, and I knew not even the joy of raising a child would change that fact."

I swallowed and nearly choked, fighting back tears. Somehow I did it though.

"I want *all* of you," I said. "I want to be your girl. Your *girlfriend*..."

The word dropped from my lips with a surge of incredible happiness that warmed me from within. It felt so good saying it. So natural. So perfect.

"I want to raise this child with three wonderful fathers, instead of none. And I want to forge a relationship with all of you, with each of you. Whatever it is you want to call this, I want it all just as badly as you do."

Two arms enveloped me, then two more. And then I was being hugged. Kissed. Picked up from the floor and lifted into arms so big and strong I couldn't help but laugh, and when the tears started to flow I couldn't stop them.

"I want to move here obviously," I sniffed, drying my eyes. "I want to work here. Build here. I want to live and love and laugh with you, and especially, with our child."

Everything went blurry. The tears of happiness were just too much.

"Of course, I'll get a place nearby. Somewhere with enough space for all of us, so that when you're in town—"

"Not a chance."

Devyn's arms were folded. He shook his head as he said the words.

"What?"

"You're staying with us," Gage explained for him. He stared at my belly. "The both of you. You're *ours* now. We're a family—"

"But—"

"Our house will finally be home," Maverick added, "and not just some place in the desert where we sit around waiting for the unknown. It'll finally have warmth. Love. Structure."

"I can't ask you to do that," I cut in quickly. "You're SEALs. You have a contract, and we all know the terms. No wife. No child. No life beyond the mission, for as long as you—"

"We canceled that contract," Gage interrupted me coolly. "Effective yesterday."

I stopped cold. For a few long seconds, his words didn't register.

"He's right," Devyn cut in. "This last mission was also our final operation. We decided this over in Somalia, before we even came back. At a certain point you have to stop rolling the dice, Jules. Eventually, you lose."

I saw him absently fingering the dog-tag around his neck. Perhaps wondering how things could've been different, but weren't.

"There are still terms to discuss, and roles we can fill," Devyn added. "But none of them will involve going away. None of them will involve taking us away from here... or more importantly, from *you*."

For a while I could only stand there, trying to soak up everything they were telling me. Eventually I shook my head. It just didn't seem real.

"But this job is your *life*," I pleaded. "This is what you do."

"No," Maverick corrected me gently. "It's what we

*did.* For ten long years, which is more than most."

Silence descended. I had to be sure.

"Just like that, you'd give it all up?" I was still incredulous. "You'd really do that for me?"

"We'd do it for *all* of us," Devyn answered. His eyes dropped to my belly. "And for him."

"Or her," I croaked.

The handsome face I'd fallen in love with over a computer monitor grinned back at me. "Or her."

Gage was smiling too, and now he stared down at me from two glassy eyes of his own. "*You're* our life now," he chimed in. "You and the baby we'll raise together."

The words choked me up all over again. I just couldn't believe them. Or maybe, I wouldn't believe them.

In my heart of hearts though, I knew they were the truth.

"You sure you're ready to be our girl?" Devyn finally teased. "It comes with certain... responsibilities."

I sniffed again, wiping away my tears as I let out a laugh.

"Why, are there tryouts?"

He shrugged. "Could be."

"Sounds right up my alley."

The heat of their bodies was making me hornier than ever, and that's because they'd inched even closer on all sides. The idea of having all three of them again was wildly exciting. I'd been fantasizing about it for weeks, and now it was finally going to happen.

"Wanna take me home?" I murmured, smiling wickedly. "Try out this shared girlfriend thing?"

"Maybe put you through the paces?" asked Devyn.

"Or I could put *you* through the paces," I replied, adding a wink. "One... by one... by one."

"Damn," Gage shifted where he stood. "You really are insatiable."

I extended my arm, staring down at my tattoo that read 'invincible.'

"Maybe I'll put that one on my *other* arm," I teased.

# Fifty-Four

## JULIANA

The streets of New York looked vaguely foreign by time I'd returned, but that of course was on me. I'd been away for far too long. Even worse I'd been cheating on Manhattan with a whole different city, and the odd way the streets stared back at me it was almost as if it somehow *knew*.

"Boss!"

Aric hadn't seen me in so long he rushed into my office with what promised to be a crushing bear-hug. As I turned sideways however, he caught my profile and stopped dead.

"Oh my God..."

His jaw dropped. He whipped off his glasses.

"You're *huge!*"

"I prefer the term well-rounded," I smirked, not really caring what my assistant called me. "But yes. I'm definitely getting up there."

My baby bump was a full-fledged hill now, and would likely be a mountain soon. Which is why I didn't have any time to waste.

"Aric, what do you think about this office? Do you like it?"

By the look on his face, it was the last thing he expected me to ask him.

"Sure, boss," he replied, glancing around at the four glass walls. "It's got a great view."

"Good. It's yours, then."

His expression was mild amusement. "Mine?"

"I'm giving it to you."

A crease formed on Aric's brow, right below his perfectly dark Clark Kent hairstyle. All he needed was that little errant lock hanging down to complete the picture.

"And where are you going to—"

"I'm not," I cut in. "I'll be gone."

The crease turned into several angry lines. *"Gone?"*

"Yes, I'm heading out," I confirmed. "Not coming back. And Aric... I'm leaving this whole place to you."

He looked stunned. Frightened. Pissed.

"You're *quitting!?*" he practically shouted. "Just giving up?"

"No, I—"

"Selling out to Skyline?" he demanded angrily. "Please tell me you're not going to let those asshats win?

After all the stuff we went through, after all the things you said—"

"Aric, I'm not," I assured him. "Shameless Marketing's not going anywhere. In fact, we'll be stronger than ever. Especially with our new Southwest office."

My last words were greeted by a long span of stunned silence. He didn't understand.

"You're taking over New York," I told him. "And I'm opening an all new branch in Phoenix. There'll be more reach, more coverage. More contacts. More everything."

His expression still hadn't changed. He looked like a man who'd been struck by lightning, but it still hadn't registered yet.

"But more than that, I'm making you a partner. Fifty-fifty. Equal votes when it comes to everything. We can work out the details and the money and the legalese, but this place will be yours now. You can shape and mold it into something all your own."

My assistant wasn't just stunned, he was overwhelmed. And on top of that, he was in tears now.

"W—Why would you do this for me?"

"Because I *love* you Aric," I told him. "You're the third brother I never had, and the only one I actually *bonded* with. I could never truly relate to that type of connection before, but I can now. More than ever."

My assistant gulped, took a step back, and actually leaned against my desk for support.

"And I also know that people like you only come

along once in a lifetime."

Now he did bear-hug me, being careful not to squash my pregnant belly. His big arms squeezed and squeezed, while I felt warm tears dripping down from both sides of his face.

When I could breathe again, I let out a chuckle. "Easy there, big guy."

I patted him on the back for a while, until he finally let go. Then we sat down, and I told him the gist of it. We made arrangements to have lunch, where I'd give him the specs of the new place and fill him in on all the finer details between Robert Valentine and I. When he finally rose and made for the door, I cleared my throat.

"Oh, and Aric?"

"Yes?"

I twirled one finger in a slow circle. "You might wanna get rid of all this glass."

My assistant's eyes widened in genuine excitement. *"Really?"*

"Oh yeah," I grinned. "It's like living in a fishbowl."

# Fifty-Five

## JULIANA

Days. Weeks. Months.

Time either flew or it crawled, depending upon what we were doing and where we were. Being with the guys though, it always seemed like one or the other. For some odd reason, there never seemed to be an in-between.

I moved in straightaway, and together we turned the beautiful house in the desert into a full-fledged home. It was amazing, having them all there at once. Devyn, Maverick, and Gage were attentive and adorable, both with me and our ever-growing unborn child. As my belly got bigger they tagged along to every doctor's visit, every sonogram. They also jumped through hoops to fulfill my every need, even when I didn't want them to, until I was shooing them away just so I could head out to the office and get some work done.

And there was a *hell* of a lot work to do.

Shameless West opened without fanfare and went

straight to work, building a client base all its own without siphoning too many resources from the New York office. Aric of course was an absolute godsend. He took care of everything over there as I knew he would, plus he took on tasks remotely that helped make our launch go smoother than a dolphin's ass.

I tried not to recruit too many people from there, but in the beginning I needed them. And they came, one by one, sometimes for weeks and months, other times permanently. Aric razzed me for some of that and pretended to curse me out, but I knew in at least some instances he was pushing and prodding those people to come help out, even offering extra money and a good chunk of his own bonus to get them out there. I appreciated the help without admitting it, while pretending he could spare more. It was all part of the little game we played. It worked for us, and it always would.

Eventually I had to spill my pregnancy to my parents and siblings, who were shocked, elated, astonished, and then angry, all in that order. After running through the full gamut of emotions however, they ended up thrilled for me in the end. Even if they couldn't understand why I'd use a sperm bank to get pregnant in the middle of opening a new branch of my business while simultaneously moving most of the way across the country.

But hey, considering they already thought I was an insane workaholic that part wasn't all that surprising.

The real confusion came when I flew mom and Mariah out to visit, and gave them a tour of the house I was 'sharing' with three incredibly ripped and handsome roommates who just happened to be military. My sister left drooling over shoulders and arms and impossibly broad chests, but my mother — always the savvy one — gave me a distinctly insinuating look before she left. It was the kind of look that told me: *I know you're with one of them.*

For now at least, she could think that all she wanted.

Devyn and Maverick were surprisingly busy, and even Gage to a lesser extent. Although no longer active for combat duty in the SEALs program, they had a vast wealth of knowledge that was still incredibly valuable. The three of them accepted all kinds of training assignments that took them to Great Lakes, Illinois for BUDS school, and back to San Diego for land warfare training. When they weren't in Norfolk they were in Jacksonville, or Corpus Christi, or way out at Pearl Harbor-Hickam.

And when they weren't at any of those places, they were home here with me.

The best part of being the center of attention for three gorgeous men was that I always had someone to come home to. I had one, two, sometimes all three of them wrapping their strong arms around me at the end of the day. There was always motion, always excitement, always stories to tell. And just as they passed in and out of the house... they were in and out of my bedroom, as well.

That part was the greatest, most intense part of being together. The guys shared me in the most dripping hot ways, emotionally and physically, leaving me spent and satiated, but always wanting more. I loved taking them on together, letting them possess me and fuck me and sandwich my body between theirs. I also found that being pregnant turned out to be the horniest time in my entire life. Or maybe it was just the fact that I was screwing three guys at once, jumping them at will. Getting bent over or shoved backward or devoured mercilessly until I came, screaming... all while the others watched, waiting their turn.

My pregnant belly seemed to turn them on as well, and the bigger it got the more eager they were to pin me down and ravage me. They were adorably careful, though. As the months went by I began missing the roughness, the speed, the frenzied desperation. But I knew all that would eventually come back. They'd even whispered such things into my ear, while sawing my body back and forth between them.

Once I'd delivered, it would open season all over again.

It was the week before I was due when Legendary Gaming finally came crawling back to us. Robert Valentine even flew out to deliver the good news himself. I showed him the finished space, then sat down with him to go over new projects and divide them between Aric and I based on which office best suited their needs. By the time he flew home we'd nearly quadrupled our revenue. He'd also brought me the softest, most incredible zombie baby-blanket on the planet as a gift. Hell, maybe the *only* zombie baby-blanket on the planet.

All three of my men stayed home in the days leading up to my due date. Our lives were busy but damn-near perfect.

And then came Erin... and our hearts melted.

She was seven pounds eleven ounces of pure unadulterated joy, wrapped in the arms of three eager dads and one proud momma. She shattered the glass ceiling of our combined dreams. Flung us so far beyond anything we ever could've thought we might love together that it both humbled and astonished us; quite a feat considering we already had so much experience in that department.

Taking her home, making her the precious little center of our universe —it was the cherry on top of the ultimate sundae. Far out in the desert, away from the crowds of New York, I'd finally found peace. Happiness. Love times three... and now four.

Weeks went by again, weeks that turned into months. We worked hard and played hard and doted over our tiny little princess, who slept in the most gorgeously *redecorated* baby nursery on the entire planet. That part was even more fun, because we got to do it together. Just like most everything else.

And then one night out in the desert the conversation turned serious, and three Navy SEALs dropped to their knees with military precision, at exactly the same time. A glimmering diamond ring was placed on my trembling finger, reflecting back the light of a million shimmering stars. I cried tears of jubilation as they kissed me slowly and tenderly, one by one, promising themselves to me forever. These were men who were accustomed to pledges; men who knew the value of loyalty and who always kept their word. They were men devoted not just to each other, but now to the woman they loved and the child they'd sired with her.

And from that moment on, the five of us were forever bonded beyond words.

# Epilogue

## JULIANA

I squirmed deeper into the coolness of silk sheets, arching my back and letting my body stretch forward like a cat's. My wrists were bound together with scarves in front of me. Or at least they felt like scarves, because without my eyes it was impossible to tell.

*Where the hell are they?*

Anticipation, I'd learned, could be a real bitch. Especially when you were bound and blindfolded on your own bed, face-down ass-up. Waiting for the inevitable sound of footsteps that would end your torment, because you were literally *dripping* with the need to be thoroughly and completely fucked from behind.

*Come* on *already!*

I grunted impatiently, letting my soft purr turn into a growl. And that's when the egg-shaped vibrator began pulsing inside me, triggered by the bluetooth connection one or more of them held in their hot little hands.

*FUCK...*

The tiny surges felt incredible, especially as the rhythmic waves of vibrations reached my clit. They started slow, with several seconds between the next pulse...

*They're really going to get it next time my hands are free.*

But slowly, tantalizingly, the toy inside me began pulsing faster and faster.

This time, the deal was for the dishes. Other times it was for even bigger chores. The game was always the same though; all three of them would come upstairs and have their way with me, one at a time. They'd blindfold me first. They'd dress me up too, right after that. But if I could guess who each of them were, and in which order they ravaged my body... well, then I would win.

And if I got just one of them wrong, *they* would win.

I almost didn't seem fair, the whole thing being three on one. But over the course of the past few months I'd gotten quite good at knowing who was who. My men were of different thickness, different sizes. They grabbed me and used me in different ways, and with different techniques too, although recently they'd wised up by switching things up a little.

Tonight had been an anniversary of sorts; an entire year since we'd moved in together. It was a year of love and laughter and sweltering, white-hot sex. Of frantically trying to raise an adorable baby together, while each of us launched our old careers in all new directions.

The guys had gone all out tonight, cooking me a

delicious five-course candlelight meal. It was romantic. It was beautiful.

But there were a *lot* of dishes.

I scissored my legs, feeling a slight catch between my stockinged thighs. They'd gone with the fishnets, I could tell that easily. They'd snapped on garter belts, too. I didn't know what panties they'd slipped over my naked, blindfolded body, but they didn't feel all that substantial. A thong, most likely. Maybe even a G-string.

Up top they'd left me totally bare-breasted, though. Which in retrospect, was probably a Gage move.

*Maybe he'll go first, then.*

It was always fun, trying to figure out the order. Even more fun was lying there half-delirious, enjoying the feeling of being wholly and completely dominated, while trying to determine which of my anonymous lovers was inside me at the time. Because in all honesty? Nothing — and I mean *nothing* — is quite as hot as getting taken blindly... while not truly knowing who might be screwing you.

At long last, the sound of footsteps in the hallway dragged me happily back to reality. The guys were just too big, their footfalls too heavy to not make any noise. No matter how many times they'd tried to sneak into the room, I could always sense when they were there. And right now, one of them was in the doorway for sure.

"You gonna stand there staring?" I demanded. "Or are you gonna fuck me?"

It had worked once before — asking them questions. In the heat of the moment Maverick had accidentally answered me without thinking, and it had been the funniest thing in the world.

Right now however, my mystery lover gave no reply. He only crossed the room, grabbed my by the ass, and began kneading and rubbing it in his big, beautiful hands. All while the vibrating egg continued thrumming rhythmically, just inside me.

*Ohhhhhh...*

I purred throatily, squirming even deeper into the sheets. Then suddenly my thong or G-string was yanked to one side, and I felt the wonderfully familiar presence of warm oil being drizzled all over my bare behind.

"So it's gonna be *that* kind of night, is it?" I sighed softly.

The guys had done all sorts of fun and amazing things to me during these blindfold sessions. They'd used distractions like ice cubes and spanking paddles, even candle wax — which really rode the knife's edge between pleasure and pain — to keep me from knowing which one of them was screwing me at the time. I always looked forward to their innovations, even as I fought hard to determine the order in which these insanely hot men drained themselves inside me.

And they were *all* coming inside me. Because yes, they were trying to get me pregnant again.

*God, that's hot.*

No sooner had I spoken than a finger began probing me back there. After rubbing along the puckered surface for a while, getting it all warmed up, it entered my tight little hole for a scandalous inch or two.

*Fuuuuck.*

I bucked forward a little, and the finger followed. When it had me pinned tightly to the sheets it pushed even further inside, giving me those exquisitely naughty shivers I always felt when one or more of them took me in the ass.

Expecting him to climb onto the bed and replace his finger with something far more substantial, I screwed my fists into the sheets. And that's when I felt the distinctly familiar feel of a smooth glass plug being pushed into my ass.

"Mmmph..."

It wasn't a big one, but I could tell it wasn't small either. Maybe it was new. Having three different horny boyfriends, I'd accrued quite the collection of toys over the past year of being their shared woman.

The plug snapped snugly into place, giving me that wonderfully full feeling back there. Whoever was behind me thumped it a few times, sending shockwaves of pleasure throughout my body that reverberated off the bullet-shaped egg. And then he removed the little egg, leaving me momentarily numb, before finally climbing onto the bed and buying his face into my pussy from behind.

*FUUUUCK!*

I was torn between rolling my blindfolded eyes back and enjoying it, or trying to feel by the stubble around his mouth who was devouring me so expertly. All three of my SEALs were equally amazing at going down on me. But one of them — Devyn — had a tongue that delved a little deeper than the others. I couldn't tell though. I was too distracted by the rush of heat from the warming oil, which was still being massaged into my ass by two calloused palms and ten spirited fingers.

"If you're Gage, squeeze once," I teased. "Or squeeze twice if you're Maverick."

The man behind me didn't change course. He continued kissing and nibbling my outer folds, while gliding his tongue up and down along my warm, wet entrance.

"Fine, Devyn it is then," I quipped.

A moment later I was pulled backwards and over to the very edge of the bed. Two hands settled over my hips, and I was pierced to the core by a thick, throbbing shaft.

*Yesssss...*

Warm euphoria flooded its way through my sex-addled brain. Being penetrated so deeply, so thoroughly — it felt like scratching a long-ignored itch. The man behind me began pumping away, fucking me hard with long, deep strokes that told me he was just as desperate to come as I was.

"Now we're talking," I purred into the sheets.

My hands still helplessly bound, I thrust my ass into the air again. My head was sideways, my hair hanging down over my face. My left cheek rocked back and forth against the sheets as whoever was behind me took complete control over my hips, my ass, my oil-soaked essence. They plowed me over and over without stopping, driving me to the brink of an unstoppable climax and straight through to the other side.

*Thank GOD!*

And then I was coming, squeezing myself around him. Milking him with my insides until I felt him go off inside me.

"Give it to me, Devyn..." I breathed, sexily. "Dump it in."

Devyn or not, whoever it was went off like a volcano, splashing their magma against my insides while squeezing my hips tightly with both hands. It was another tell, maybe. Another little piece of information I could use at the end, when the blindfold came off and all three of them stood over me, grinning, daring me to guess who was who.

*SLAP!*

With a grunt and a push my first lover was gone, slapping my ass playfully on his way out of the room. It felt like a Gage-slap, or maybe it really was Devyn. Maverick's spankings were always a little awkward, as he never got that perfect palm-to-flesh contact that left a bright-red handprint that glowed up a minute or two later. As much as those handprints stung, I loved seeing them in the mirror. They made me feel torridly naughty, like getting fucked in the ass did.

I lay there on the bed for a minute, squirming and leaking, until I heard the sound of someone else. Or maybe even more than one person.

"Hi Gage," I guessed. "You wanna take your turn now?"

Thrusting my ass in the air again, I waved it back and forth obscenely. I could feel a warmth and wetness, running down the insides of my thighs. With my stockings on and the plug in my ass and my panties pulled to one side, I imagined I must've been quite a sight.

"No?" I sighed, as I was met only with silence. "Want me to turn over then, or—"

Someone grabbed me, flipping me onto my side. My arms were still overhead, but now one of my legs was pointed upward at the ceiling, held by the ankle in a strong, sure grip.

"I was hoping you'd—"

Whoever it was straddled my other thigh scissoring their way against my come-soaked crotch. A second later it felt like I was being split deliciously in half, as they shoved themselves all the way inside me.

*OHHHHHHHHHHH...*

The hand clutching my leg bounced up and down, as my newest lover pistoned themselves in and of my body. The bed rocked forward and back as he drilled me deeply, taking me all the way to the core with every stroke.

*It's gotta be Maverick!*

It was his favorite position for sure... or maybe they were just trying to fool me. Whoever it was didn't stop as he bottomed out, but pushed that extra glorious inch or two at the end. Each time our bodies came together he screwed his balls tightly against the base of the plug in my ass, adding another dimension of pleasure to the whole sordid experience.

*This is crazy.*

Harder and faster my latest Navy SEAL went, screwing me sideways until I was practically begging to come again. The whole thing felt amazing and exhilarating. Like fucking through a countdown timer to the end of the world.

"Holy—"

The word slipped out from my lovers' mouth, and I

strained to make sense of it. It was whispered instead of said, and gasped more than anything else. The grunt — or curse of pleasure — had been an unavoidable slip-up, but a slip-up nonetheless.

Suddenly I felt a face near mine, as the man fucking me leaned over my body. My hair was brushed aside, and a pair of warm lips slid against my ear.

"I love you Jules," the man whispered.

It was Gage's voice... but also it wasn't. He was the only one who called me by that pet name, though. Unless one of the others were trying to throw me off again, and make me guess incorrectly. As far as sneaky went, that would be pretty damned devious.

*Or maybe it's just Gage disguising his voice. Trying to trick you into thinking it was someone different...*

My mind wrestled with the voice for another moment or two, which was fading in light of my soon-to-be second onrushing orgasm. But then the man began grunting as he exploded inside me. He grunted primally rather than speak, as the enormity of his climax eclipsed all reason.

*Mmmmmm...*

His body was warm and heavy across my back, and felt immeasurably good against my naked skin. Still spilling his seed deep in my womb, his hot breath raised goosebumps all along my neck and shoulders.

*He's not tall enough to be Gage.*

The revelation made me grin, even as a pair of lips closed over mine. The man kissed me firmly but without revealing too much, then exited the bed at almost the exact moment another hopped on from the other side.

*Knew it!*

Whoever was about to take me last had also watched my second tryst. And when it came to voyeuristic tendencies, no one loved watching more than Gage did.

"Whoever you are," I teased, "you'd better make me come."

There was a low chuckle, followed by two powerful hands that maneuvered me swiftly and easily. I was placed onto my back, legs spread, with my arms stretched high overhead. One big palm closed over both my wrists at once, pinning them to the bed, while my final lover propped himself over my body with his other arm. A second later he was kneeing his way insistently between my thighs.

"Somebody's desperate to get laid, huh?" I smirked proudly beneath my blindfold.

There was no answer, only movement. My last boyfriend clenched his ass and thrust his hips forward all in one motion. As he sank into me with all the fury of an angry warrior, I'm pretty sure my eyes crossed.

*This isn't going to take long...*

I knew the statement was true for the both of us. My last climax had been cut abruptly short, and this next one wouldn't be far behind. I also knew that by being so warm and wet and filled with hot seed, the poor guy who'd drawn the third straw didn't stand a chance.

"C'mon," I urged, trying to hook my ankles behind his hard, thrusting body. "Give me something."

Prodding him did no good, because this lover was taking things at his own speed. He plundered me slowly but deeply at first, churning his hips and digging me from the inside out. There was love in his movements. Building arousal in the slow but dreamy way he rotated his hips.

At one point he let go of my wrists, and I reached forward to caress his outstretched arm. It was scrumptiously big and thick. So incredibly long and beautiful, especially with the muscles flexed tight from supporting his body weight.

Eventually he pinned my hands again, then began really going to town. My lover's breathing changed drastically. Little grunts began escaping his tightly-sealed lips, and then he was pounding me fast and hard, bearing down as he impaled me over and over again.

"I'm... I'm going... to..."

I was talking to no one. Speaking for no reason at all as my mind was wiped utterly and completely clean of everything except my surging, brain-erasing climax. The blindfold meant nothing. Silvery-white stars shot across a field of pale shimmering grey so awesome, so breathtakingly beautiful, it felt like every last color flung together at once.

I must've passed out, because when I came to my wrists were untied and the blindfold had been pulled off. The plug was gone too. I was lying there spent and exhausted. Stretched out across my own bed, in a room permeated by sweat and sex and all things manly.

Down below however, I was still wet and throbbing. I laid there a few extra minutes to recover, then addressed those problems with a twenty-minute shower filled heat and soap and steam.

I found the guys downstairs, by following the sound of bells and the whir of electronics. All three of them were gathered around a pinball machine in the arcade.

"You okay?" Maverick grinned. "Seems we lost you there for a moment or two."

Gage chuckled. Devyn smiled but kept on playing the flipper buttons.

"Oh I'm fine," I said happily. "And I'm not doing the dishes either."

At that even Devyn looked up. There was a distinctly sad 'womp-womp' sound effect as he let his ball drop into the exit chute, but then a new one popped up near the plunger.

"That, my pretty princess, remains to be seen," he taunted. "So... what's your guess?"

I considered pausing dramatically, maybe even leading them on and teasing them for a bit. Instead, I folded my arms in triumph and leaned into the wall.

"It was Devyn, Maverick, Gage. In that order."

Gage smiled and whistled, while Maverick's mouth dropped open. Devyn pounded the glass top of the pinball machine with his fist.

"Damn!" he swore. "But how?"

Beaming on the inside, I gave up a casual shrug.

"She got lucky," suggested Maverick.

"Yeah right," I snickered.

"You mean you didn't?"

"Nope."

"Then how'd you know?"

I paused for a moment, then shrugged again. "You all have your own little tells," I told them. "Like poker players. But with sex."

They looked at each other, shifting their heads one by one. It was obvious they still didn't believe me.

"Okay I'll bite," said Devyn. "What tells?"

I let out a sharp, barking laugh. "You think I'm giving them up? Look at how many dishes I just got out of!"

They still looked skeptical, but a lot less so. This time it was Gage who stepped up.

"Tell you what," he said. "Give us one tell each. If we agree that you're not making them up, you don't have to do the dishes for a month."

My smile widened. "A month without dishes, huh? What else?"

"What else do you want?"

I thought for a moment. "How about you boys wait on me hand and foot?"

Maverick frowned. "*Wait* on you..."

"That's right. You bring me things. Do stuff for me. That sort of thing."

"Fine," he grumbled. "We'll bring you things. Now go ahead. Give us these so-called 'tells.'"

I cleared my throat. "Alright," I said, pushing off the wall. "Well for one, you all have a habit of grabbing my hips, right before you let loose."

"That's not a tell!" exclaimed Maverick. "Every guy in the world does that."

"Did I say I was finished?" I smirked back at him. The trio fell silent again. Slowly I walked around them in a circle, like a detective examining his three main suspects.

"So yeah, you all grab my hips right before, well, you know... except that one of you doesn't tighten your fingers all at once. One of you actually *drums* your fingers against my ass one at a time, pinky to thumb, before *really* digging in..."

Maverick and Gage looked at each other curiously. Devyn however, had turned a shade redder.

"You?" Gage swore.

"Yeah, I suppose I do that," Devyn admitted sheepishly.

Maverick shook his head, then folded his arms. "Alright fine. What else?"

"So you've all screwed me sideways," I said, glaring back at him. "But *you're* the only one who grabs my ankle and points my toes at the ceiling." I chuckled gruffly. "I love it of course, but it makes me feel like a ballet dancer. Or at least, a very dirty one."

Maverick's face scrunched up in defeat as I turned toward Gage.

"By process of elimination that would've left you as the third man," I explained, squeezing his bicep, "even if I hadn't reached out to touch your arm. But your arms are way longer than the others, by the way. Fingers to elbow,

elbow to shoulder... I knew it was you the moment I measured how long that taut, beautiful arm was. Not to mention you entering the room early because you *always* like to watch."

Gage tried on his best expression of mock anger, but he failed miserably. In the end, he just laughed and shrugged.

"Next time we're tying your hands to the bedposts," Devyn stepped in. "So you can't get any tactile advantage."

"Then I'll get *another* advantage," I beamed back at him. "Trust me. I'm resourceful."

I strutted in the direction of the living room, and all three of them followed. Dropping into my favorite spot on the couch, I held out my hand and grinned back at them.

"Someone remote me?"

After some muttering, Devyn handed me the remote.

"Popcorn?"

There were a pair of sighs, followed by the sounds of rock paper scissors between the other two men. A moment later, Gage disappeared into the kitchen.

"I get to pick the movie tonight, right?"

I was pushing it now and I knew it, but I wanted to see just how far they'd go. When they balked again I grinned, then motioned to either side of the couch.

"Oh get down here," I chuckled. "The three of you can pick the movie. You can even pick the snacks if you want, and the drinks too."

Extending my tired legs, I plopped them into Maverick's lap and playfully wriggled my toes.

"As long as you rub my feet..."

## ★ BONUS EPILOGUE ★

Wanna read the ULTRA-HEA, sugary-sweet,
super-sexy, flash-forward
BONUS EPILOGUE?
Of course you do!

TAP RIGHT HERE TO SIGN UP!
Or enter this link into your browser:
https://mailchi.mp/kristawolfbooks.com/bonus-epilogue-sbns
to have it INSTANTLY delivered to your inbox.

# Need *more* Reverse Harem?

Thanks for checking out *Secret Baby for the Navy SEALs*. Here's hoping it rocked your socks off!

And for even *more* sweltering reverse harem heat? Check out: Secret Wife to the Special Forces. Below you'll find a preview of the sexy, sizzling cover, plus the first several chapters so you can see for yourself:

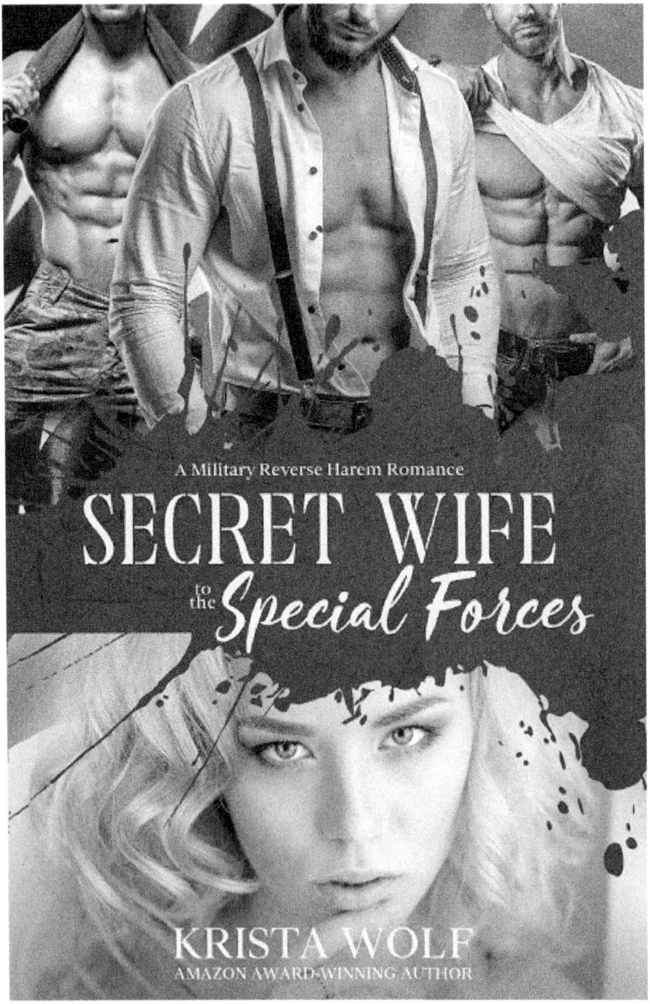
A Military Reverse Harem Romance
SECRET WIFE
to the Special Forces
KRISTA WOLF
AMAZON AWARD-WINNING AUTHOR

# Chapter One

## DAKOTA

Brian dropped into his chair, but not before swiping something on his phone and sliding it deep into his front pocket. His smile was perfunctory. His expression, as always, read like his mind was somewhere else.

"Sorry I'm late," he non-apologized for the twenty-minute delay. "Damn. You ordered a whole bottle, huh?"

I grinned sweetly, pouring him a generous portion of deep red merlot. He was paying for it, after all. And once he saw the price of the bottle I'd picked out, he'd want to drink every last drop.

"Thanks babe."

"You're very welcome," I grinned, raising my glass. He toasted me awkwardly. "Can't have my man thirsty. Besides, you'll need it for all the double-talking."

"Double what?"

I'd muttered the last part into my glass, while tipping

it back. It was a miracle he'd heard me. "Oh, nothing."

He wore his grey shirt, the one that shimmered to black in an almost ombré way. It clashed violently with his purple tie, but at this point who was really keeping score? As we picked up our giant menus, it seemed suddenly odd how attracted I'd once been to the man sitting across from me. It was hard to believe I'd ever considered a future with him, even briefly, during the past year we'd been together.

"What's that?"

Brian's gaze was fixed on the empty glass off to one side, in front of an empty chair. He chuckled. "You planning on doing some double-fisting?"

"I probably should be, but no," I told him. "That's for our guest."

He laughed again. "We're having a guest?"

"Oh yeah."

He shook his head dismissively, as his attention dropped to the menu. If he cared, he might've noticed the small red dot at the bottom of that glass. Or the merlot residue still clinging to the side of it, had he really looked.

But Brian didn't really *look* at anything. He wore the blinders of someone so selfish and truly self-centered, nothing else really mattered unless it pertained to him.

*God, he's so oblivious.*

I took an emboldening sip of wine. Not that I needed emboldening, really. I made a hand signal, and my accomplice approached the table. She slid into the empty chair while Brian was busy behind the wall of his menu, and

I poured her a new glass of wine.

The payoff came when my boyfriend finally dropped his menu. The look on his face was so priceless, so abruptly panicked, I wished I could've bottled that look and kept it forever.

"Hello, baby."

In the span of less than three seconds, Brian had gone as white as a ghost. Every ounce of color was now drained from his face.

"What's the matter?" Naomi chuckled musically. "Nothing on the menu you like?"

My soon-to-be ex-boyfriend's mouth opened, closed, then opened again. He almost actually said something, but whatever it was got stuck in his throat.

"This isn't quite the threeway he wanted, is it?" I laughed, and Naomi laughed with me.

"No," she agreed. "It *definitely* isn't."

Brian finally dropped his head into his hands. The comically oversized menu flopped to the table.

"That's too bad, too," I shrugged, turning to Naomi. "If he'd been the right kind of boyfriend I might've gone for it. I'm actually pretty adventurous."

"Oh totally!" she agreed. My newfound friend jerked a thumb in our victim's direction. "But with *him?*"

We both broke into hysterical laughter, and the laughter felt cathartically good. It was such a relief to finally be through. To be putting an end to all the lies, all the scheming, all the deception.

"T—The two of you planned this?" Brian finally spoke. "You set me up?"

"I know, pretty crazy right?"

"Like something out of a movie, really," Naomi agreed.

"It wasn't hard though," I added, "finally figuring it out. All those times you abruptly canceled plans, then turned off your phone. All the holidays you couldn't be with me, because you were spending them with her."

"Ditto," my accomplice nodded. "Dakota and I went over our dates together, and in retrospect it seems so obvious now. Still, it must've been logistically hard, seeing us both." She eyed him skeptically. "Or you know what? Scratch that. For someone like you, it was probably all too easy."

Brian sat there silently, taking it all in. He looked half dejected, half pissed off at all the laughing we were doing. I realized his anger was probably my favorite part.

"So yeah, we're both obviously through with you," I told him, matter-of-factly. "We're done with the lying, the sneaking around, and the super lame sex."

"*Especially* the super lame sex," Naomi groaned, tipping her glass back again. With her free hand, she made an obscene jerk-off motion. "Wasn't even that good in the beginning, to be honest."

I shrugged, trying to remember. "Maybe passable."

"Maybe," she squinted.

"Except for that one thing he does where he—"

"ALRIGHT, enough!" Brian cried suddenly. "I get it

already, okay? I'm the asshole."

"Oh I don't know if you're *the* asshole," Naomi purred. "But you're definitely *an* asshole. Just one of many."

She was certainly cute, I'd give Brian that. Dark hair, mocha brown eyes. The physical opposite of me, right down to being short where I was tall. As far as two-timing assholes went, my ex had good taste at least.

Naomi caught me looking her over and shrugged. "So what do we do now?"

"I dunno. Throw our drinks in his face?"

My raven-haired accomplice considered it for a moment, then shook her head. "Nah. We're classier than that." She giggled. "Besides, this wine is too damned good."

"It better be," I smirked. "It was at the very bottom of the menu."

We toasted — the two of us — and drained our glasses together. By the time we set them down on the table, Brian's face had regained all of its color and then some.

"Word of advice," I said, looking into my ex-boyfriend's eyes for what I knew would be the last time. A tiny pang of sadness threatened to rise up, but I shoved it down. "You *might* want to think about other people before you do this next time. And not just yourself."

We rose together, gathering our things. At the other end of the table, Brian looked very small and very defeated.

"Hey look, it's not *all* bad," Naomi said in consolation. "You've still got some delicious meals coming — all to yourself."

This seemed to snap our cheating boyfriend out of his trance. "I–I do?"

"Sure," I answered, delivering my brightest, million-watt smile. "We ordered tomahawk steaks before you got here. Three of em, in fact."

We waved back at him in tandem on the way out.

"Hope you're hungry."

# Two

## DAKOTA

The phone rang yet again, and for the fourth time in a row my car's bluetooth intercepted the potential connection. This in turn interrupted the song, and it was a hell of a good song. Maybe even a great one, if I could only settle back into my heated leather seats to enjoy it.

*Fuck off, Brian.*

I closed my eyes, trying to relax as the heat from the vents washed over me. My ex had been calling me non-stop for the past five days, and today was no exception. I had no idea what he wanted. My voicemail was too full to leave a message. I'd deleted any and all texts he sent without reading them, which had been fun at first, but now it was growing tiresome.

The ringing eventually stopped and the song came back on. I rode its melody all the way to the chorus, and just when it got to the best part... the phone rang again.

*Dammit!*

I banged the steering wheel in frustration. It was bad enough to be stuck in a ditch on the side of the road, waiting for help. But it was even worse when that help would arrive only to chastise me for not switching over to snow tires by now.

*Knock knock knock!*

The sharp rapping against my window nearly jolted me out of my skin! My father's smiling face greeted me through the frosted glass and blowing snow, as I popped the door a few inches open.

"Stuck huh?"

"Yep."

He glanced down and shook his head, but it was mostly for effect.

"Should've put on the snow tires, Dakota. You know better than this."

I accepted my reprimand and stepped out into the cold Minnesota wind. The snow was mixed with sleet now, pelting the exposed skin of my face and hands like tiny daggers as I squinted into the darkness.

"Swing around," I told him, jerking my head in the direction of my father's truck. "I'll unravel the winch and—"

"I can do it, honey. You stay inside and keep warm."

I raised an eyebrow in mock disgust. "Are you kidding old man? Get back in your truck. You don't even have a jacket on!'

For as long as I could remember my mother and I were always yelling at him for going out without a coat, but my father never seemed to care. He'd wear the same flannel shirts summer or winter, day or night. You could always tell how cold it was by how many layers he had on, though.

Eventually we got the winch hooked up, and it was a simple thing to pull me free. Relief flowed through me as my car rolled back onto the road where it belonged.

"Thanks dad."

Again he'd come through. Just like clockwork.

"You sure you don't want to switch vehicles?" he jabbed, wiping his frozen hands on his dirty work jeans. "I could take it down to the shop first thing tomorrow. Get those tires all changed up for you."

"That's tempting," I scrambled, "but I really need to run. I've got work tonight."

"Ah, yes," he grinned. "Work."

My father never could — and probably never would — understand what I did for a living. But it put food on the table, whether he understood it or not.

"Plus I have groceries in the back," I continued. "And also—"

"Come by during the week," my father said sternly. "Or I'm going to tow this thing to my shop when you're not looking and do it myself."

I flushed and stared back at him, noticing the tiny changes as I always did. His cheeks were a little more sunken, his once-blond hair flecked with a little more grey. It was somewhat heartbreaking, watching time catch up to this man who raised me and loved me. Wrinkle by wrinkle, it changed him in all the ways I wished I could stop.

"Yes daddy."

My father smiled back at me warmly. "Now *there's* my ankle-biter."

He kissed my cheek before driving off, eventually leaving me to my thoughts. The ankle-biting nickname went way back to when I was a little girl, laughing and playing and biting my father's ankles to get his attention whenever he wasn't working. Unfortunately, that wasn't very often.

Another song came on, but not for long. I hadn't even put the car in drive yet when the bluetooth was interrupted by another phone call, this time from a number I didn't recognize. Most likely Brian using a friend's phone, trying to trick me into picking it up.

This time I pressed the ACCEPT button and did it anyway. Enough was enough.

"What!?" I shouted into the empty car. "For fuck's sake, what could you *possibly* have to say to me!?"

There were three of four seconds of complete and utter silence. Then: "Ummmm.... hi?"

The voice at the other end of the connection wasn't Brian's at all. It was deeper and more baritone. Velvety and delicious.

"Dakota?"

"Yes?"

"It's Jace."

*Jace...*

It didn't register for a few seconds. That's how long it had been.

"Jace..." I squinted, as the heat warmed my pink skin. Then, a revelation: "Oh, JACE!"

Images of my brother Tyler's best friend popped immediately to mind. I could envision his tall, slender frame. His deeply tanned skin, accented by that beautiful white smile.

"Jace!" I repeated again. "Oh, I'm so sorry! I was just —"

"Thinking I was someone else?"

He chuckled, and the visual solidified. I hadn't seen Jace for nearly a decade. I knew he'd entered the military, and I knew he was doing some very badass stuff. The last I'd heard from Tyler, his friend was somewhere on the other side of the world, getting decorated for something amazing he couldn't fully talk about.

"Yes, I thought you were someone else," I told him, before adding: "and nobody very important, believe me."

"Good," Jace answered smoothly. "Because although we teased you a lot in high school, I can't imagine you'd hate me *that* badly."

He was referring to him and Tyler, of course. When I was a sophomore and they were both seniors, they spent a lot of their time teasing and pranking me mercilessly. But that also meant I got to hang out with my older brother and his friends a lot, which was never a bad thing.

"Nah, we're good," I sighed happily. "So how've you been!? Where are you now? Most of all, what the hell have you been up to? Last I heard you were—"

"All good questions," Jace cut in, "but right now I have a favor to ask of you." He paused awkwardly. "A really *big* favor."

"I can do favors," I reasoned, saying the words slowly. "Shoot."

"Well it's actually part favor, part proposition."

I shook my head. "Can't be worse than *some* of the propositions I've been getting lately."

"And you can totally say no if you want," he went on. "But you can also say yes. At least I *hope* you say yes. Even though what I need is a little... unorthodox."

God, what the hell could it be? Jace had always been straightforward: totally cool and confident. He was a good-looking lacrosse player, with tons of friends and even more in the way of girlfriends. It just wasn't like him to beat around the bush.

Then again it had been a while, and people changed. Everything *around* you changed too, as I found out from remaining home these past several years. The changes usually happened when you weren't looking, whether you liked it or not. It was an unfortunate fact of life.

"Okay," said Jace finally. "Here goes nothing..."

I sat there with both eyebrows arched, staring into the phone. Just inches in front me, wave after wave of frozen sleet blasted against my windshield.

"How would you like a free trip to Hawaii?"

# Three

## DAKOTA

The descent was a little bumpy, but the views were outright spectacular. I saw fluffy white clouds and yellow sand beaches. The turquoise waters were broken by swirling, colorful reefs, and dotted with little white sailboats here and there.

Of course our landing approach also included the big city itself: Honolulu. Its streets and avenues seemed almost cast against the lush green mountains like an oversized throw-net, punctuated by rectangular hotels and skyscrapers that, oddly enough, didn't seem out of place in such a paradise.

For any Minnesota girl slogging her way through mid-December, a trip to Hawaii was a no-brainer. But a *free* trip to Hawaii, to do a special favor for one of my brother's closest friends?

Well that was an instant and enthusiastic YES.

It didn't hurt of course that I was getting over a breakup. Or that my personal life had been in a bit of a rut lately, even with all the success I'd been having at work. Getting away for a couple of weeks would definitely clear my head. It might even help soak some much-needed vitamin-D into my sun-starved skin as well, as long as I located some sunscreen and aloe plants straight away.

I'd told my parents I was taking off on a last-minute vacation, the details of which I'd fill in later. I realized trading a free trip to Hawaii for a 'favor' might not sit well with them, especially when I couldn't yet explain what that favor was. All I knew was that Jace had asked me to be his date for an extremely fancy, *very* important military dinner. Beyond that, the only other detail he promised was that it would be strictly platonic.

Besides, of all Tyler's wacky friends my father always had a soft spot for Jace. The two bonded on levels that rivaled his relationship with my brother, and I didn't want to mess that up.

Any explanation I might've owed Tyler himself was preempted by the fact he was thousands of miles away. My brother was an incredible hockey player who rocked the collegiate circuit and fell just short of going pro, but being a coach turned out to be his true calling. For the past several years he'd been criss-crossing the country with various triple-A teams.

No, everyone could learn all about my trip *after* I'd taken it. Between helping out at my dad's shop and freezing my ass off through sub-zero temperatures, for once I was finally doing something for me.

"Dakota!"

I was just through the arrival gate, and the voice

reached me before I even recognized the face. I scanned the crowd twice and suddenly there he was, standing a full head taller than anyone else in the crowd.

*HOLY.*

*SHIT.*

"Jace?"

I could barely believe my eyes. Gone was the lithe, almost skinny version of my brother's best friend. Standing in his place was a hulking, well-muscled giant in a tight green shirt and camouflage cargo pants.

"Right here!"

We ran to each other, and he swept me up in a spinning bear hug. I dropped my carry-on and marveled at how impossibly *hard* his body felt. He wasn't just big, he was enormous! I could barely get my arms around him!

"How was your flight?"

He put me down in a daze, still blinking up at him in disbelief.

"M—My flight?"

"Yes."

"Jace... forget about my flight! Just look at you!"

"Look at me?"

"Yes!" I cried, taking a step back. "What the hell *happened* to you!?"

He laughed at my dismay, and his laughter was deep and resonant. His childhood face had matured into the strong cheekbones and angular jaw of a man, and an astonishingly good-looking one at that. He sported a well-trimmed beard that was a hundred-percent brand new. The smile beneath it however, was exactly the same.

"The Army happened to me," he answered. He dropped his gaze to his massive arms and chest, as if discovering those things for the first time. "I guess it's been a while, huh? You haven't seen me since... well..."

"Since you were some skinny beanpole punk, running around with Tyler," I jumped in. "Short-sheeting my bed. Stretching plastic wrap over the toilet bowl—"

"Oh man," he swore, "your mother was *so* mad at that one!"

"And let's not forget putting glitter all over the fan blades in my bedroom during my fifteenth birthday," I finished. "I was cleaning that up for months. Years, maybe."

Jace laughed again and held up his hand. "Guilty."

"Damn," I swore happily. "How long has it really been?"

He slung my carry-on over one giant shoulder and pointed toward the baggage carousel. "Too long."

A few minutes later we were hopping into a Ford Bronco with oversized tires; a beautiful green-and-white relic from the mid 1990's. We took off with the windows rolled down, and I gawked shamelessly at the scenery. The Hawaiian air was sweet and fragrant and pregnant with a thousand open-ended possibilities.

We made small talk at first, mainly because there was so much to say. We asked about each other's jobs, lives, and what we'd been doing since the last time we'd laid eyes on each other. Even with Tyler as common ground, the time gap was so big it seemed almost insurmountable.

"So tell me," I finally asked, as the beautiful palm trees raced by. "What kind of favor requires sending all the way to Minnesota for little old me?"

Jace bit his lip. "A... pretty complicated one."

"Really?" Now I was little more than intrigued. "Do tell."

"Well, I sort of got myself into a little white lie..." said Jace. "And it eventually snowballed into something bigger."

The big arm guiding the 30-year old steering wheel flexed casually with each turn. That arm was ripped and tan. Exquisitely wonderful. As we picked our way through the streets, I couldn't stop looking at it.

"We'll go to my place first," said Jace, "so I can fill you in. But yeah, I messed up and things quickly got out of hand. I'm in over my head now," he turned to me and smiled, "but I appreciate you coming to help."

*Help.* I still couldn't imagine what kind of help this man needed. He looked like he could lift the couch with one hand and vacuum under it with the other.

"As a matter of fact—"

His sentence trailed off as we pulled into the driveway of some cookie-cutter house in a cookie-cutter neighborhood. Jace killed the engine, just as one of the neighbors raised an arm cheerfully from the porch next door.

"Ah, shit."

Jace's handsome face had suddenly gone red with worry. Putting on his most plastic smile he returned the gesture, but not before circling around to help me out of the Bronco.

"Jace, what are we—"

His hands felt electric on my hips. For a split second I was weightless in his two big arms, and then I was standing on the pavement... holding his hand.

"I'm so, so sorry," Jace whispered back to me. His fingers squeezed gently as they interlaced with mine. "For now, just please—"

"JACE!"

The young woman from next door bounded over happily, now with her husband at her side. Their smiles were so big, so bright, they seemed almost painted on.

"At last!" she cried. "After all this time!"

The woman extended an enthusiastic palm my way. Still clasping Jace in my right hand, I reached out awkwardly with my left and shook it.

"We finally get to meet Jace's *wife*."

# Four

## DAKOTA

*Wife...*

The word dropped right out of the clear blue sky. I couldn't have looked more shocked if it hit me on the top of the head, which I guess it did.

*WIFE?*

It was another squeeze of the hand by Jace that jolted me back to reality.

"Umm, hi!" I said finally, trying to sound as casual yet cheerful as possible. "So nice to meet you. My name is..."

"Dakota," the woman interrupted with a grin. She shook my hand vigorously. "C'mon, you don't think we've already heard all about you?"

*Dakota.* Well that part was easy, I guess. Whatever 'little white lies' Jace had been telling, at least the name was right.

"I'm Zach, and she's Annie," the husband said,

shaking my hand next. He was young and well-built, with close-cropped hair and dark, bushy eyebrows. Another soldier no doubt. "You both need to come over for drinks. You know, once you get settled in."

"Dakota's tired I'm sure," Jace jumped in. "And probably a little jet-lagged."

"A little," I smiled.

"I'm going to rest her up for a while, but maybe in the next day or two—"

"*Definitely* in the next day or two," Annie replied. "But yes, okay. So nice to finally get to meet you Dakota!"

Zach grinned, nodding his agreement. "We were starting to think you were just a myth. Like Bigfoot!"

The neighbors turned away, leaving us to awkward looks and heavy luggage. Jace took most of it upon himself, then handed me his key. I unlocked the house and we dragged everything inside, closing the door behind us.

"What in the world—"

"Dakota I'm so sorry!" Jace interjected, his face wrought with apology. "I had no idea they'd even be home, much less come running over the moment we pulled up."

"Yeah," I quipped, "well a husbandly head's up would've been nice."

"I know, I know."

"Wife, Jace?" I said incredulously. "I'm your *wife?*"

As strange as it sounded, the word also sat like a hot little ball in the pit of my stomach. Jace stood there looking down at me, his hard, fit body not even heaving slightly from the exertion of carrying all four of my bags. I still couldn't believe how incredible he looked.

*Wife...*

Holy shit, the word seemed more and more exciting every second that ticked by.

"You want coffee," he asked. "Or something stiffer?"

I grinned my way through the double-entendre. "Both, I think," I replied. "But coffee for now."

He led me through an arch and into the kitchen, which was brightly decorated and immaculately-kept. For a bachelor, his house was certainly big. But Jace wasn't a bachelor anymore. Apparently, the two of us were married.

"Sit down and I'll tell you everything."

I pulled up a chair as his giant stainless coffee machine went through a noisy but delicious-smelling cycle. A few minutes later I was cradling an expertly-made latte, foam and everything.

"Wow," I offered. "This is nice."

"Yeah," he chuckled. "We take our coffee pretty seriously around here."

"We?"

He let out a low whistle. "Damn Dakota, there's so much you need to know. So much has happened."

After fixing himself a mug, Jace crossed his arms and leaned back against the counter. Which was good, because it gave me an excuse to stare at those arms.

"Why don't you start at the beginning?" I told him.

"Last time I saw you was at my house, if you remember."

He nodded slowly. "My going away party." The grin beneath his beard widened. "That whole night was pretty fucking legendary."

"Sure was."

"I passed out cold, and you all shaved my head so Uncle Sam didn't have to."

I laughed as my mind traveled back in time with him. "I can still remember plugging in the buzzer," I murmured. "I also remember being really depressed."

"What? Why?"

"Because you were a hell of a lot of fun," I told him, "all through high school. And it sucked that you weren't going to be around anymore."

Jace took a long, deep breath and let it out as a sigh. "Things always change, don't they?"

"They sure do."

He smiled again, and I felt that familiar pang of nostalgia. I could tell he felt it too.

"I remember you as Tyler's little sister, always around. Always underfoot."

"And I remember you as the tall, goofy kid who always got my brother in trouble," I replied. "I was shocked when you said you'd signed with a recruiter. But I also figured the Army would straighten you out."

"Oh, it straightened some things out," Jace nodded. As he sipped his own mug I could see his eyes were still distant, still far away. "My God, boot camp seems like a thousand years ago."

"It *was* a thousand years ago," I agreed. "Or thereabouts."

The sound of the front door unlatching echoed through the foyer, followed by cheerful voices that preceded their way into the kitchen. The first man through the archway was tall — even taller than Jace — and carried himself with a rock star's swagger. His companion was equally well-built, with sprawling shoulders and a V-shaped body that only came with long, hard hours in the gym.

In fact, both men were covered in sweat. Their shirts stuck to their hard bodies in places I would've loved to spend more time looking at, if I weren't already being introduced by Jace.

"Dakota, meet my housemates: Aurelius and Merrick."

Merrick smiled and nodded politely, then began rifling through the fridge for something. But it was Aurelius, the exceptionally tall and goateed one, who took my palm and planted a kiss on the back of my hand.

"Congratulations on the wedding," he winked.

# Five

## JACE

I didn't plan on overwhelming Dakota with everything at once, but keeping her in the dark wasn't doing her any favors either. It also didn't help that Aurelius and Merrick knew. Yet as my brothers-in-arms they knew everything, and always would.

"Sorry I didn't get you guys a gift or anything," Aurelius teased. "But if you give me a few days, I'm sure I'll come up with something."

Merrick dug one of his pre-made protein shakes out of the fridge and chugged it down. Wiping his mouth with the back of one arm, he jerked a thumb at me.

"Whatever you do, make sure he doesn't skimp on the honeymoon," he told her. "Jace has a tendency to half-ass everything, if you let him."

"Is that right?" I challenged glibly. "Did I half-ass pulling your *own* ass out of the fire, back in Al Fallûjah?"

Merrick grunted and went silent, as I knew he would.

It was his only option.

"Thought so."

I turned my attention back to Dakota, who was sitting there sipping her coffee. In the span of just eight or nine years so much had changed! Gone were the braces, the freckles, the last remnants of baby fat. The long-legged blonde sitting before me was a full grown woman now, and a gorgeous one to boot. She could've easily been a total stranger, if not for those piercing, arctic blue eyes I'd grown up with for so many years.

*God, she's beautiful.*

She really and truly was. That part might come in handy, of course. But when it came to the favor I needed, I had to push everything — including appearances — to the side.

"So two weeks before every Christmas there's an officer's ball," I began finally. "It's the most important off-duty event of the year. Especially this year, and especially for me, because I need something very specific from my CO."

She wrinkled her nose. "CO?"

"Commanding officer," said Merrick. "The big guy."

"Oh. That's right."

"See, I shouldn't even be there," I told her. "At the ball, I mean. I wouldn't even be part of this whole ridiculous thing, but for my CO who insisted I come."

"Why shouldn't you be there?" Dakota asked innocently.

"Because I'm not an officer. And I'll never be one."

I saw her avert her eyes for a moment, almost

uncomfortably. But she had the wrong idea.

"Dakota, I'm a Green Beret. Highly decorated. I've completed dozens of successful missions, across eleven different countries and seventeen conflicts."

Her eyes flitted to the others, perhaps expecting them to interject some kind of sarcastic response. There was none, of course. Both Merrick and Aurelius knew the validity of every single one of those conflicts. For more than a few of them, they were right there beside me.

"After Special Forces training I rose through the ranks fast," I explained. "In fact, I got promoted quicker than anyone in recent Army history."

"Why aren't you an officer then?"

"By choice," I replied simply. "I've been a Sergeant Major for a lot years now. I must've turned down advancement half a dozen times, most of them from my increasingly pissed-off CO."

"*Very* pissed off CO," Aurelius agreed.

"But as angry as he is that I won't accept a commission, he's also a man I deeply respect. General Burke came out of Vietnam a genuine hero. He earned two Silver Stars and the Distinguished Service Cross, plus countless other citations too. And shit, I don't even know how many Purple Hearts."

"Four," Merrick chimed in. "I think."

"He was there for Desert Storm," I added, watching Dakota's reaction. "Just as your father was. And though he's pushing past seventy, the old man's still got it."

Dakota's father was another man I respected all throughout high school, but even more now after my service. He'd been a heavy equipment mechanic throughout the conflict, working on everything from Abrams to Apaches. He served all the way through the Gulf War, and was there for the liberation of Kuwait. I knew these things because I'd looked them up. I'd seen his file.

"I still don't understand what this has to do with me," said Dakota. "Or why we're supposedly married."

The guys joined her in glancing expectantly at me from across the kitchen. Eventually, I shrugged.

"Over the past year or so, throughout all the many conversations we had about life, family, and future... I might've told the old man I was married."

Aurelius snorted. "*Might've?*"

"Okay, fine," I admitted. "I did. I told my CO I had a wife, and that wife is you. It has to be you."

"Me?" Dakota asked, arching an eyebrow. "Why me?"

"Because... well..." I winced. "I might've shown him a photo or two."

"Of me?" she asked, surprised. "Oh God, which one?"

"Just some pretty one I pulled off your Instagram account."

"You follow my Instagram account?"

"Uh... sure."

My face was turning undeniably red now, especially

since the guys were thoroughly enjoying this. As awkward as it was, I had to get through it.

'Which one did you take?" asked Dakota.

"That bachelorette party you went to last year? Sometime around the summer?"

"Amber's?" Now *she* was turning red. "Oh God. I got so drunk that night! Which one did you use?"

"One of the early ones," I grinned. "You were standing outside, with the lights of the city behind you. Your eyes were shining. You had the most beautiful smile."

I realized I was rambling, but I didn't care. The photo had been amazing, really — the one silent thing that bridged the gap between the girl I once knew and the woman Dakota had become. I felt shitty using it. I felt even more shitty lying. But the photo itself...

Man, I'd admired that one little photo so many times.

"Alright, that one's not bad," Dakota said, finally remembering. "I can let that one slide."

"Good."

"What else?"

I paused to pull my phone from my pocket. After swiping left a bunch of times, I held it up to show her.

"This one."

It was a photo of a photo, or maybe a scan. In it, Tyler and I stood with his sister between us. We were all so young, mid-teens maybe. The three of us had our arms draped happily around each other.

Dakota stared into my phone and slowly shook her head. "You told him we were childhood sweethearts, didn't you?" she asked flatly.

"Yes."

The kitchen went silent as Dakota and I just stared at each other. My housemates stood there innocently, watching the show.

"Look, it just came out one day," I explained. "I don't know what the hell I was thinking. The old man kept wanting to hear about my personal life, and I was floundering, so eventually I made one up. I told him I had someone from back home, someone who I grew up with. I kept building the relationship up more and more every time I talked to him, fleshing it out, giving it details. Then one day he wanted to see a photo. And I realized that this woman I'd been building up this whole time; the one who was strong, and fiery, and independent, and beautiful... this woman was *you*."

Dakota stared back at me blankly, and the complete lack of expression made her somehow prettier. It was hard to tell if she was pissed or flattered or—

"So your boss thinks I'm your wife?"

"Yes," all three of us said at once.

She bit her lip. "That shouldn't be *too* hard to pull off, I guess. Especially for just one person, over a single night."

The others exchanged sideways glances with me. Glances that were awkward enough to notice.

"What?"

"Well, like I said the whole thing snowballed," I confessed. "The general likes to talk, and for some reason he likes to talk me up."

"So?"

"So people over me, people under me, my entire company..."

"Just about everybody on the joint base thinks this guy is recently married," Aurelius finished for me. "He made up a wedding *and* a honeymoon. He even wears a ring."

Sheepishly, I held up my left hand. The simple gold band that still felt so alien on my finger glinted playfully in the dying light.

"Well then I guess congratulations are in order," Dakota declared, taking a long, casual pull of her coffee. She stared back at me again with those big blue eyes, and her mouth curled into a sardonic smile.

"I sure hope our honeymoon was a good one."

## SECRET WIFE
## TO THE SPECIAL FORCES
## IS NOW ON AMAZON!

Grab it now — It's free to read on Kindle Unlimited

# About the Author

Krista Wolf is a lover of action, fantasy and all good horror movies... as well as a hopeless romantic with an insatiably steamy side.

She writes suspenseful, mystery-infused stories filled with blistering hot twists and turns. Tales in which headstrong, impetuous heroines are the irresistible force thrown against the immovable object of ripped, powerful heroes.

If you like intelligent and witty romance served up with a sizzling edge? You've just found your new favorite author.

Click here to see all titles on
Krista's Author Page

Sign up to Krista's VIP Email list to get instant notification of all new releases:
http://eepurl.com/dkWHab

Printed in Great Britain
by Amazon